NO REGRETS

NO REGRETS

*A Novel of Love and Lies
in W.W. II England*

THE FIRST IN THE THORNTON TRILOGY

MARY CHRISTIAN PAYNE

Published by TCK Publishing
www.TCKPublishing.com

Sign up for the newsletter to get news, updates and new release info
from Mary Christian Payne:
http://bit.ly/MaryChristianPayne

To Dia for getting it right.

1

Mᴀʏ 1940

Sloan Thornton was a flight lieutenant in the RAF, fresh from Military College, when he found himself among an enormous crowd of people trying to reach the safety of British soil, after the Battle of Dunkirk. His plane was shot down, just past the small village of Bergues, France. Sloan managed to parachute safely from his crippled aircraft, but was wounded when bullets targeting the plane hit his leg. Once on land, he found the Luftwaffe strafing the ground continually. He tore his shirt, tying it round his leg to stem the flow of blood. He wasn't far from the English Channel where, if fortunate, he'd be picked up by a ship and returned to his English base. As the queue proceeded toward the beaches, he crawled off the road onto farmland and woods lining the side. It was raining. Through the downpour he saw a small farmhouse, painted white and well kept. There was a fence surrounding the structure. A few wide steps led to a covered veranda.

Pulling himself up the steps, Sloan lay on the porch. Soaking wet and shivering, he feebly knocked. There was no reply. Then he called out. After several minutes, the door was unbolted. Although nearly unconscious with pain, Sloan was stunned by the beautiful girl who stood before him. He wondered if he'd already died. She looked like an angel. He was totally speechless, and, in that instant, everything in his life changed. She was the ideal lady he'd been waiting for, as long as he could remember. Standing there, she made his heart beat as it never had before. In spite of his wound, he couldn't concentrate on anything except her face. She was young, tall, slender, and fair, with a sweet face – inexpressibly lovely. She had a complexion like rose petals, long, dark lashes and sensitive, soft lips. Her hair hung in long golden ringlets, and the expression on her exquisite face was shy.

"My soulmate" he almost said aloud. He'd murmured those same words to himself hundreds of times throughout his life. Now, on the porch of a small farmhouse in rural France, he believed, with all of his heart, that fate had brought her to him. Sloan couldn't remember a time when he hadn't dreamed about such a woman. Even though he'd proposed to Anne Whitfield, the girl back home, on the evening before leaving for war, Sloan hadn't forgotten the lady of his dreams. He'd never believed he'd find her, because it was ludicrous to think such perfection existed. If he'd painted her portrait, it would have been identical to the young lady who stood in the doorway. Sloan struggled to come to his senses. Closing his eyes for several moments, he was afraid she might be gone when he opened them. But she was still there, looking fretful, waiting for him to speak. He was nearly trembling, trying to understand what had happened. He didn't even know her - had only seen her face. Yet she'd touched something deep inside of him. He gathered himself together, realizing he was probably frightening her.

"*Parlez vous Anglais?*" he asked, hoping she spoke English.

"Yes. Yes. That's no problem. Have you been wounded?" she asked.

"Yes, The Luftwaffe shot me in the leg. I'm RAF. I had to ditch my aircraft. I need to reach the beaches, but I'm not able to stand or walk. Will you be kind enough to help me? I know it's dangerous. I'm not sure what your beliefs are. If you're not Resistance, I won't bother you."

"Yes. Of course I'm Resistance. All patriotic French are Resistance. But if Germans come, I do not argue with them. You understand?"

"Of course," he smiled. "No one argues with a Nazi."

She reached down and guided him though the doorway. Not strong enough to lift him, she took hold of Sloan's arms and dragged him across the threshold. Lying him on the wide plank flooring, she ran to fetch a pillow and blanket. Then she gathered medical supplies, bringing them to where he lay.

"May I ask your name, Mademoiselle?" Sloan enquired.

"My name is Elise Lisak. I apologize for being wary before I opened the door. I'm here alone. My brother, Josef, joined the Resistance Forces. I hope he's safe in England now."

"When did he leave?"

"This morning. My neighbour tells me there've been ships, boats, and all sorts of crafts rescuing your military men and French Resistance fighters, as well as refugees. When I last saw Josef, he came home and told me he was going to the beaches, hoping for a chance to escape to England. He couldn't take me. He's going to join the forces and fight against the Nazi's."

"I imagine he's accomplished his goal. There've been watercraft picking up people by the score. I saw them from my plane. That's where I'm going too, if I can make it on this bloody leg. Excuse my language. Sometimes we military men forget ourselves in front of ladies."

"I know. I have a brother." She smiled. "Now, just lie still, Lieutenant. I'm going to try to remove this bullet," she said, He didn't move, and instead stared up at her lovely face.

"Elise is a pretty name. I've never heard 'Lisak' before. Are you French by birth?" he said, trying to get his mind off the pain of the bullet extraction.

"No. My parents were Russian. My mother died in childbirth, and my father died in the Revolution. My brother has taken care of me since I was a young girl. He brought me from St. Petersburg. That's where I was born in 1918."

"And now you've found yourself in the French countryside."

Elise continued to work on his leg, while she chatted.

"Yes. We were in Monte Carlo and Paris. When the trouble started, my brother used money he'd saved to move us to this region. He's a trained chef, so he opened a small restaurant in Bergues. He hoped it would provide a more tranquil life, and he was right. It has. But, the Germans have come, and nothing is tranquil anymore. There's general belief that the Nazis are going to conquer our land." She finished cleaning the wound, and began to splint and bandage it.

"I'm afraid that looks quite possible. France hasn't put up much fight. My Country will do all it can, but we all foresee a terrible conflict. It appears that the French will surrender to the Germans."

"Oh, *Mon Dieu*! Do you think there's any way I might escape to England?"

"Did your brother leave instructions for you?"

"He told me to use my common sense. He thought I'd probably be safe in this house, but I don't feel safe. That was before word started to circulate that the German's want to occupy France permanently."

"I'd try to get out if I were you. It may be your last chance for a long time. Wait until night falls. You'll be less conspicuous. The boats are definitely taking refugees, from what I've heard and seen. To be honest, I think the biggest problems are your youth and beauty. When events like this occur, law and order break down. There's looting, vandalism, rape – even murder. You should try to camouflage your appearance. Some of these Nazi men aren't safe to be around."

"Yes. I understand," she murmured, as she leaned over to wrap the bandage round his leg. The bullet had travelled through his knee and had fractured the bone.

"Now, do you think you might be able to stand?" Elise asked.

She put out her hands, firmly taking hold of his. As she gripped tightly, he came to his feet. The discomfort had subsided, probably because she'd given him two pain tablets from her cabinet, left over from Josef's bouts with migraine headaches. After Sloan stood, she helped him limp to the kitchen, where she heated onion soup and crisp bread. She sliced a slab of cheese and tossed a salad. It was the best meal he'd eaten since leaving Dover. They continued to chat while he ate, and his attraction grew. He wished he could tell her his feelings, but was frightened she'd be turned away by his impetuosity. Still – still – she *was* the embodiment of everything he'd ever dreamed. How could he leave without telling her his feelings?

As she stood at the old kitchen sink, her long, golden curls falling to the side of her face, Sloan speculated on what it would be like to hold her, and to keep her safe forever. Time was limited. He'd have to leave if he had hopes of being rescued by one of the vessels in the Channel. He shouldn't linger. Who knew how long the rescue effort would continue? But perhaps – perhaps he could stay just a bit longer. Surely the ships in the Channel would be there quite some time. Thousands of people were waiting to be evacuated. An hour wouldn't matter.

"Would you like some coffee in the parlour?" she asked.

Sloan knew he should refuse, but what if he never saw her again?

"Yes. I'd like that. I feel rather weak. Perhaps a cup of coffee would help," he answered.

"Do you take cream or sugar?"

"A bit of cream usually. But, I think some sugar too, if you have enough. It might give me energy."

"You're right. I was a nurse before the war. I trained in Paris. I wish I'd had the proper instruments to care for your leg. I did remove the bullet, and the wound looks clean. Have it checked when you arrive back in England."

"Did you practice nursing long?" he asked.

"No. Not very. The war began. I wanted to stay and help with possible casualties, but my brother insisted upon moving to the country. I'm glad we did."

"So am I," Sloan smiled.

She looked at him, with a puzzled expression in her blue eyes and a slight smile on her lips.

"Lieutenant, are you implying that you're glad you've met me?"

"Indeed, I am. I know that sounds forward, but let me explain. Since I was a young man, I've dreamed of finding the perfect girl. I've fallen asleep almost every night thinking about her – what she would look like – what she would *be* like. When you opened your door, I saw her for the first time. The girl I've dreamt about is you."

Elise smiled and nervously giggled.

Please don't laugh. It's true. I was overwhelmed by your remarkable resemblance to my dreams. I wish I had time to become acquainted with you. I can almost guarantee that you're exactly as I expected you'd be."

"And what exactly have you expected?" she asked, shifting position on the camelback sofa, where she daintily sat. "How can you possibly know what I'm like?"

"Because, I'm telling the truth when I say I've known you all of my life," he answered.

"I'm finding that difficult to believe. So, all right, then. Describe me."

"I believe you're an innocent – naïve – sweet – tender hearted girl. I suspect you love animals, and babies. You're slow to anger, and then only if someone hurts you, or someone you love. You're very kind.. You dream of a house by the sea, and you love to grow and tend flowers. You're somewhat dreamy, but also blessed with good, common sense."

"*Mon Dieu*! Have you been reading my journal?" She laughed, softly. "I must admit, you describe me quite well."

"You see. I really *have* dreamed of you my whole life. Furthermore, I believe you're my soulmate."

"I think you go a bit too far with your fantasy. No matter how well you may think you know me, the truth is that we're scarcely acquainted."

"I wish we could change that, Elise."

"But, we can't, Lieutenant. The war takes precedence over all else. Two people who meet in a farmhouse in Bergues, France will be nothing more than a memory when this war is over. If the time were different, perhaps we'd be able to learn if there's any truth to your pretty dreams."

Sloan sighed. "Perhaps someday. But, can you honestly say you feel nothing unusual when near me? How can I be so certain that you're my soulmate, yet see no evidence that you share those same feelings?"

"I think you're attractive, and you seem kind. I like the sound of your voice. You're obviously intelligent, and well-spoken. But I've never had such dreams. I don't doubt your sincerity. I've just never given any thought to soulmates."

"Elise, I'm not making this up. I swear. I believe that people who're unhappy together are those who refuse to wait until the right person comes along. How do you explain the fact that I knew exactly what you'd be like?"

"You have an ideal, that's all. Whether I truly match your ideal would remain to be seen. My appearance makes you think this way."

"That's part of it, I admit. But it's who you are on the inside, too. I'm certain of that."

"Well, we won't ever know. It's growing late, and if you're going to be lucky enough to find a way back to England, you must go."

Sloan stood and tried his weight on the injured leg. It hurt, but he was able to walk. He approached Elise and took hold of her hands. They were lovely hands – slender and smooth. They felt cool.

I know I'm sounding awfully forward. I'm sorry for that, but you can't know what it's like to finally come face-to-face with someone you've dreamed about for so long. Is there – is there any chance that I could have a photograph of you? I'd carry it with me for good luck, when I'm flying lonely missions."

Elise looked surprised. She wasn't used to strangers asking for her photograph. But, he was a soldier. If she could ease the fear of battle in some, small, way, then, of course, she'd give him a picture. It was a small enough thing to ask. She dashed to the parlour, opened a drawer and returned with a small, black and white snapshot, probably taken by her brother at the farm. In the photo, she was standing on the front porch, her curls blowing in the wind, wearing a pretty, print frock. She held a small dog in her arms, and there was a lovely smile on her face. She handed it to Sloan.

"Elise. This is beautiful. I'll treasure it. I'll keep it next to my heart. I'll always remember your kindness. I'll always remember *you*, Elise. You'll be in my thoughts and prayers."

She looked down at the floor and blushed. Her long lashes nearly touched her cheeks.

"I'll remember you too, Lieutenant. What a strange conversation. I don't even know your name." She paused. "God speed and travel safely. I'll pray for you."

"I'm sorry. My name is Sloan. It's an old family name," he answered. He couldn't take his eyes from her exquisite face and was concentrating on memorizing her features.

"Thank you so much for your help. Until we meet again," he murmured, kissing her hand.

She looked at him, and their eyes met. Sloan knew he'd never forget her expression. Those stunning features sent desire through his heart.

"I shall see you again, Elise. There's no question about that. Please remember me with fondness, and keep safe." Then, he paused. Placing his arms round her, pulled her close and kissed her passionately. She was taken aback, but the emotion was so strong, she kissed him in return. Then, quickly turning, Sloan limped toward the entrance. He would have given anything to stay, or to take her with him.

Elise stood in the doorway, watching him go.

"Sloan," she murmured to herself. "Sloan." She felt exceedingly sad.

She would remember his name.

2

Soon after Sloan limped from the farmhouse, there was a second knock at Elise's door. She hesitated a moment, thinking perhaps the handsome Lieutenant had come back. Gingerly opening it a bit, she peered out. Three burley, intoxicated Nazis forced their way inside. They reeked of Schnapps and were boisterous. Speaking French badly, they shouted at her.

"You're in serious trouble. As representatives of the Third Reich, we're here to enforce the law. You've aided and abetted the enemy. We saw an English airman leave this house. Do you know the penalty for such a crime?"

"I did nothing wrong. I couldn't send him away. He was wounded by your guns. I bandaged his leg and sent him on his way. Anyway, you have no jurisdiction over me. I'm a French citizen," Elise stood taller and tried to keep her composure.

"We're taking control of this area. Soon we'll rule all of France. The English airman should have been turned in to the Bergues police," shouted one of the brutes. They all had swastikas on their shoulders. "You'll pay for this," he went on.

Elise didn't know what to believe. She'd heard nothing about the Germans having seized control of France, or even her Province. But what good would arguing do?

"I couldn't turn him in. I have no telephone in this house. I thought the best thing was to give him aid and ask him to leave."

"You were wrong, and you'll pay."

"What are you going to do to me?" Elise asked, trembling.

"We'll mete out your punishment ourselves. Be glad we aren't going to send you to an internment camp."

"What are you going to do to me?" Elise repeated.

"Come," said another of the men – a blonde, heavyset swine. "Follow me," he demanded, making his way toward the stairway.

"No. I'll not willingly go up those stairs with you," she answered firmly. Were they only trying to frighten her? Were they lying about her having broken the law?

"Then we'll take care of you here," shouted the third man, who was clearly, very, drunk.

He threw Elise onto the floor, and then, one by one, the disgusting creatures had their way with her. She'd never been touched by a man before, and what they did was savagery. First one, and then another ravaged her body, while two stood, watching and cheering. She was screaming and sobbing, but they had no empathy. On and on it went, until Elise wished she were dead. She willed her mind to a different place, hovering outside of her body, as if the assault were happening to somebody else. Finally, the attack ended. They buttoned their uniform pants and left. The last one out of the door kicked her in the ribs. She'd heard their names – Dieter, Wolfgang, and Pieter. She even knew which was which, if the time ever came to identify them. But what good could that do? They wouldn't be punished.

She lay on the floor, bleeding and weeping. It was inconceivable that such a thing had happened. Just an hour before she'd been sipping coffee with a kind Englishman, and now she'd been mauled by disgusting, filthy Nazis. She'd never feel clean again. Slowly, she stood. Her legs were shaking. She felt faint. All that mattered was being able to soak in a tub - to wash away the remnants of her attackers. She climbed the staircase, holding tightly to the banister, pulling herself from step to step. At last, she reached the top, unsteadily making her way to the toilet. She stripped off her clothing, mostly in tatters, and threw everything into the waste. When the bath was ready, Elise stepped into the tub, letting herself sink into the warm water. She was in shock and was terribly frightened. If she remained in the house, the three monsters might return. She had to leave. But where could she go? Scrubbing herself until nearly raw, Elise formulated a plan. When the water began to cool, she stood, dried herself and left the bath, walking in the direction of her brother's room.

Sorting through his clothing, she found everything she needed - one of his caps, a pair of over-all's he'd outgrown, a shirt and a jacket. Her own riding boots would suffice. Elise also packed a small bag – just enough for a few changes of clothing after she arrived in England. Having gathered all of the items, she took them to her own room and dressed. Pinning her hair into a knot, she tucked it beneath Josef's beret. When everything was complete, she looked into the mirror. If one didn't look too closely, she could pass for a male refugee. Darkness had fallen, and that was an advantage. If she could make it to the beaches, Elise was certain she'd be able to board one of the watercraft plucking people from the sand and water. It didn't matter if it was discovered that she was a woman once on British soil. Her camouflage was only necessary to prevent being accosted while in France. She moved outside to the yard and removed the dirt covering a hole. Josef had dug it, near the small stable. He'd hidden money and valuables there. Elise removed everything, and put it into a bag. Glancing toward the road, she saw that it was less crowded than it had been earlier. There were still many people, but the throng had thinned quite a bit. Then, she thought of her brother. What if he returned and found her missing? Shouldn't she tell someone her plan? Thinking for a moment, she ran to the farm adjacent to her own. An elderly lady lived there with her husband. Knocking on the door, she waited impatiently for a response. Brigitte, the owner of the farm, opened the door. When she saw Elise, dressed as she was, her hand flew to her heart, and she looked astonished.

"What in the world...."

"I know I look strange, Brigitte. I haven't time to explain. Something dreadful has happened. I'm going to try to get aboard one of the ships in the Channel and escape to England. I have to get away from here. I only wanted to let you know. If my brother should return, he won't know what's become of me. Please tell him where I've gone. "

"What – what's happened? Why are you leaving in such a rush?" Brigitte asked.

"Three German beasts crashed through my doorway. Need I say more? I was assaulted. It was the worst experience of my life. I have to leave. What if they come back? They may even tell their mates that a young woman is living alone at the farmhouse. I know it's supposed to be strictly forbidden for German soldiers to assault French women – in fact, the penalty is hanging – but what woman in her right mind would take the chance of reporting such swine to the police? I don't trust the authorities. I'd be terrified. And, of course, the monsters would deny everything anyway."

"Yes, yes, of course. I understand. Oh, God help us. What next? You poor girl. Is there nothing I can do to help you?"

"No. Nothing. Just watch for my brother. Oh, and please take my horse, Sasha. She's in the stable. You can take anything you want from the house, too. Now, I have to go. Pray I can board one of the vessels rescuing soldiers and refugees."

"Elise. When you reach England, go to Brighton. It isn't far from Dover. I have a dear friend who operates a boarding house there. Her name is Violette Beaulieu. I haven't seen her for years, but we knew each other in Paris, long ago. Give her my name. She'll help you. Can you remember that?"

"I can remember, yes. Violette Beaulieu. But where will I find her?"

"The name of her establishment is *Maison de Violette*. It's on the beach. God bless you, my dear Elise. You'll be in our prayers."

Brigitte hugged her. Elise turned and ran toward the Dunkirk beaches.

⚊⚊⚊

She didn't try to hide that she was a young lady. Although dressed in her brother's clothing, Elise knew her voice would give her away. But, she didn't advertise it either. She didn't expect to speak often, and her appearance blended with the multitude of others standing on the beaches, or wading into the water. Miraculously, it was only a short while before she was picked up by a large fishing trawler. Rescued people were packed in like sardines. There were about fifty others, but she found a corner and curled up, keeping to herself. Guns were being fired from Luftwaffe planes circling above, but because it was dark outside, there were less than there'd been earlier. What was, in reality, a rather short crossing, seemed to take forever.

Finally the vessel docked at Dover, and she set foot on English soil. She was so overcome with relief that tears fell from her eyes. Thank God she could speak English. That would make it much easier to navigate. People were being guided to trains. She boarded one intended for Brighton Beach, which she learned was less than 100 miles. It was very dark outside, as she climbed up the steps and entered the carriage. She pondered what to do about changing her clothing. Arriving at the boarding house dressed in such an odd way would look very strange. The answer was obvious. She stood, grasping her small valise, and made her way to the ladies' toilet. As the train rocked to and fro, she quickly took a frock from her bag. She stripped off her brother's clothing. Next came the boots, which would have to be abandoned, since there was no place to stow them. She had packed two pair of shoes - white sandals and black, patent slippers. The sandals would be fine with the floral print of the sleeveless chemise. Elise knew Brighton was a beach town, so the clothing would blend in perfectly. Looking in the tiny mirror, she saw that her hair was a snarled mess. There was a small brush in her bag, and she ran it through the tangled curls. They were damp from the sea breeze. Brushing the locks up into a knot, she secured them with a clip. She looked a bit more presentable. She stuffed the male clothing into the waste bin and set the boots under the sink. Perhaps someone would find them and put them to good use. Returning to her seat, Elise settled in, pretending to read a periodical someone had left behind. She was much too anxious to concentrate upon anything, except arriving at her destination.

When the conductor called out, "Brighton, next stop," she gathered her bag and walked to the front of the car. She waited until it came to a complete stop, and then exited the train. She felt confused about which way to go. Looking right and left, Elise tried to gauge if there was one area that looked more populated than another. There were lights on both sides. A porter on the station platform asked if he could be of assistance.

"Yes, please. Can you tell me where *Maison de Violette's* is located?"

"*Maison de Violette's*? Are you certain that's where you want to go?" he asked.

"Oui. Yes. I've come from France to stay there."

"You look like such a nice girl," he replied.

"Of course I'm a nice girl. Please, just tell me where I can find *Madame Violette's*."

"All right," he answered, rather sullenly. "Go to the walkway to the right." He pointed in that direction. "Keep walking until you come to the buildings. Go past the old chain pier. The house is painted lavender. There's a sign. I'd say it's ten or twelve houses down the beach."

"Thank you so much. You've been a great help."

He nodded his head and abruptly turned away. His manner surprised Elise. Were all of the people in Brighton so unfriendly? Finding the walkway, she began her trek. Counting the buildings, while moving along, a pretty, lavender house came into view. It was just as the man had described. Three stories, with lights in most of the windows, vines climbed the sides. Elise was almost certain they were morning glories. "What an enchanting place," she thought to herself. There was a white picket fence surrounding the front, with a lovely arbor over the gate. Unlatching the gate, she approached the doorway. Music and laughter could be heard. The boarders must have been having a party. Rapping gently, Elise waited. It wasn't long before the door was opened by a platinum-haired, sophisticated-looking woman.

"Are you by chance Violette Beaulieu?" Elise asked.

"Yes. Who, may I ask, are you?"

"My name is Elise Lisak. I've come from France. My neighbour, Brigitte Meursault, told me where to find you. She said you would give me a room and protection."

"Ah, my old friend Brigitte. I haven't heard from her in a long while. We knew each other as innocent girls in Paris. Do come inside. Forgive the loud noise. Sometimes my house becomes a bit unruly."

Elise followed the woman inside. She was dressed in deep lilac and wore a necklace of large amethysts, with matching drop earrings. Elise could see, in the light, that Madame Violette was quite lovely. The room adjacent to the entry was filled to over-flowing with young men and lovely, youthful ladies. They were all dressed in elaborate evening wear. A tune was playing on the Victrola, and couples were dancing very close to one another. It was the strangest boarding house Elise had ever seen. Violette took her to a small room, resembling an office, although it was decorated with purple velvet chairs and wallpaper with violets scattered upon it. She motioned for Elise to sit in one of the gilt-edged chairs.

"So. Brigitte suggested that you come to me? You're certainly a stunning creature. I'm sure you have the potential to increase my profits considerably. Have you any experience?" she asked.

"Experience? Living in a boarding house? No Madam. I have escaped from France because of the Germans. I had my own home, shared with my brother. I was forced to leave. I was - I was assaulted by a group of Nazi soldiers – right in my own home. I was frightened they might return. I went to the beaches at Dunkirk and joined the refugees. Before I left, I spoke with my neighbour, Brigitte. She told me she knew you and that you had a house in Brighton."

"She said nothing else?"

"Just that she was certain you would offer me refuge."

"My dear young lady, I'm afraid you've misunderstood. My home is not a boarding house. I do, however, run a business here. It's for the entertainment of gentlemen. Do you understand what I mean?"

Elise's face turned scarlet. The pieces of the puzzle fell into place. No wonder the porter at the railway station had looked at her suspiciously. No wonder the people whom she thought were boarders were dancing so closely and dressed in such a risqué manner. The house was a brothel.

"Oh, Madame Violette. I am so sorry. I wasn't told the full story. Did Brigitte know of your - your business?"

"Perhaps not. I may not have made that perfectly clear. I hope you aren't too shocked. I run a very upscale establishment. You'll not see any riff-raff here. My employees are of the highest caliber. I don't suppose you wish to join my working girls?"

"Oh, no, no. I apologize. I don't mean to insult you. What you choose to do is your own private concern. But I could never be - well - I simply couldn't."

"I understand perfectly. You look very young and inexperienced. Quite shy, in fact. I'm terribly sorry you endured such an ordeal with the soldiers. I wouldn't welcome such vile pigs to my establishment. Of course you felt the need to run. I'm a kind woman and will be happy to help you. I have extra space. You're welcome to a room here, and I don't need your money. Stay as long as you like. I'll explain to the other ladies. You'll find they're not such a bad lot. Some have experienced tragedies similar to yours. If you don't want to be bothered, I'll make it clear that no one should annoy you."

"I wouldn't want to hurt anyone's feelings. I'm not certain I'd be welcomed by your other - um - guests."

"Elise, they're not guests. They work here. But they aren't monsters. They have a need to earn an income, and they do very well here. It isn't easy for a woman to make a decent wage in our society."

"I understand. I'm grateful for your offer of help. I'd like to accept it, at least for a short while, until I can sort myself out. You're being very generous to me. I don't know where else I would go. I do have money to pay for my room and board."

"That isn't necessary. I'm a French woman, too, although I've been an English citizen for years. I'm patriotic. I'd like to do something to lend support during this dreadful war."

"Then I do accept your offer. Thank you. I'll try not to be a bother. Can you tell me the routine of the house, so I'm aware of how to behave?"

"Certainly. Breakfast is quite late. The girls generally don't wake early, due to entertaining until the wee hours. The dining room table is set from nine to eleven o'clock; luncheon is served, buffet style, from noon until two; we dine at six o'clock in the evening. Festivities generally begin later. We welcome visitors any time after eight o'clock at night. Tea is also served at three o'clock in the afternoon. I'll show you the layout when I take you to your sleeping room. Of course, you're free to come and go as you please. I expect that you not to speak about the sort of business I operate. It's well-known in town, and the authorities even avail themselves of my services, but it's not spoken about. I simply say that I operate a gentleman's club, where men can find a place to smoke cigars, play poker, drink fine whiskey and dance with lovely women."

"I understand," Elise gulped. "I would never say anything to harm your business."

Violette smiled. "It would be difficult to harm my business, *Mon Cherie*. My house is considered one of the finest in all southeast England. But I appreciate your consideration. Have you any other questions?"

"I can think of nothing at the moment. Again, thank you. If you could show me to my room, I'd appreciate it. I'm very tired. It's been a long, arduous day."

"Of course. Come with me," Violette answered, rising from her chair. Elise followed, feeling a bit strange as she passed the drawing room again. There were fewer couples than before. She and Madame Violette climbed the staircase and walked down a long hallway. The house was quite large. Violette led her to an empty room at the very end, decorated in the same lavender as the house's exterior. The cover on the bed was a duplicate of the wallpaper in Violette's office. Draperies matched. A bath was connected to the room, which pleased Elise greatly. She wouldn't have to worry about sharing with one or more of the working ladies. She smiled and turned to her hostess.

"This is lovely. I feel very fortunate. I'll be most comfortable here. You're so kind."

"I'm glad you like it. It's actually my best room. I keep it for special guests. I thought you would prefer your own loo, as they say in England."

"Loo?"

"Yes. You need to learn their little colloquialisms. Loo is an oft-used word for toilet."

"Ah — I'll remember that. Yes, I *do* like having my own, private loo," Elise smiled.

"Right then. Have a good rest. I promise no one will disturb you. I'll explain the situation to my girls. Don't be frightened. They'll be kind to you."

With that, Violette turned and left the room. Elise took a deep breath and folded back the bed covers. In a moment she'd run a bath and then collapse under the soft, down-filled comforter. She'd worry about everything else in the morning.

3

Elise had been living at *Maison de Violette* three months when she realized she was pregnant. At first she attributed the lack of her monthly curse to the trauma of the assault, followed by the stress of relocation to England. However, other symptoms started to pop up. She'd come to view Violette as a mother figure – caring, concerned and understanding of Elise's deep-seated pain. So, she was the obvious person to talk with about pregnancy fears.

After teatime she tapped gently on Violette's office door. She was immediately told to enter. Violette was dressed in a variation of her usual colour – a purple gown with soft lace ruffles at the neckline. Elise wore a simple, yellow linen frock, with long sleeves and a loose waistline. She had replenished her wardrobe with a shopping trip, shortly after her arrival in Brighton. Thank goodness, the frocks she'd purchased were mostly chemise-style. There wasn't a hint of pregnancy, yet, but if her fears were realized, she would need clothing that wasn't form-fitting. After she sat down in Violette's office, she was hesitant about how to broach the subject. However, from the moment Violette had heard about the attack, she'd been worried about just such an outcome. If Elise hadn't found the words, Violette would have.

"Violette, I may be in a terrible predicament. I'm so uninformed. I lost my mother at an early age, and no one has ever explained things I should know. I'm afraid I'm pregnant. Until what happened to me in the farmhouse, I'd never been intimate with a man. It never crossed my mind that a baby could result from such violence. I'm terrified. Oh, Madame Violette, please tell me I'm being an innocent fool."

"All right, *Mon Cherie*, let's chat. Obviously the beasts who assaulted you didn't use any protection. Do you know what I mean?"

"Yes, I do. No - no - none of them did."

"The filthy swine! Well, then it *is* entirely possible that you're going to have a baby. Do you remember when you had your last monthly?"

"I'd have to look at a calendar. It was before those men attacked me. I'm sure of that. Perhaps about two weeks before. I remember running out of necessary supplies. I'd intended to go to the village to buy more. My curse never came. I was so anxious about everything else, it completely slipped my mind. But all of a sudden, today I remembered."

"How are you feeling? Are you at all ill?" asked Violette.

"For the last few weeks, I've been rather nauseous in the mornings. Sometimes I feel a bit dizzy. Oh - and my, my, breasts…"

"Yes, dear. Your breasts. Are they tender and swollen?"

"Oh yes. Is that a sign, too?"

"Yes, I'm afraid so, Elise."

"What am I going to do? I'm so frightened."

"We have to find out for certain. You need to see a physician."

"A doctor? Oh - I couldn't. How perfectly revolting."

"It's the only way you can be absolutely certain. After we have the answer, we can discuss plans."

"But where would I find a physician?"

"That's no problem. I have a man who calls regularly to check my girls. This sort of establishment calls for very strict health assessments. Each girl is examined monthly. The doctor is a very kind gentleman. You needn't be frightened. I'll ring him, and he'll pay a visit. I'll stay with you. You were a nurse, Elise. Surely you know what a gynecological examination is?"

"Yes. I do. It's just that I've never had one. It seems so – so – embarrassing."

"Dr. Rice is very professional. You won't be embarrassed. Go back to your room. I'll let you know when he'll be here."

Elise left Violette's office, relieved to have allowed the older woman to help her, but still terrified. Having a baby, when she wasn't married, was bad enough. But to have become an expectant mother in such a deplorable way – not to know which of three men had impregnated her - was repugnant.

By nightfall, Elise knew with certainty. Violette had been right. Dr. Rice was a kindly, older gentleman. Violette made it clear to him that the lovely, French girl was not one of her employees. With Elise's permission, she shared the tragic story of how she'd come to be in such a wretched state. It was clear that the doctor was infuriated when he learned about Elise's dreadful ordeal. He was very gentle and didn't make her feel ashamed. Unfortunately, he couldn't alter reality. She was pregnant, nearly thirteen weeks. She tried to keep her composure, but when he left, she turned her head into the pillow, sobbing pitifully. Violette sat beside the poor girl, trying to calm her.

"You aren't alone, Elise. I'm here with you. You'll get through this. I know it's a terrible situation. But we have to talk calmly. We must make plans and decisions."

"What sort of decisions? What plans?" Elise sobbed. "Why is God doing this to me? What did I do to bring on his wrath? I'm not a bad person. Why, why Violette?"

"There aren't any answers. You need to accept that there are reasons for all things – even something as frightening as what you're going through. You have to move beyond the past. What do you want to do about this?"

"What do you mean? What *can* I do about it? I'm going to have a baby. It seems impossible, but that's the way it is. I don't know how I can bear it."

"Would you want to do something to rid yourself of this child?" Violette asked.

"Rid myself of it? What do you mean? You aren't speaking of – of –an operation?"

"Yes. Women *do* have them. I can make certain you'd be cared for by a physician - not a butcher."

"Oh, but Violette, that's murder. I'd be condemned to Hell for eternity."

"Some people believe that, yes. Others don't. Because of the way you became pregnant, I'm not certain the church would think you should be forced to carry the baby to term. Would you want to speak with a Priest?"

"No. Even if it weren't considered evil, I just don't think I could ever do such a thing. It isn't the child's fault. The baby is innocent. My God, Violette, I know enough from my nurse's training. The baby already has a tiny heartbeat. Why should it be destroyed because it was conceived in such a crude, wicked way? All babies deserve to be loved. The poor little one in my womb will face a hard enough life as it is - never knowing who its father is — not being wanted. But I don't believe I have the right to choose whether it lives at all. Do you understand?"

"Yes, *Mon Cherie*. I do understand. I'm not telling you what you should do. I simply want you to be aware of your options."

"No — let's move on to other options. I don't want to consider that one."

"All right. Then I want you to know that you're perfectly welcome to stay here as long as you wish. I told you that when you first came to Brighton. It's more important now. You certainly can't be alone. You'll have the best care."

"What will people say? What will they think? I know the ladies who work here will be kind. But, how can I walk down the street?"

"You'll wear a wedding ring. You haven't been here long enough to have met many people. I've already told others that you're a niece of mine from France, who escaped the Nazis. Now, I'll add that your husband was killed at Dunkirk. With a baby on the way, the fictitious husband will be added. No one will think you're one of my girls. Don't fret about that. Remember, you're my niece. I know most everyone in this town. Believe it or not, most are friendly to me. While wives don't invite me for tea, they don't turn their heads when I walk by, either. It's very unlikely anyone would believe you're anything but what you appear to be— a sweet, innocent girl, whose life has been turned upside down because of this ghastly war."

"Thank you, Violette. I'm so fortunate to have found you. Now that this pregnancy has happened, thank God I got out of France. I can't imagine what would have become of me."

"Yes, that's true. So. The next question is what to do when the baby is born? I'd understand if you didn't want to keep it."

"But where would it go, if I didn't keep it?"

"There are always families who can't have children of their own. You could make arrangements to have the child adopted. The Catholic Church is known to work with such families. I don't think you'd have much difficulty finding loving parents for him or her."

"Oh Violette. It's so difficult to know, isn't it? While I loath those men who assaulted me, I wonder if I can carry a baby inside of me for nine months, and then just pass it over to someone else, like a piece of merchandise? Have you ever had children?"

"Yes, I have. I was married before I opened my business. My husband was killed at Ypres, during the Great War. I had a son, Yves. We lived in Paris. I was a designer of hats. When he was three years old, he came down with the deadly flu sweeping the globe in 1918. I lost him, and it broke my heart. I went to London. I was a pretty, young girl, not yet twenty-three, but nothing mattered to me anymore. It was easy to find work in an upscale house. I became a great favorite. French girls always find favor. Brighton was a popular get-a-way. I knew I could establish my own business here, making a good income. I'd learned a lot, of course. That was in 1934. I'd reached an age where I was able to assume the responsibilities of ownership, and that's what I did. Anyway, *Mon Cherie*, yes, I know what it's like to give birth. I understand how a woman feels when she becomes a mother. There's nothing to compare with it. I'm like you. Giving a child up would have been awfully hard for me. Of course my situation was different. Only you can decide what's right for you."

"I suppose I don't need to make that decision right now. I have many months ahead of me. This is all so shocking. I'm very frightened."

"There's nothing to be frightened about. One way or another it will work out. Whatever you decide, you'll know in your heart it's the right choice."

4

1940-1941

Besides the terror associated with learning that she was expecting a baby, the war became more frightening and real. In June, Paris had fallen to the Germans. Elise found it nearly impossible to imagine the German flag flying over the Place de la Concorde. She was so pleased about having made the decision to escape France. It was hard to picture the village of Bergues, so near their little farm, under Nazi occupation. She wondered if the monsters who'd stormed the house now held positions of authority in the area that she and her brother had once considered a haven of peace.

In midsummer, terrible air battles began. English and German planes fought for supremacy in the skies over the English Channel and eventually London itself. What became known as the Blitz turned the capital city into a nightmare of carnage. Whole blocks were completely destroyed. Businesses and homes became piles of rubble, and streets were filled with shattered glass. On Sunday, December 29th, there was intense firebombing in the East of London. St. Paul's Cathedral stood in the midst of the wreckage, but amazingly, it escaped severe damage and became an inspiration to residents of the besieged city. Lives were lost, and hospitals overflowed with the wounded. The stories filtering back to Brighton were heartbreaking. Citizens lived in constant fear, and Anderson shelters became their second homes. Air raids often began as soon as darkness fell and continued throughout the long, dark nights, until dawn appeared in the eastern sky. The odor of cordite filled the air, and no one was allowed to venture out of doors without a gas mask draped over their shoulder. Elise read every line in the newspapers. It was ghastly and terrifying. She wondered if her brother, Josef, was a part of it.

Other cities in England also experienced horror. Only fifty miles from Brighton, where Elise suffered her own anxiety and despair, Southampton was struck. The entire High Street was completely obliterated. The worst came at the end of November, when fires from detonated bombs were easily seen at *Maison de Violette*. It was said that the flames were visible as far away as the coast of France.

As months rolled by, Elise's pregnancy advanced. She wore a gold wedding band and held her head high. She also changed her surname to one sounding more French. She called herself Elise de Baier. The people of Brighton grew to know her, and everyone was instantly attracted to her beauty and sweetness. She became involved with the war effort, knitting socks and jumpers for soldiers. In addition, she was active in her local parish, taking part in jumble sales and helping prepare meals for the poor. People admired Elise's obvious kindness and compassion. No one questioned that she was a grieving widow, facing motherhood alone. The tale was told so many times, Elise began to believe it herself. The first time she felt the baby move, she knew she couldn't give it up for adoption. The circumstances surrounding the child's conception became more and more insignificant. Elise believed that although the rape was the worst nightmare she could have imagined, God had created the tiny life in her womb as a reward for such terrible degradation.

Deep inside, she wondered if she could ever stand the touch of a man again. There was no question that the awful, physical attack had left deep scars on her psyche. She had no desire to ever marry, nor to feel the warmth of a decent man's embrace. She was wary of men, believing they all wanted the same thing from a woman. She reflected on her brother, Josef, and thought he was the only man she could ever trust. Living at a brothel didn't help. She witnessed men coming and going, and was well-aware that many were supposed to be upstanding husbands in the community.

Occasionally, she thought about the handsome RAF pilot who'd come to her home the same day the German soldiers paid their visit. She still remembered his name. Sloan. She always smiled when he came to mind. He'd been so absolutely certain they were soulmates. It was a silly fantasy, yet he'd been unequivocally definite. She wondered if she'd shy away from him, too, if they ever met again. There wasn't any doubt in her mind that if he knew what had happened to the virginal, shy girl he'd met on a rainy day in the French countryside, he'd be repulsed. That hadn't figured into his whimsical illusion. Obviously the man was a dreamer. But the grim reality of her assault would strip away his delusions of perfection. She firmly believed it would leave him, or any man, with feelings of distaste toward her. He was clearly the sort who worshipped perfection and hated defects or flaws. So when Sloan entered her mind, she chased away his memory. She'd shrug her pretty shoulders and imagine the look on his face when told how she'd been defiled. It was good that they would never meet again.

***

Ironically, during the times Elise was thinking about Sloan, she was on his mind, too. In fact, she was on his mind a lot of the time. He could scarcely get her out of his thoughts. He carried her picture with him, always in his breast pocket, close to his heart. Finally, in the early months of 1941, when it had been nearly a year since he'd so briefly and randomly met her, Sloan decided he could no longer go on pretending he hadn't changed as a result of their encounter.

Therefore Anne Whitfield received a letter from him in the summer of 1941. He'd been back at his base in England after Dunkirk, but was now stationed in Africa. Anne wondered how long it would be before she saw him again. She expected this latest letter to be another of his usual missives, filled with talk of aircraft– spitfires and hurricanes – but this one was vastly different. He was releasing her from their engagement. Her hands shook as she read.

He told her that he'd purposely waited over a year to write. It wasn't fair, he said, for her to continue believing they had a future together after the war. His thoughts had taken a completely different turn. He admitted that what he was about to tell her would undoubtedly cause Anne to think he was reckless and immature. Nonetheless, he believed that he was honourable, and the feelings he had were so strong that he had to share them with her. All he could do was hope that the years they'd spent as childhood companions would keep their friendship intact. He said he didn't want to lose what they'd always shared. But, he didn't love her the way a man should love the woman he wanted to marry. He thought of her as a sister – nothing more. Certainly a beautiful, sweet sister, but a sister nonetheless.

Then he launched into an account of the day he'd wounded his leg near Dunkirk and of a beautiful French girl who'd provided aid. It was a romantic anecdote, but Anne found it difficult to believe that he'd alter his life's plan because of something so trivial. Her heart ached when he described the girl – Elise – and try as she might, she couldn't help but feel intense envy when she read his description of golden curls and an angelic face. Anne had always been told that she was a rare beauty, but now she was reading a letter from the only man she'd ever loved, telling her he'd found a girl he thought even lovelier. He said Elise was his soulmate. Anne put her head down and sobbed. It didn't seem possible that such a thing was happening. Not once in her entire life had she thought of marriage to any man besides Sloan. She'd met many men in her life – had gone through a London Season and been presented to the King. There'd been no shortage of suitors. But never had she been remotely interested in the multitude of young men who'd worn a path to her parent's doorway.

Sloan's letter spoke of love, as though she didn't know what it was. Of course she did. When Sloan returned from Oxford, the childish admiration she'd always felt, had subtly changed to a deeper and different sort of feeling. She knew what love was, because it was what she felt for Sloan - what she would always feel for him. And now he was throwing her away, for a fantasy about a French farm girl. The entire muddle was rubbish. She tore the letter to shreds and stuffed it in her waste bin.

Anne fell upon her bed and sobbed hysterically. She felt as though someone had opened her chest and ripped out her heart. Heartbreak turned to anger, and anger to rage. She pounded the pillow with her small fists and mumbled words to herself.

"How dare he? How *dare* he? He wants to throw me over for some farm girl from the French countryside. My God! Has he lost his mind? This can't be happening. I have to think this through. I can't let anger get in the way of intelligent thinking. I need to find a way – develop a plan. I'll do whatever it takes. He'll pay for what he's doing. I want him to hurt as much as I'm hurting. I want his life to be ruined. He'll be begging my forgiveness someday."

Sloan sincerely cared for Anne. But, love had become a very serious matter. He didn't view it lightly. He'd always had the dream about his soulmate, never quite believing she existed. But, now fate had placed him at that small farmhouse near Bergues, and everything had changed. He knew that when he told his parents what had happened they'd consider it immature and senseless. "Such things don't happen in the real world," he'd be told. He'd been fond of Anne as a child, with the sort of affection often existing between small children. But he'd never told her he loved her. She'd been a sweet playmate. Nothing more. He was not in the slightest degree in love with her. Anne was dark-haired, and he preferred blondes; brunette beauty held no charm for him. He liked gentle, fair-haired women. A tender-heart was essential. Anne would never be described that way. She was strong-willed and a bit self-absorbed. Why, oh why had he proposed to her?

Before leaving for the war, he'd visited Anne at her home, *Meadowlands,* to say goodbye. He remembered she'd been charming and picturesque as she stood next to the lilac trees. He told her he'd never see a lilac again without thinking of her. But that didn't mean he loved her. He'd bent down and brushed her cheek with his lips, but it was not a lover's kiss. He felt he was saying goodbye to his sister. Yet – yet, he was leaving for the war and had no idea how long he'd be gone. He was well-aware that she cared deeply for him. He didn't want to go away with nothing to look forward to. Sloan knew it was foolish to continue thinking about his soulmate. So, in a moment of weakness, he'd asked Anne to marry him. She'd immediately responded with genuinely thrilled acceptance. On that day, wedding plans seemed far, far away. She promised to wait for him, no matter how long it took and to write every day. It felt good to know he had a girl at home, whose letters would follow him into battle. She was still a child then – only seventeen years old.

One of the girls who worked at *Maison de Violette* became Elise's friend. Although they were from vastly different backgrounds, they bonded. Most of the others were nice to her, and only a few made her feel uneasy. There were two she didn't like very much. She suspected it was jealousy on their part, because Madame Violette gave her free room and board. She didn't have overt trouble with them and simply stayed out of their way. Her friend's name was Giselle Dupris, also an escapee from German occupied France. Giselle, however, had already been a 'working girl' when she left France. Her parents were deceased and, unlike Elise, who had a brother to depend upon, Giselle had no one. Hence, she'd found a home in a Paris pleasure palace when only sixteen. Despite her occupation, she was a deeply spiritual person. She attended Mass daily and wore a lovely gold cross round her swan-like neck. Giselle had her own beliefs when it came to the way she earned an income and felt no shame.

Both girls loved the countryside and were passionate animal-lovers. They each dreamed of a cottage by the sea, where they could surround themselves with shelves of books, and a garden filled with flowers. While Elise was privileged to have more education than Giselle, the latter was by no means unintelligent. On quiet days they could be found sitting side by side on the bench behind *Maison de Violette,* reading poetry, or discussing the meaning of bible passages. Elise's faith had always been strong. However, after the shock she'd endured, her belief was shaken. Giselle helped her sort through many doubts.

As their friendship progressed, Elise divulged the wretched details of her assault. Giselle said if she ever came face-to-face with one of the disgusting men who'd committed the crime, she'd neuter him. It was the first time Elise had laughed when speaking about the ordeal. Giselle longed to find a good man, who wouldn't judge her poorly. At heart, she'd always wanted to be a wife and mother. Because of her striking appearance, if a person had met her in an upper-class environment, they'd never guess she earned her living in a disreputable way. She had long, dark hair and blue-green eyes. Her skin was like creamy porcelain, with cheeks the colour of baby-pink roses. Elise thought she resembled the English cinema actress Vivien Leigh, although her hair was darker. Occasionally Giselle would share her fantasies with Elise, admitting her greatest wish was to immigrate to America, abandon the life she'd lived since the age of sixteen, meet a respectable man and marry. She would be a virtuous and proper wife. Elise would smile, telling her friend that nothing was impossible.

Elise's baby was due at the end of February. Madame Violette treated her with the utmost kindness and made certain she followed all of the doctor's orders. Arrangements were made for the child to be born in hospital, and Elise kept a small bag packed with all necessities, so she'd be fully prepared when the time came. She'd grown quite large and was uncomfortable, but made every effort not to complain. She was so grateful not to be facing childbirth alone. Even with support, she was still afraid and couldn't imagine being a mother. Since making the decision to keep the baby, Elise had read everything she could find about child-rearing. It seemed like a difficult task. Not having a husband only made the prospect more frightening. It was important that she do it well. She also prayed the infant wouldn't resemble its sire. She absolutely couldn't use the word 'father' for the monster who'd contributed to the baby's conception. All three of the brutes were fair-haired, and so was Elise. Thus, she expected a blonde child. Unless, by some miracle, her own father's genes were inherited, since he'd had very dark hair, brown eyes, and olive skin. It wouldn't be long until she knew.

5

1941

On February 10, 1941, Elise gave birth to a healthy, baby girl. She had flaxen hair and beautiful brown eyes. So, while she'd not inherited her grandfather's dark tresses, she *had* become heir to his warm gaze. She was named Chloe Arabella de Baier. The moment the nurse placed her into Elise's arms, there was no question about whether she'd made the right decision. She could never have allowed anyone else to be the precious infant's mother. It didn't matter in the least how Chloe had been given life. Her sweet face nearly erased Elise's bitter memories, and she could only see the present and future.

After three days in hospital, she brought the baby back to *Maison de Violette.* While that had always been the plan, and Elise hadn't worried about raising an infant in such surroundings, suddenly her viewpoint shifted. What the blazes had she been thinking? The first few months wouldn't be so worrisome, but she abruptly came to the realization that her little girl shouldn't be brought up in a house of ill-repute. She was hesitant about discussing the matter with Madame Violette, who'd been so kind and caring throughout the pregnancy. The last thing Elise wanted was to offend her. But the welfare of her child was of paramount importance. She would do whatever was necessary. Even more upsetting was the fact that Elise had no idea where she and Chloe could go. She had some money, but not enough to pay for anything beyond a low-cost bed-sit. That was no way to raise a child.

She went to Giselle. Her friend immediately understood and agreed wholeheartedly that Chloe couldn't begin life surrounded by ladies of the night. The two talked at length, and Giselle told Elise to wait a few days before she spoke to Violette. Giselle had an idea, but wanted to think it through carefully. She had to make certain it was plausible. Elise agreed, but tossed and turned trying desperately to think of some alternative. She considered finding employment, so she could pay for a better place to live, but who would care for Chloe? She could send her to board with a kind family, but she had such deep love for the baby and hated the idea of being forced to part with her.

Finally Giselle came to her room with a proposed solution. She'd decided to find a different, respectable way to earn a living, away from Brighton. As soon as she found employment in another village, Elise and Chloe would join her. They could all share a small cottage wherever Giselle found work. Elise was dumbfounded. It was hard to fathom that her friend might change her entire life to ensure Chloe had a proper upbringing. She voiced her feelings, but Giselle shrugged them off.

"Elise, I'm more than ready for a new life. I was a foolish child when I went to Paris. Then, I found myself trapped. I never should have become involved in this sort of work. But what could I have done? I was poor, with no one to guide me. It happened slowly. At first I was simply a sort-of maid. Then, they offered me a way to make a lot of money. I was stupid. But things have changed. The war has made an incredible difference. A lot of women have gone to work in factories and the like. Personally, I'd rather find work in domestic service. I believe that's possible, because now women have other options. Ladies who were employed in great houses have left for more lucrative jobs. I know factories pay more, but I can't picture myself doing that sort of labour. I've always loved beautiful things and, if I can't own them, I'd enjoy working among them. I'd also learn a lot." Giselle laughed. "I might even add some refinement, which would further my dreams of finding a respectable husband."

"You don't need refinement, Giselle. But, it's awfully hard for me to agree to this plan. How can I allow you to support Chloe and me? I *do* have some money and, of course, I'm willing to share what I have with you. Perhaps we could make it work until Chloe is old enough for school. Then I could find a job too – at least part-time."

"Yes. You see, I think it's a fine plan. Even if you don't agree, I'm going to leave *Maison de Violette*. I've been thinking about this for a long time. But, I'd so much rather have a friend come with me, to share a cottage. Perhaps we could find the one we've dreamed about. Who knows? Perhaps even near the sea. Oh say you'll do it, Elise."

"Of course I'd love to. How will we go about it?"

"I'll go first, and search for a position. When I've found a job and a cottage, I'll post you. Then, you and Chloe will join me."

"It sounds so wonderful. Where are you thinking of searching?"

"I've already researched the locations of some of the large estates on the southeast coast. I could enquire by letter but, to be perfectly honest, I think it would be wiser to present myself in person. I don't mean to sound self-centered, but since God has blessed me with attractive features, I'll put them to good use." She laughed again. "That's what I've been doing for years now, isn't it? I'll just present myself in a different way. The hair will go into a bun, and I'll be plain and modest in my dress. I know the aristocracy prefers an employee who gives a pleasant, subdued appearance. And, I should think a French accent might be attractive. I'll take anything they offer – parlour-maid, whatever."

"Giselle, I don't think you'll have any trouble finding a position. You may be surprised. The only problem I can see is your lack of a reference. The sort of employer you're talking about usually wants a recommendation."

"Well, I've only recently come to England from France. Because of the war. How does anyone know that I didn't have a fine position in my own Country? Perhaps my former employers were sent to an internment camp. That would explain why I don't have a letter from them."

"I've told you before that anything is possible," Elise smiled. "I think your explanation is excellent."

"All right, dear friend. I'll speak to Violette and begin to pack my bag. We'll start a brand, new life together.

By June 1941, Giselle Dupris and Elise de Baier were firmly ensconced in a small, stone cottage. It sat in a quaint village named Thornton-on-Sea. Neither of them had ever heard of it before. Giselle had made a journey around the entire southeastern coastline, stopping at every house of a size to employ a staff of servants. It hadn't been easy. There were a couple of residences offering the position of cook's helper, and she wasn't above accepting such work. But, she wanted to make certain something better wasn't available. Finally, she'd come to Thornton-on-Sea. It was a charming seaside town, about one hundred miles past Brighton. The ancient manor of *Highcroft Hall* dominated the picturesque hamlet. It was built of red brick, covered in thick, green Ivy and wisteria. The main house was massive, with a pillared veranda that ran the length of the façade. At either end there were wings extending to the front. Giselle had never seen anyplace so beautiful. It sat high on a hill, over-looking the sea, and there were acres and acres of rolling green parkland, with rolling mounds in the distance. The moment she'd seen the exquisite mansion and its bucolic setting, she'd been enchanted and wondered if she might be lucky enough to find employment there.

A very proper English gentleman opened the door when she knocked. His name was Richmond, and he was the butler. He was dressed in the traditional black, suit all butlers wear. Giselle wore a grey, shirtwaist dress, with a belted skirt that fell to her calves. She'd also donned short white gloves and a simple hat. Richmond asked her to enter. Then he summoned Mrs. Littleton, the housekeeper. He introduced Giselle and said she was searching for employment in a great house. Mrs. Littleton was very kind. She took Giselle into her small office and offered a cup of tea. Once they were settled, a discussion ensued about Giselle's previous experience. Giselle managed to answer the questions with her previously rehearsed lines, followed by the fact that she had excellent skills in a wide variety of tasks, including housekeeping, care of fragile items, setting a formal table and the personal toilette of ladies. The latter appealed greatly, as Lady Celia Thornton, the Countess at *Highcroft Hall,* was searching for a lady's maid. The lovely, young French woman, sitting in front of Mrs. Littleton, was a rare find. Mrs. Littleton knew Lady Celia would adore having a French accent in her boudoir. While neither Lord

Rowan nor Lady Celia put on airs, they weren't above adding a pretty, French girl to their staff. Mrs. Littleton made arrangements for Giselle to speak privately with the countess.

The day turned out to be a long one, but in the end, Giselle walked away from *Highcroft Hall* over-the-moon. Lady Celia had hired her, at better wages than she'd anticipated, and told her she could begin in two weeks. That allowed Giselle time to find a place to live and to summon Elise and Chloe.

She rose early the next morning and set about looking for a cottage to lease. There were no advertisements in the local newspaper, so she visited a property agent's office. While standing on the street, outside of the large window, displaying pictures of homes, she spotted a photo of a sweet cottage. It was surrounded by a picket fence. A typical English garden dominated the entrance. It resembled the cottage she and Elise had day-dreamed about. Giselle was certain it wouldn't be available to them, because it was probably not for lease, or the price would be prohibitive. Before Giselle had left Brighton, the two friends had put pen to paper, figuring how much they could afford. Giselle's wages had turned out to be much better than hoped for, but the cottage looked as though its price would be very dear. Entering the office, she spied a middle-aged woman, sitting behind a desk, doing paperwork. She glanced up and smiled. Giselle introduced herself, and the other woman acted in kind.

"My name is Paula Jordan. I'm the manager here. I'll be happy to help you. I'm very familiar with the cottage you're talking about — the one in the window. It's a little jewel."

"I don't suppose it can be let?" Giselle asked.

"Yes — yes, it can be. It was owned by an elderly lady. She's passed on. Her heirs are quite flexible. They'd let it, or it can be bought. Would you like to see it?"

"Not until I know what the cost would be. I'm interested for a widowed friend of mine and her daughter — and, of course, for me. We're on a rigid budget, so there's no point in seeing it, if it isn't in our price range."

"I understand," replied Mrs. Jordan. "Let me get the folder with particulars. We can go over them."

She opened a drawer and, after a moment, pulled out a file with the cottage's address printed on a label at the top. Instead of a street number, it simply had a name – '*No Regrets*'. Giselle laughed. She liked the name. Mrs. Jordan chuckled along with her.

"Everyone around here is familiar with the cottage. For as long as I can recall that's been the name. As I said, the previous owner was older. She and her husband originally purchased and named it. I suppose it could be changed, if you wanted something else. I don't think the heirs care one way or the other."

"Actually, I think it might fit us perfectly," Giselle smiled. "Since we're starting a new life, it seems appropriate."

"From your charming accent, I suspect you're from France?" Mrs. Jordan said.

"Yes. We both were fortunate to escape during the Dunkirk evacuations. How horrible it's all become. My friend lost her husband. She was in early pregnancy. Since then, she's had a lovely daughter, who's taken away some of the anguish. I didn't leave any family behind. We met in Brighton, and now I've accepted employment at *Highcroft Hall,* as a lady's maid. It seems a charming home, and I feel fortunate."

"*Highcroft Hall.* Yes, it is a splendid estate. You'll find that the Thorntons are extremely nice people. They have a son, but of course, he's away fighting, as are all men between eighteen and forty. I believe he's in Africa. I should think it would be a lovely place to work. You'll find the village very welcoming. Of course, it's small, but we have most everything one needs. What with rationing, there isn't too much one can buy anyway, is there?" she exclaimed, ruefully.

"No. I think the village is charming and quaint. I like the size, and I'm certain Elise will too. That's my widowed friend's name."

"Ah, here's the information on pricing details and the like," Mrs. Jordan said, as she thumbed through the file. "Actually, it looks quite reasonable, for such a location, close to the sea." She quoted Giselle a figure that was well below what both she and Elise had in mind. She could scarcely believe it.

"Yes, that's very much in keeping with our budget. I'd definitely like to see it, if that's possible."

"Yes, of course. The cottage is unoccupied, so we can pop over there right now, and have a look. Let me get the key."

It was captivating. Stone, with a thatched roof, it sat adjacent to the beach, next to dunes and a nature reserve. The front yard was densely planted with delightful flowers, ranging from larkspur, to roses and foxglove. There were three bedrooms – two double and one twin, two bathrooms, a cozy parlour with fireplace, dining alcove and roomy kitchen. The cottage had clearly seen better days, and Giselle immediately understood the modest price. Everything looked to be in good working order, but the décor was terribly dated. So were the kitchen appliances. On the other hand, the floors were flagstone, there were no cracks of major proportion on the ceilings or walls, and the baths were decent. It needed elbow grease, but that wasn't problematic. Giselle walked through the rooms several times, noting how three people would fit. Just as she was thinking about how much furniture they'd need to buy, Mrs. Jordan remarked that for a small, additional fee the cottage could be bought or leased furnished. That definitely sealed the deal. Not everything was what Giselle would have chosen, but it would suffice until the day she and Elise could do some refurnishing. The important rooms – those that guests would see – were furnished in faded, chintz-covered sofas and chairs, and there was a pretty dining set with a refectory table. Giselle loved the fact that there were French doors from the living room to a terrace, where another garden was in full bloom. After a thorough look-through, she told Mrs. Jordan she loved it and wished to sign a lease.

They returned to the office, where a lease was drawn-up. Mrs. Jordan suggested a three-year lease, bringing the price down a bit more. With Giselle's offer of renovation and updating, the agent knocked off another ten percent. Giselle was thrilled. Since she'd made no arrangements for a place to sleep that night, she asked if it was possible to take possession immediately. Mrs. Jordan said that normally their office liked to go in and do a deep cleaning before new tenants moved in, but if Giselle didn't mind, they'd schedule it for another time. Giselle told her she would do the deep cleaning herself. Five more pounds came off the rent. Giselle accepted the key and handed over a cheque for the first and last month's rent. By nightfall, she was tucked into one of the double bedrooms, where sea-breezes filled the house. She could hear waves lapping on the shore.

The next morning she sat at a table on the terrace, drinking a cup of tea and writing a letter to Elise. She had the property-office brochure, so it was included, along with her own description of their new home. She knew Elise would be thrilled. After posting the letter, Giselle made a list of chores that needed to be done. First, she made a trip to the village and purchased necessary items. Then, she put fresh linen on all of the beds, cleaned both bathrooms and scrubbed the kitchen until it was spotless. By the end of the day, the cottage was as clean as a whistle. She was proud of what she'd accomplished.

It only took Elise two days to reach Thornton-on-Sea. One of those was spent packing all of her possessions. On her last night in Brighton, she dined out with Violette and several other friends. The few girls who weren't close to Elise didn't attend. Two women, Adele and Lana, were Elise's only true adversaries, but she'd quickly learned to avoid them. They scarcely spoke to her anyway and didn't seem the sort with whom she would want to be friendly. They were quite rough around the edges, but Violette kept them on because she needed ladies to entertain men who weren't as distinguished as most of her visitors. They were undoubtedly happy Elise was leaving. During dinner there was a lot of talk about the town to which she was moving. A few girls knew the village. They raved about the heavenly location – the quaintness of its streets and lanes. Elise showed the brochure Giselle had sent, and everyone oohed and aahed at the cottage's charm. She was so anxious to see her new home. She promised to write to Violette and instructed her to share letters with everyone.

The following morning, the porter from the railway station came to collect her bags. He said he'd meet her at the depot. They'd become friends since the summer night she'd arrived from France, seeking *Maison de Violette*. That subject was hilarious now. Just as Elise was about to leave for the station, Violette took her into the private office and handed her an envelope.

"I want you to have this little gift, to carry you and Chloe through. Put it aside, if you don't need it now. The time may come when it will be useful."

Elise opened the flap and saw that there was a great deal of money inside. Enough to live on for more than a year. Tears welled in her eyes.

"You've been so wonderful to me. I wish I could repay you. I promise I'll never forget you, Violette. You're like a mother to me. Thank God I found you. I'll put the money away and use it for Chloe's education. It's important to me that she have the best of everything. I'll tell her, of course, who it came from. I hope you'll come to visit. You need to watch Chloe as she grows up."

"Don't count on that. I'd never take the chance that someone might see me coming or going from your cottage. I can never know who might recognise me. You and Giselle are starting a new life. You need to put me, and anything connected with me, far behind you."

Elise began to weep. "I'm not ashamed of you. I could never be anything but loving to you. Please say you'll come for a visit.

"Elise, you're such an innocent. Giselle will explain it all very clearly. Please remember, I don't want you to ever mention where you lived while in Brighton. Even though you didn't work here, there are people who'd never believe that's true. You can't make any reference to me or to my establishment. You know Brighton well enough by now. You can name any of several boarding houses where you might have lived. Don't ever mention my name. Promise me."

"All right. I promise, but only to make you feel at ease. I don't care what people think. I know in my heart what a good, kind person you are. I'm not ashamed of you. But for Giselle's sake, as well as yours, I'll do as you ask. You can't keep me from writing to you though. I'll not promise that."

"All right, Elise. Write, and send pictures of Chloe. I do love her and want to see her grow into a fine, young lady. If you ever need anything, let me know."

The two hugged and exchanged kisses on each cheek. Then, Elise lifted Chloe and began the trek up the beach to the depot. She was excited at the prospect of a new life, but there was a lump in her throat when she looked back at the lavender, three-story house, covered with morning glories.

6

Giselle met Elise and Chloe at the station. Mrs. Jordan, from the Property Management Office, drove her, making it easier to transport Elise and Chloe's possessions to the cottage. The two were like young girls, chattering incessantly. As soon as Giselle finished a sentence, Elise began a new one. It was as though they'd been parted for ages, when, in reality, it had been less than two weeks. Elise had never heard of Thornton-on-Sea, nor did the name Thornton ring a bell. If the RAF pilot, upon whom she'd made such an impression in May 1940, had mentioned either the name of the town, or his surname, she only remembered that his Christian name was Sloan. Mrs. Jordan parked the car in front of the cottage and placed Elise's bags on the kerb. Then, she hugged each of the ladies and said goodbye. They all promised to see one another again soon.

Elise threw her hand over her heart and gasped. She could scarcely speak and was flooded with emotion.

"Giselle! It's the place we dreamed about. Identical. Everything about it is the same – even the garden and the pretty fence. I can't believe you found it! Even better, that we could afford it! Oh, you dear, dear person."

"I knew you'd love it. The moment I saw it, I was mad for it. It needs a bit of work on the inside, but nothing dreadful. I've done all of the deep cleaning. Chloe's room is ready for her. I think we'll be very happy here."

"I know we will. It's more than I could have imagined. And right on the sea! Oh Giselle, there's nothing I love better than falling asleep to the sound of ocean waves."

"Yes, I've been keeping the windows open at night, and it's heavenly. We'll have to learn to keep the garden in proper order. I don't know a thing about gardening, but I'll be surprised if you don't."

"Oh, I do, I do. Remember, I lived on a farm in France. My brother did the heavy things, but I was the gardener. I'm very familiar with what needs to be done to keep it in good form. Isn't it pretty now?"

"Yes. I was scarcely able to believe my eyes when I saw how enchanting it was. That was the *piece de resistance*. Come. You need to look inside. Then we'll get sorted out," said Giselle.

They unlatched the gate and entered the quaint structure. Chloe was gurgling and babbling, as though she also gave her approval. Elise was enthralled. The size was perfect for two adults and a child. When they reached the baby's room, she was once again speechless. Giselle had managed to find a delightful baby cot, very old, made of wrought iron and painted white. It had once been in a French orphanage. An antique shop in the village had displayed it in the window. Giselle said she'd lost her head and purchased it. Elise immediately told her about the money she'd received from Violette. She said she'd pay Giselle for the cost of the cot. Giselle waved her hand, telling her that it was meant as a gift for Chloe.

"You have to accept it," Giselle declared. "It was so perfect for her. I wanted her to have it. I have a good bit of money put aside. It wasn't that expensive anyway. But, it's my special treat for Chloe."

"I won't argue, but please remember we have this windfall. I think it should be kept for Chloe. I thought perhaps a savings account in a bank. But, if we find ourselves in dire straits, it's there for an emergency."

Giselle hugged Elise. "What good news, and how generous of Madame Violette. Yes. I agree. It should be Chloe's, except in the case of an emergency."

There was also a large, old cupboard in the room. It had been scarred and chipped, but Giselle had sanded it and painted it white. It was perfect for Chloe's clothing, with a side door which opened to a large space for toys. The baby cot was covered with a white eyelet comforter. Matching curtains hung at the windows, and a rocking chair sat in the corner. Elise was overwhelmed at what Giselle had accomplished in such a short time.

"This gives you an idea of what we can do with the rest of the cottage. Eventually, I think it might be lovely to put up wallpaper in here. What do you think?"

"Oh Giselle, yes. Perhaps something pink and white. Is there a shop in the village?"

"Yes. I've already explored. We'll have to measure. Do you know anything about that sort of thing?"

"Yes. I'm not an expert, but I've done it before. If the pattern isn't too difficult, I'll be fine."

They both laughed. After a complete tour of the cottage, they carried the few items Elise had brought with her into the hallway. Then Giselle suggested they sit down and catch-up. Elise sat on the chintz sofa in the parlour, and Giselle curled up in a comfortable chair across from her friend.

"So," began Elise. "Tell me everything about the village. It's absolutely charming. What have you discovered? Have you met anyone? Also, I want to hear all about your new employers."

"Well, yes, the village *is* charming. Not just in appearance, but everyone has been very friendly and helpful. I was a bit frightened about whether they would be welcoming to strangers – particularly foreigners – but everyone I've spoken to has been extremely cordial. They seem to think we were very brave to escape the Nazis.

I've told them that you're a widow – the whole tale. There's great sympathy for you. I've said we met at a boarding house in Brighton. I haven't come across anyone who knows Brighton well – only its location, of course. Thornton-on-Sea is such a pretty place and, being directly on the sea, there aren't a lot of reasons why anyone would visit Brighton for a holiday. Of course, I've not met a lot of people yet.

There's a school very close to our cottage. Only two lanes over, which will be convenient for Chloe, when the time comes. I haven't located a Catholic church, but there's a very pretty Anglican, called *St. Martin's by the Sea*. I'm rather taken by it. While I'm not Anglican, the services are very similar, and I think I can make the adjustment. I've already attended. It's what's known as a 'high church', so I feel at home. I know there's a difference in some beliefs, but I'm not terribly concerned about them. They have a Mass every morning, so I can attend before reporting to work."

"That's perfect, Giselle. I need to have Chloe Christened, too. I'll have to talk with the rector and make arrangements."

"We'll go this Sunday. I think you'll like it. It's important to be a part of a church in these small villages. No matter. I want to go anyway."

"Yes. I do, too. It's important for Chloe to have a Christian upbringing. Now, tell me about the house you'll be working in as a lady's maid."

"It's incredible. It's called *Highcroft Hall*. The family name is 'Thornton'. The town is named for them. They're an earl and countess. He's Lord Rowan Thornton and his wife is Lady Celia. Of course the family goes back eons — to the 1600s. I went to the library and looked up information about them. Needless to say, they're very posh. The house isn't absolutely ancient, since it's been re-built and added onto as years have passed. But, it still dates to the seventeenth century. I've never seen anything like it, but where would I? Unless you count having visited Versailles, when I lived in Paris. It isn't as grand as Versailles, but it's awfully spectacular. There are so many rooms, it will be hard to learn all of them. I suppose I shall, eventually. Lord and Lady Thornton seem like good people. He's quite a handsome old gent, with white hair and a trim form. She's one of those people you want to put your arms round and cuddle. She's very aristocratic, but still approachable. One seldom sees her without her knitting. She dresses sensibly and has white hair, worn in a neat updo. I already like her immensely."

"And what will your duties be? I know your title is 'lady's maid', but what exactly does that entail?"

"I'll be her personal maid, responsible for her clothing — making certain it's in top shape at all times. No buttons missing, no tears, no seams requiring a mend. I'll tend to her personal needs, too. I'll do her hair and anything else that's part of her toilette. I don't think she wears any cosmetics — perhaps a bit of light lip rouge. She always looks immaculate. I'm told I'll advise her on what frocks to wear, if they're entertaining, or even just for daywear."

"Aren't you a bit frightened?" Elise asked.

"Not really. Naturally, I'll be somewhat nervous. But Elise, I did so many of those things when I worked in Paris. When I first began, I was very young – sixteen. Well, you know that. I was trained to assist the older girls with their toilette. I became very accomplished at hair dressing, and also took charge of keeping wardrobes in perfect condition. I even made some clothing. The moment I was offered this job, I searched out the village library and found several books on the duties expected of domestic help. One was particularly helpful regarding proper etiquette in a great house. I've read it so many times, I practically have it memorised," she smiled.

"You'll learn everything very quickly. I think your accent adds to your charm. Your command of the English language is wonderful. I've never heard you make a mistake. I'm sure you'll be a great addition to the staff."

"We're both fortunate we were taught English. I'm very comfortable with it."

"Yes. So am I. In fact, I've thought about teaching French someday, when Chloe is older. You're going to be very successful, Giselle. They're lucky to have you."

"I do hope so. I liked everyone I met. The housekeeper, Mrs. Littleton, has apparently been with the family forever and a day. She seems very kind, but I imagine she can be strict. One would have to be to oversee such a massive home. The butler, Richmond, is exactly what you'd expect a butler to be. Tall, dark haired, somewhat stern-looking and exceedingly proper. I'm sure he's very nice, but it's hard to tell about someone in that position, until one gets to know him. The only other person I met was the cook, Ruth. I imagine she's quite talented. What with the entertaining called for in a large house, she'd need to know how to prepare extravagant meals. Just cooking for the family is probably an event. There are parlour maids, kitchen helpers, upstairs maids – I'll get to know them in time."

"Have the Thornton's any children?"

"Yes. Only the one son. He's away fighting, of course. RAF. Lady Celia said he's in Africa. I don't recall his name right now. She may not have told me. Since his father is an earl, he's a viscount. I learned that at the library, too. These things are very important to the gentry. *Mon Dieu*! I never dreamed I'd find myself working in this sort of position. It will be a whole new experience, but I'll adjust. I want to start over. I want to forget the past and become a decent lady."

"You've always been a decent lady, Giselle. You made some unwise choices, but so does everybody in one way or another."

"I feel that way too. As long as no one from my past pops up and ruins everything."

"I think that's highly unlikely. Where would people like the Thorntons meet someone from a brothel in Brighton, or even Paris? That's very improbable."

"Let's hope so."

"I have to worry about that, too. After all," Elise said, as she turned the gold wedding band round and round on her finger, "there are things I'm not being completely honest about either."

"Elise, there's no way anyone would learn that you didn't lose a husband at Dunkirk. There are hundreds of women who've had the same thing happen to them. If anybody wants to hear details, which would be very cheeky, simply tell them that you never talk about it."

"Yes. I've already decided to say that. I *don't* want to talk about what really happened to me, so it won't be hard to resist speaking about myself at all. When will you begin your new job?" Elise asked, changing the subject.

"Not for another week. It gives us time to explore the village a bit more and to make some decisions about what needs to be done to the cottage. I'll also have plenty of time to spend with Chloe, which I always love. Isn't it nice that she'll be growing up in this precious village, in a cottage by the sea?"

⚬⚬⚬

The next week flew by. Each day they took Chloe and went on another excursion. By the time a few days had passed, they'd been on every street and lane in the village. They had taken a bit of Violette's gift, and purchased an old automobile. It wasn't pretty, but it ran well. As soon as they had it, Giselle took Elise to see the outside of *Highcroft Hall* and, of course, Elise was overwhelmed. She couldn't imagine her friend actually going there to work each day. Giselle was fortunate she wasn't expected to sleep at the mansion. Most of the staff were. At first that's what the Thorntons had in mind. But,

44

when she explained that she had a widowed friend, with a small child, who shared a cottage with her, they said that if Giselle didn't mind working until Lady Celia dressed for dinner, it would be fine if she lived away from *Highcroft Hall.* Giselle wasn't concerned about the hours. In return for putting in such long days, Lady Celia told her she could have Sundays and Mondays off. The arrangement was perfect. After the two friends talked further, Elise decided that, since Giselle would be free on Mondays, Elise could add to their income by giving French lessons. She wouldn't have to wait until Chloe was school-age. Giselle would be free to tend Chloe, while Elise taught. By the time Giselle started work, Elise had placed an advertisement, and she already had three little girls, whose mothers wanted them to speak fluent French. She planned to start a class on Monday afternoons.

Giselle reported to *Highcroft Hall* early on a lovely, summer morning. She'd purchased a bicycle and rode the short distance to the country house. The only difficult part was climbing the hill that led to the Hall. She enjoyed the ride, since the pathway was leafy and lined with wildflowers. When she reached the steepest part of the journey, she walked beside her bicycle, enjoying the sunshine and views of the ocean. Her heart was very light. How incredible that her life had changed so abruptly. She'd attended Mass before setting out and asked God to bless the house where she'd be working. She thanked the Lord for giving her the opportunity to start anew and promised she wouldn't do anything that wasn't kind or good.

When she arrived, Mrs. Littleton took her into the office and gave her a cup of tea. She also offered breakfast, but Giselle declined. She'd eaten a croissant before leaving the cottage. Her duties were explained in detail, and Giselle realized that what she'd read in her library book matched perfectly with Mrs. Littleton's expectations. After they'd chatted a bit, Giselle was taken to Lady Celia's boudoir.

Since they'd met before, she didn't feel uncomfortable with the countess. Lady Celia sat in a chair by the fireplace, inviting Giselle to join her. They enjoyed another cup of tea, and Lady Celia spoke of how she hoped they'd grow to be companions. Her last lady's maid had been with her for many years, but had retired. She hoped Giselle would also be with her for a long time. She talked about her son, whose name was Sloan, and of how she worried for his safety. He'd been in Syria and Lebanon since the Allies had invaded those countries on June 8. She went on to tell of his engagement to a lady named Anne Whitfield, who was the daughter of a Duke. She explained that they'd known one another since childhood and that she and her husband loved Anne as if she were already their daughter. Both were impatient for the war to end, so Sloan would return and marry his lovely fiancée. Lady Celia told Giselle she'd undoubtedly meet Anne, since she often stopped by *Highcroft Hall* to visit with her prospective in-laws and to share letters from Sloan.

Finally the day truly began. Giselle was proud of herself for performing duties with no mishaps. Lady Celia was most satisfied with the way her hair was arranged. She also thought Giselle made excellent choices for wearing apparel. Giselle was actually surprised at how simply the countess dressed. Most of her day-clothing consisted of twin sets, or modest dresses with a cardigan. Evening frocks were a bit more formal, but not nearly as lavish as those worn at *Maison de Violette*. She didn't find any of her assigned tasks overwhelming, and the hours flew by. When it was time to leave, Lady Celia said she was happy with her performance and looked forward to seeing her the next day.

Giselle sailed down the hillside just before the sun fell beneath the horizon. It had been a wonderful day. When she rode up the lane to the cottage, Elise was in the garden, with Chloe in a basket.

"Was it a success?" she called to Giselle.

"Absolutely. From start to finish. I'm going to love working there. Lady Celia is so pleasant. We spoke at length."

She parked her bicycle and gave Chloe a cuddle. Then, the three went into the cottage. Elise had supper prepared. The aroma of roast chicken wafted through the cottage. While they set the table, Giselle chatted about her day. She told Elise about the Thornton son who was away fighting in the war, and about how he was engaged to the irreplaceable Anne.

"I think that sounds like a wonderful love story," Elise responded.

"Yes. I suppose. I don't know why, but I don't think I'll like Anne very much. I'm probably being unfair. I've no reason to have such feelings. She sounds almost too good to be true. Maybe I'm jealous."

"Oh, Giselle. You? I don't think so. In any event, you'll get to meet her. Then you can decide. What did you say the son's name is?"

"Sloan. Sloan Thornton. A different sort of name. I've never heard it before."

Elise's face paled. "Sloan? I've known someone named Sloan. It's an unusual name. I don't suppose it could be the same person."

"Where did you meet someone named Sloan?"

"Do you remember the RAF Lieutenant I told you about? The one who came to my farmhouse needing help, after his plane was shot down? It was the same day the loathsome Nazis came to call."

"Yes. Of course I remember. Do you mean to say his name was Sloan?"

"It was. I never knew his last name. Nor did he say where he was from. He did say 'Sloan' was a family name. You don't suppose...?"

"As you've often said, anything is possible. But you told me that the 'Sloan' who came to your house believed the two of you were soulmates? This 'Sloan' is engaged to be married to a childhood sweetheart. Surely they aren't one and the same?"

"No, it doesn't seem likely. It's just the similarity in names."

The two friends sat down to eat. Chloe was placed in her basket by the table's side.

"Still," said Giselle, "I'm going to see if I can find out more about Sloan Thornton. I'll ask Lady Celia if he was at Dunkirk, or injured his leg. Also whether 'Sloan' is a family name. Let's see how many coincidences there are."

7

The opportunity to ask more about the Thornton's son didn't present itself for nearly two weeks. Lord Rowan and Lady Celia took a short trip to London. That called for sorting through clothing and making decisions about which outfits were appropriate for the journey. It wasn't a particularly sensible time to visit the Capital, due to the war-footing, but they were attending a funeral and didn't feel they could decline. Thankfully, by the summer of 1941, the air raids over London had become much less intense, since the RAF had begun to take control of the skies. That, undoubtedly, influenced Lord and Lady Thornton's decision to attend the service of a life-long friend's son. He'd died in London, from war wounds.

When they returned, both were tired. Giselle spent the majority of her time sorting through garments earmarked for contribution to the war effort. Thus, she didn't see much of Lady Celia, who spent a lot of time resting. Finally things returned to normal. On a rainy afternoon Giselle and her employer took tea in Lady Celia's boudoir. As the countess once again settled on her favorite topic, Lady Anne Whitfield and her son, Sloan, Giselle saw a perfect opportunity to investigate whether or not Sloan Thornton was the same person who'd paid a visit to Elise's farmhouse in May 1940. She began by asking about his name.

"Lady Celia, I find Sloan an interesting choice for a Christian name. I've known several English people whose surname is Sloan, but I've never heard it used as a given name. I'm curious about how you chose it for your son."

"That's an easy question," Lady Celia smiled. "Sloan was my maiden name. My husband's mother's maiden name was Rowan, which is how he came to be called that, so when we had a son, we decided to follow the same tradition. We used my maiden name. Sloan loathed it as a child, but I think he's rather fond of it now. At least it isn't ordinary," she smiled.

"No. I like it. I've never asked, but did Sloan go into the RAF as soon as war was declared?"

"Yes. He couldn't have been held back. Just like all of his chums. Not all chose the RAF, of course, but he was fascinated with the idea of flying."

"I imagine that worries you. So much of this war has been fought in the air. If it weren't for the RAF, I wonder if there'd be much left of London. He hasn't ever been wounded, has he?"

"Yes, as a matter of fact, he was. Early on. At Dunkirk. His aeroplane was shot right out of the sky, and he was wounded in the leg. He found his way to a rural house and asked for help. Apparently a very kind, young lady, who'd been trained as a nurse, rendered first aid. He was able to get to the beaches, and a British ship picked him up. When he returned to England, the flight surgeon told him the French girl had done an excellent job on his wound. She probably saved his leg."

"How remarkable!" Giselle exclaimed. "And how very fortunate."

"Yes, it was. So, you see, we owe the French a debt of gratitude."

<hr>

Giselle was bursting at the seams when she arrived at *No Regrets* that evening. Elise could tell by the look on her face that she had something important to say.

"All right, Giselle. What is it? You look like you have a giant secret," Elise laughed. She'd just finished feeding Chloe and had come downstairs after having tucked the baby into her cot.

"Well, I found out that 'Sloan' of the farmhouse, is the same 'Sloan' who's heir to *Highcroft Hall*"

"Unbelievable!" exclaimed Elise. "I had a strong suspicion. So, we have another example of a scoundrel. You know, I really took him for a decent sort. I did think it peculiar that a man who I'd only just met, would go on and on about this 'soulmate' thing, but he was so convincing. I could have sworn he meant every word he was saying. He had such a sincere demeanor. That does take the cake, doesn't it? There he was, engaged to the girl back home. I should tell her what a cad she's planning to marry."

"On no, Elise. Don't do that. I agree. He's a rogue, but don't get involved with his personal life. It could put my job in jeopardy. The Thorntons think he hung-the-moon. They'd never listen to anything negative about him, and, of course, would take his side. They adore Anne. If you said something that caused her to question the engagement, it wouldn't be their son who'd be blamed. It would be you. From what you've said, he's quite a smooth talker. He'd get out of it someway – probably by denying he ever said such things."

"Of course. You're right. I guess she'll have to find out for herself. I do feel sorry for her though."

"Perhaps it was some momentary lapse of judgment on his part. You know, he'd been wounded. Perhaps he was in shock. Don't people sometimes say strange things when they're in that condition?"

"Yes, I suppose that could be, but he seemed very rational. No matter. It isn't really any of my business. I'm sure he never thought he'd see me again. I doubt I *will* see him, even though I'm living in the town named for his family. I certainly don't *want* to see him. You know how wary I am of men. *Mon Dieu*, Giselle. Are they all liars?"

"It seems so, doesn't it? I think it's good to be wary of men. Better safe than sorry."

"Do you think you'll ever fall in love, Giselle?"

"I'd like to. It's hard to imagine though. I've known so many men and wouldn't have considered any of them as a future husband. Of course, if I'm honest, the sort of man I'd want wouldn't be found in a brothel. At least I hope not," she smiled ruefully.

"No, that's probably not the ideal place to search for a mate." Elise couldn't help but laugh. "I'm not sure there *is* an ideal place. Look at poor Anne. She's known the rascal all of her life – grew up with him –knows his family. Yet, apparently she still doesn't *really* know him."

"That's a sobering thought, isn't it? She probably trusts him implicitly. If you can't trust someone you've known all of your life, who can you trust? Perhaps it's better to spend your life alone, than to have your heart broken by a cheat."

"You might be right, Giselle. With what I've been through, I much prefer being alone. I suspect, however, that someday *you'll* marry. You'd make a wonderful wife and mother. And, of course, you're beautiful. Surely there's some decent man in the world who'll be good to you and make up for the sad times in your life."

"That would be nice. But he'll never know about the sad times, I can promise that. At least not all about them. I was such a little fool, Elise. I don't know how I could have been so spiritual and not have known I was committing the worst sins."

"You were very young. And foolish, yes. There are people in the world who take advantage of a young girl's innocence – especially one with no parents. You were searching desperately for love."

"I wasn't raised with the religious values I grew into. When I was in Paris, I believed I wasn't hurting anyone – that what I did with my own body was my business. That's the way most of the girls I worked with thought. By the time I found God, I'd already made a mess of my life."

"But Giselle, our religion teaches forgiveness of sins. I know you've been forgiven. You really need to try and believe you're a new person."

"I *do* believe that. But I'm afraid if I ever meet a good man, he won't understand. How could I tell him such a thing?"

"Don't worry about it now. You haven't met him yet. If he's truly good, then I think he'll be understanding and forgiving."

"Do you think you could ever forgive the men who hurt you?"

"That's such a different thing. They were evil – pure evil. I think I'll let God do the forgiving."

"What about this 'Sloan' person?"

"He was a ship that passed in the night. There's really nothing to forgive. He didn't hurt me. It was all a bit of innocent flirting. He probably thought all French girls expect that sort of behavior. I don't think very highly of him, now that I know he was engaged, but compared to what came later, he didn't do anything so terrible. He made me feel special for a few moments. I guess that isn't so awful, really."

"I think you're right. People do odd things at times like that."

"No matter, Giselle. I hope he marries the divine Anne and has a happy life. I won't interfere."

•••

The very next day, Giselle met the divine Anne. She'd expected the girl would eventually visit *Highcroft Hall,* and that Lady Celia would introduce them. She'd pictured Anne as a rather snooty young lady and had no great desire to meet her. But, of course, Giselle would be deferential, in keeping with her position in the household. She was sitting in the morning room, mending some clothing for Lady Celia. It was a pretty autumn day, and her mind was far away, thinking about how she'd spend her off-days that week. Suddenly her reverie was interrupted by the sound of voices. Glancing up, she saw the countess enter the room, followed by a very striking, dark haired girl. She had one of the loveliest complexions Giselle had ever seen. When she smiled, deep dimples showed, and her eyes were filled with kindness.

"Giselle, I want to introduce our son's fiancée to you. This is Lady Anne Whitfield, of whom you've often heard me speak."

Giselle stood and dropped a small curtsy. She knew it wasn't strictly necessary, but it seemed the appropriate thing to do.

"I'm so happy to meet you, Lady Whitfield. I've heard such charming things about you."

"And I have heard nothing but praise of you. Lady Celia thinks of you as a daughter."

"Oh, I'm flattered, Lady Whitfield, but it's you who has that honour. As I understand, you'll truly be her daughter when this dreadful war ends."

"Yes. That's the plan," she replied, casting her eyes toward the floor.

Giselle thought she seemed ill-at-ease at the mention of marriage.

"I understand you came from France when the war began," Anne continued. "I think you must be very brave. I can't imagine what courage that took."

Giselle smiled. "I don't think I was courageous. When you're desperate, you just act and think later. I'm sure you'd have done the same thing."

"Perhaps. I've never found myself in that sort of situation. How fortunate that all went well, and you weren't captured. One hears horror stories about what's done to people interred in camps."

"Yes. That's one reason I decided to leave. Everyone I knew would have left, if given half a chance."

"Well, I still think you're marvelously brave."

"Thank you, Lady Whitfield. I'm only glad to be in England now."

"Oh, do call me Anne. I detest such formality. I suspect we're about the same age."

"I'm twenty-one. Sometimes I feel much older," Giselle smiled.

"Then we're exactly the same age. There are so few girls in this town with whom I have anything in common, because of age. Either they're much younger, and quite silly, or much older." She turned to Lady Celia. "Oh don't misunderstand," she smiled at the older woman. "I love spending hours with this dear lady, but there are times when I long for someone my own age to laugh with and share secrets. I don't have a sister, and I was educated at home by a Governess, so I've never had the chance to meet a lot of girls my own age."

Giselle's heart went out to the young lady. Perhaps she'd judged her too harshly. Now that they'd met, she found Anne awfully charming. She seemed sweet and unaffected. In other circumstances, Giselle would have suggested that Anne meet Elise, and the three of them do something fun on an off-day, but she knew that would be completely inappropriate.

"Lady Celia tells me that you share a cottage with a widowed friend and her small child. I know the cottage well. I think everyone in Thornton-on-Sea knows it. Did you keep the name '*No Regrets*'?"

"Yes," Giselle laughed. "It was a fit. We love it there. Elise came over from France too, during Dunkirk. Her husband was killed. She was carrying his child. We became fast friends, and now we're more like sisters."

"Is she employed?" asked Anne.

"She teaches French. I'm off on Mondays, so Elise has me watch her baby, Chloe. She has several children from the village in a class. They come to our cottage and sometimes, on warm, sunny days, they sit under an old Chestnut tree in the back, conjugating verbs."

"What a pretty picture. I wonder if she'd consider taking an adult student. I've never been as fluent in French as my mother would like. My Governess wasn't particularly strong in languages. I'd love to learn from someone who's truly French."

"I don't think there'd be a problem, but I can't speak for her. There are only so many hours in her day, and I'm not certain how many students she has on her schedule now. If you're serious, I'd be happy to ask her. She's well-educated and has a fine, aristocratic manner of speaking, so you'd be learning the French of your peers."

"Oh, do please ask. Of course I'd pay whatever she charges. I'd rather have private lessons, if possible. Since I'm an adult, I can't imagine being in a class with children," she giggled.

"Of course not. I'll ask her. I'll tell Lady Celia tomorrow. She can give you Elise's answer."

Impulsively, Anne reached over and hugged Giselle. "I appreciate that so much. It gives me something to look forward to. Oh, I hope she'll agree to take me as a student."

***

Just as the name 'Sloan' had struck a chord with Elise, the name 'Elise' startled Anne. It was impossible to forget the girl Sloan had described in his heartbreaking letter. He'd clearly referred to her as Elise. It was typically French, although Anne had never known anyone of that name. But, she also remembered that Sloan had mentioned meeting her near Dunkirk. Obviously this girl was from that area, too. He'd said nothing about a marriage, nor a pregnancy, but then, as far as Anne knew, he'd only spent a short while with her. Anne looked forward to meeting Elise. Somehow, she would learn whether Elise was the girl who'd ruined her life.

It didn't take long to get her wish. The following day, Giselle told Lady Celia that Elise would be happy to take Anne as a student. She suggested that Anne ring Elise to set a time for a meeting. Later that day, Lady Anne, once again, appeared at *Highcroft Hall*. She was filled with excitement at the news that she'd be able to learn French from a woman who'd actually lived in France. Giselle gave her the number of the cottage, and Anne immediately placed the call.

Elise answered on the first ring, sounding very professional. She had a sweet voice and a fetching laugh that sounded like a pretty, silver bell. The two got on well during the conversation. They made arrangements for Anne to visit the cottage at four o'clock on Monday. Anne wished she hadn't found the girl so likeable on the telephone. She was fully prepared to dislike her, if what she suspected was true.

On the other hand, Elise had no ill will toward Sloan Thornton's fiancée. It wasn't Anne's fault that she was in love with a probable cad. She and Giselle had discussed the entire incident, and Elise had firmly reached the decision not to tell Anne anything about having met Sloan. But she was still curious about the girl Sloan planned to marry. After all, the man had said that *Elise* was his soulmate. Would Anne resemble her?

At four o'clock on Monday, a knock sounded at the cottage door. Elise knew who to expect. She wore a simple dress of white piqué. Her golden curls were pinned on top of her head, and she wore dainty pearl earrings. Elise never needed any cosmetics to enhance her beauty, but she'd added baby-pink lip rouge to her pretty mouth. Opening the door, she was somewhat startled by the lovely girl who stood there. She was nothing like Elise. She had very dark hair, lovely skin and beautiful eyes. They were very different types. Elise was demure and angelic, while Anne was sophisticated and well... sexy. Her mouth was painted crimson, and her hair tumbled to her shoulders in soft, sultry waves. She didn't look cheap. Elise knew the difference. There was nothing wanton about her appearance, but she did look worldly and sophisticated. *Chic* was the word she was searching for.

"You must be Lady Anne," Elise exclaimed. "Do come in. I'm so pleased to meet you."

"Thank you so much. I can't tell you how much I appreciate your making time to take me as a student. I'm anxious to begin my lessons," Anne answered. Her heart was racing as she gazed at the girl who'd opened the door. She'd never set eyes upon anyone so incredibly beautiful in her life. She was certain this was the girl Sloan had written about. No wonder he'd been spellbound. The girl looked like a serene angel. She immediately despised her.

How was she to compete with such an ethereal beauty? Surely she couldn't be as innocent and pure as she appeared. Could she? Anne immediately made up her mind to learn everything she could about this French cherub. There had to be more there than met the eye. 'Oh God', Anne thought. What would happen when Sloan returned and discovered that his so-called ideal woman was living in Thornton-on-Sea? Something had to be done. Perhaps she could keep him from finding out that Elise lived in the village, until she'd won back his heart. No matter that Elise appeared to be all he'd described. She was still nothing but a refugee from a foreign land. She surely wasn't the caliber of woman someone like Sloan should be considering as a future countess. All of those thoughts, and more, raced through Anne's mind, but she kept a charming smile on her face, giving no hint that she thought of Elise as a rival.

Elise, similarly, kept her feelings well-hidden. She wasn't the sort of person who would think poorly of another woman. She found Anne very attractive and warm. She immediately thought that they might become friends. She could understand at once why Sloan was in love with his childhood sweetheart. She believed, all the more, that what had taken place at her farmhouse in France had been some sort of odd occurrence. She vowed to put it out of her mind forever.

8

Elise didn't know how to be anything but genuine. As a result it didn't take long before she and Anne were seemingly friends. Just as Anne had done with Giselle, she asked Elise to stop calling her 'Lady Whitfield'. Elise wasn't so naïve as to believe she could ever be a companion to a titled aristocrat, but as time went on, the two *did* begin to share thoughts and feelings. She had no idea that Anne wasn't being forthright with her. Every Monday at four o'clock, just after the children's class ended, Anne arrived at *No Regrets*, and the two spent two hours speaking only French. Anne found that by not being allowed to speak English during the lessons, she was forced to remember how to say what she was thinking in French. She made wonderful progress. During the lessons Giselle would tend to Chloe. If it was a nice day, she often took the infant out in a pram. If it were threatening rain, or too cool, they stayed upstairs, while Giselle rocked the baby and played little games with her. Anne's lessons didn't end until six o'clock, so it was a full day for Elise. It soon became a regular occurrence for Elise and Anne to share a cup of tea after lessons were over. They'd sit in front of the cosy fireplace and chat. At first the conversation wasn't personal, but as time went on, Anne began to speak about deeper feelings.

The important thing to Anne was that she learn as much as possible about the naïve, guileless Elise. The ultimate goal was to erase her from Sloan's mind. There was also an outside chance that Anne could find a way to remove the angelic beauty from close proximity to *Highcroft Hall,* but such a task would be difficult. Lord and Lady Thornton adored Giselle. They'd become quite fond of both Elise and Chloe, too.

Before Giselle had worked at *Highcroft Hall* for less than a month, the middle-aged couple had taken an interest in her. They'd even made a special effort to meet Elise and Chloe. They were invited to tea in the drawing room of the country house, which had thrilled and delighted Elise. She was astonished that members of the aristocracy would entertain someone of a much lower class. Although the Thorntons were noble and genteel, they didn't seem to view Giselle and Elise as down-market. Lady Celia, in particular, seemed interested in their French upbringing, and that obviously played a part in her acceptance of them. Because the young ladies' manners were beyond reproach, and their command of the English language as fine as any aristocrat's, Lady Celia didn't see them as common. She understood that many refugees from France, and other European nations, had come from high-born families, but found it necessary to begin again after they reached England. Lady Celia also adored babies, so Chloe charmed her. Giselle had given Lady Celia no indication that Elise was the girl who had saved Sloan's leg. She'd been hesitant to do so. But, when the two visited for tea, the subject again came up. Elise acted astounded, and admitted that she had been the girl Sloan had met in France. Lady Celia and Lord Rowan were dumbfounded. The news only served to cement their relationship further. Of course, Elise knew that Lady Celia would tell Anne what she'd learned. Therefore, she decided to tell Anne herself, before she heard it from the Thorntons.

The very next day, Anne had a lesson with Elise. Before they started, Elise told her that she had something important to tell her. Anne listened intently.

"Anne, I need to tell you something. I don't want you to think I haven't been honest with you. You know that Giselle and I took Chloe and went to tea at *Highcroft Hall* yesterday, don't you?"

""Yes, of course. Did you enjoy yourselves?"

"Yes, very much. During the conversation, Lady Celia brought up the fact that her son had been injured in France, and had found aid from a French farm girl. The moment she told the story, I knew that she was referring to me. I can't believe the astounding coincidence. I had no idea that he was the son of Lord and Lady Thornton. He never gave me his surname. It wasn't an important event to me, and I'd never even mentioned it to Giselle. That was the same day I escaped to England. I had much bigger things on my mind."

Elise felt dreadful about lying, but there was nothing else she could do. Anne took the news well. She smiled and said it was a small world. Then, she asked what Elise had thought of Sloan. Elise hesitated, and then replied that she didn't remember a lot about him — she'd been nervous because there were so many Germans in the area. She was just glad when he left.

Anne was pleased. So, although Sloan had written to her, raving about having found his soulmate, nothing had taken place between them. Obviously, Elise didn't have any feelings for Sloan. That was a relief. It didn't erase her worry about what would happen when Sloan returned to Thornton-on-Sea and learned that Elise lived there. It was still going to be necessary to think of something she might do that would cause Sloan to change his feelings for the enchanting Elise. Anne decided to focus on finding Elise's Achilles heel. The question was, where to begin? Anne hadn't the faintest notion about how to research a person's background. Especially when that person had come to England from a foreign land. And the foreign land was France, now occupied by the Third Reich. The only way she could imagine learning anything about Elise's past, was to become her dear friend. Friends shared even the darkest secrets. So, she began to work even harder to accomplish that goal.

The lessons continued through the autumn, and into the beginning of winter. On Sunday, December 7, 1941, the news reported that Pearl Harbor had been bombed by the Japanese. It was a horrendous tragedy. The American Navy was stationed there, in the faraway Hawaiian Islands. On a sleepy Sunday morning, ghastly Japanese aeroplanes flew in from the sea and slaughtered the poor, young men who slept in bunks aboard their ships. The airfield was also nearly destroyed. America immediately declared war on Japan. Before anyone could blink an eye, Germany and Japan were foes of the Americans. England was appalled at the attack, and many people shed tears for the slain naval fleet, but they couldn't help but be happy that they'd no longer be fighting alone. Everyone hoped it would be a turning point in the war. When Anne arrived for her French lesson that Monday, it was impossible to think of anything but the war. Chloe slept in her cot, while Elise, Giselle, and Anne sat in the parlor, going over and over what had happened and pondering the changes in store for Great Britain.

"I suppose we'll have American military here now," Giselle said.

"Yes. I wonder what they're like. I've heard Americans are very forward. Has either of you ever known one?" asked Anne.

"I have," Elise replied. "When I was much younger. We lived in Monte Carlo. Americans visited the casino there. They seemed nice enough. Some were a bit unruly, but for the most part they acted decently. I was too young to see them socially, but knew girls who were older. A lot of them thought Americans were very good looking."

"I've never known one," Giselle lied. While working in Paris, she'd had occasion to meet *many* young men from the United States. They were generally doing the Grand Tour of Europe, after completion of Ivy League educations. She'd known some *very intimately*, but wasn't about to reveal that information.

"I wonder if there'll be a base anywhere near the southeast coast," mused Anne. "It would be fun to meet someone from America."

"I think they're pretty much like men anywhere," Elise said.

"I think Englishmen are more proper and gentlemanly. At least aristocratic Englishmen," Anne replied.

"Is Sloan proper and gentlemanly?" Giselle asked.

Elise shot a look of warning. There'd been no conversation about Sloan, and she didn't want for there to be. But the question hung in the air.

"I think he's the most proper, dear man in the world," Anne answered. "The epitome of an English gentleman. What do you think, Elise? You've met him."

"He seemed very proper to me, if I recall. It was all such a rush," she answered. "I wonder if the American's joining the fray will speed the war's end. It has to make a difference," she added, changing the subject.

"Yes, I'd think so," Anne answered. "We can surely hope so."

"I think it will definitely give weight to an Allied victory," added Giselle.

"When that happens, will the two of you return to your homeland?" Anne wondered aloud.

"We've never discussed it," Giselle said. "Frankly, I doubt it. We've put down roots here now. What do you think, Elise?"

"No. I don't think so. I've grown to love England. My little girl knows nothing of France. I have sad memories from there. Our move was meant to be a new beginning, and Great Britain has been good to me. Chloe was born here. It's home to us."

"Well, I'm very glad to hear that," answered Anne. It was a hard sentence to speak. She would have given anything to hear that the two would be returning to France after the war.

The chat continued until the sun set over the sea. Then, the three young ladies stopped talking and made plans for a resumption of their regular routine the following Monday. After Anne left, Giselle and Elise talked between themselves.

"I like her so much," said Elise. "I hope I'm doing the right thing by not telling her the entire truth about Sloan. She seems to love him so much. It would be cruel to break her trust in him."

"I like her too," Giselle agreed. "But you know, Elise - I wouldn't say this to anyone except you – I don't trust her completely. I wish I could say why. Something about her doesn't seem genuine. You're so good. So trusting. Perhaps I'm more suspicious than you. You don't trust men, and I don't trust a lot of women."

"What has she said, or done, to make you feel that way?"

"Nothing. I can't think of a single thing. That's the problem. It's just a feeling I have. I'm probably being unfair. I was prepared to dislike her before I met her. I thought I'd gotten over that. I truly thought I had. But there's just some strange feeling I get."

"I think you're wrong, Giselle. She seems honest and straightforward. She genuinely seems to like both of us. I think we're lucky to count her as a friend."

"We probably are. Pay me no mind. I'm probably wrong."

As it turned out, the entire southeast coast of Britain was filled with airbases where Americans were stationed. From East Sussex, to Kent, to Hampshire, there were many, many airfields. Everyone had known about the locations, for they were RAF bases first and foremost. When the 8th Air Force of the United States came in January 1942, they were stationed with the RAF. Towns like Thornton-on-Sea and Whitfield Cove, where Anne's home was located, became accustomed to seeing RAF chaps, as well as American boys in the pubs and Inns.

Anne finally got to meet an American man. Her parents, the Duke and Duchess, Lord and Lady Whitfield, were acquainted with the president of a large bank in America. Lord Whitfield had known him since his days at Oxford. Now his friend's son was in the U.S. Air Force, stationed at RAF Ashford. His friend's name was John Cabot, and he was a distant relative of the famed Cabot family of Boston, a very wealthy, aristocratic clan. John's son was Major Theodore – Ted – Cabot. John Cabot wrote to Lord Whitfield, asking if he'd invite Ted to *Meadowlands*, and keep watch over him while he was stationed in England. Lord Whitfield was delighted to do so. Thus, a dinner was planned, when the young flier had a free evening, and it was a festive affair. Lady Celia and Lord Rowan were invited. Of course, the Whitfield's daughter, Anne would be there, too. It was made clear from the beginning that she was engaged to marry an RAF Captain, serving in the Middle East, so the Major was well-aware that she wasn't free. Sloan had been promoted by that time, but Anne wished she could say that he was a Major, like Ted Cabot.

Anne decided to engage in a bit of innocent flirting. She found the handsome, rugged airman very attractive, with his auburn hair and deep blue eyes. Of course that didn't mean she'd forgotten Sloan – such a thing could never happen. But it had been a long time since she'd had the chance to bat her eyes at an attractive gentleman. After all, she thought to herself, she needed practice in order to be prepared to win back the adoration of the only man she'd ever loved. Sloan had apparently done his share of flirting – or at least *thinking* about another woman. Although no one was aware of it, Anne and Sloan weren't even engaged anymore. She was seated next to Major Cabot, which afforded ample opportunity for sly little glances and downcast eyes that showed her long lashes. It was apparent that the Major found her intriguing.

"Tell me about your home, Major Cabot," Anne said. "I'm afraid I know little of America, but I'd like to familiarize myself with your country. You've arrived at such a frightening time in Great Britain. I hope you know how much we longed for your intervention. We desperately needed help. Now you're here, and I think we owe it to your fine people to learn all we can about them."

The Major appeared to be pleased at her interest in America.

"The United States is like England in many ways. After all, we were a part of you for more than a century. A lot of our beliefs and customs are based on English traditions. But we're much more diverse. They call us a 'melting pot', and that we are. In the beginning, the majority of our people came from European countries, but mostly England. There were Dutch, Spaniards, French, and early Germans too. Then other nationalities began to immigrate, and soon we had Irish neighborhoods, Italian, Polish, and Russian. People from every country in the world can point to relatives in the States. We're still a young country by your standards. As a result, I'd say we're less inclined toward holding to a class system, which has continued in England. In America, a person who's lowborn can become very wealthy and be accepted into society."

"Oh, but isn't it dangerous to allow mixing of the classes like that? Would you marry a girl who came from a low-born family, or any down-market part of your country?"

Major Cabot laughed. "We don't think that way, Lady Whitfield. Oh, I should say some people do. I'd be much more inclined to marry a girl who shared my values and interests. Of course, I'd want her to be presentable, but I wouldn't be concerned about what her father did for a living."

"Well, that's very interesting," Anne answered. "I *do* have friends who aren't aristocrats. Two are from France. Refugees from the Nazi occupation. One is a lady's maid. In fact, she works for Lady Celia," she remarked, glancing at the Countess. "The other teaches French. She's a widow, with a small child. We don't exactly socialize though. It wouldn't be the 'done thing.'"

Lady Celia chimed in. "Oh, but Anne. In this case, Elise, my lady's maid's friend, actually saved my son from permanent impairment from a war injury. I'd invite both of them anywhere. Wouldn't you Rowan?" she enquired of her husband.

"Absolutely. They're both fine young ladies. I admire their spunk. They escaped from the Nazi's and came to England to start a whole, new life, with only the clothes on their backs. That poor Elise was also going to have a child. They're remarkable young ladies."

"You see, Lady Whitfield, in my opinion, your way of thinking would mean that you're ashamed of them. Are they prone to making social blunders?"

"No, no. Not that. They both know etiquette and speak perfect English. I just don't think they'd feel comfortable outside of their own niche."

"Have you ever asked them how they'd feel?" he asked.

"Well, frankly, it's never crossed my mind. You've given me something to think about."

Anne was embarrassed. Lord Rowan and Lady Celia's quick defense of Elise and Giselle made her seen petty and narrow-minded.

The conversation shifted to other topics, but Anne *did* think about what had been said. Major Cabot had looked at her rather dubiously. Perhaps she'd prove him wrong. She'd invite him to meet Elise and Giselle for tea. After all, her parents hadn't raised her to be full of herself. She *did* believe in the concept that all people were equal. But, in the sphere she'd been raised in, while the concept was a rather nice one, it wasn't practiced often.

9

1942

It was quite a while before the Major got furlough again. He kept in touch with Anne's father, and when she learned he had a free weekend, Anne wrote a note, inviting him to *Meadowlands* to meet her friends from France. Ted was no fool. He saw through her little charade, but having enjoyed himself at her parent's home before, it beat spending the weekend drinking ale in a pub. It was quite obvious she was trying to impress him with her liberal views on class-structure.

Giselle and Elise were dumbfounded when they received their invitation. While Anne had always been very nice, at no time had they expected to be invited to her parent's estate. Being asked to tea at *Highcroft Hall* was one thing. After all, Giselle knew the Thorntons, and it wasn't unheard of for a lady's maid to have tea with her employers. Plus, Lady Celia gave full credit to Elise for what she'd done to help Sloan. But Anne's parents were a Duke and Duchess. Outside of royalty, there was no higher social class in England. Anne had mentioned the dinner with a handsome American, but there'd been no hint of the two French women meeting him. Elise took down her *Emily Post Etiquette Book*, and copied the correct way to RSVP a formal invitation. Thank goodness she had some heavy, crème-colored vellum stationery that

Madame Violette had given her before leaving Brighton, as well as a black ink-pen. Once the reply was posted, both young ladies eagerly looked forward to seeing Anne before the designated date, three weeks away. They couldn't imagine what had prompted her to act so out of character.

On the following Monday, Anne appeared for her usual lesson. It was April, and in spite of having lived in Paris, Elise ardently felt that there was no more beautiful place on Earth than England in the spring. Hedges were covered with pink and white Hawthorn, apple trees were in bloom, the meadows were filled with white lambs, and leaves were turning into green, misty veils. Giselle took Chloe on a long outing, so only Elise met Anne at the door. It was difficult to believe that, on such a day, the brutal Nazis were beginning air raids on cathedral cities in Britain.

"Isn't it a grand day?" Anne exclaimed, as she removed her hat. "There's the fragrance of violets in the air. This is my favorite month."

"Mine too," answered Elise. "The world is starting over again. Do you want to begin lessons right away, or perhaps a cup of tea on such a pretty day? We could take it on the terrace."

"That sounds divine. I'm not in any rush, if you aren't. It might be nice to have time for a chat."

Elise set about preparing the tea, while Anne sat at the old table adjacent to the kitchen. "I received your RSVP. Thank you, Elise, though it wasn't necessary. You could simply have told me you were coming."

"Yes, Anne, but then you'd never have known how well-versed Giselle and I are in proper etiquette," Elise laughed.

"That you are. It was beautifully written."

"May I be rather nosy and ask why we've been given the privilege of tea at *Meadowlands*? Really Anne, we've never expected such treatment. Giselle and I don't fancy ourselves in your league."

"I only thought it would be nice. You've heard me speak about my home and, of course, Major Cabot. I thought you'd like to meet him, that's all."

"Well, it's a lovely thought. Of course we'd like to meet him. And your parents. It was very kind of you, Anne."

Anne waved her hand, dismissively. "It's only tea. I hope you enjoy yourselves. Major Cabot is looking forward to meeting both of you. I've mentioned you before. He thinks you sound fascinating."

"I scarcely think we're fascinating," laughed Elise. "He'll learn that soon enough."

"Well, I've always thought you're very interesting, too. Not everyone has the experience of escaping from the Nazis."

"Believe me, that's very fortunate for most people," Elise continued, as she prepared a tea tray to be taken to the terrace. In spite of the fact that Giselle occasionally made small remarks about lingering mistrust of Anne, Elise thought she was a wonderful friend and felt lucky to have met her. The invitation to tea, at what people said was one of the most glorious homes in all of England, was proof that Anne treasured their friendship, too.

After lessons were finished, Elise did something she'd never done before. When she looked back on it, she supposed it was because spring had arrived. She suggested to Anne that they open a bottle of wine to celebrate the change of seasons. Anne was only too happy to comply. Elise fetched two glasses and poured one for each of them. They continued to sit at the outdoor table, shaded by a large Beech tree. Roses bloomed next to the flagstone terrace, and daffodils flourished on either side. Giselle had mentioned a plan to attend an evening class and dinner at the church. She would be taking Chloe with her. So, she wouldn't be home until a bit later. Anne seized the opportunity, as a perfect time, to loosen Elise's tongue and learn more about her past.

After finishing one bottle of wine, they opened a second. It was so enjoyable to sit outside and chat, and there didn't seem to be any harm in letting their hair down. Elise was accustomed to drinking wine, and the entire scene was reminiscent of lovely days spent in France before the war. She said as much to Anne.

"You must miss France," Anne replied.

"Seldom, really. But days like this can't help but make me remember happy times there."

"It had to be very, very difficult to lose a husband. I can't imagine going through something like that. And to think, you were carrying his baby."

"Oh, Anne, I shouldn't tell you this. In fact, I don't know why I am, other than we've grown close. I think it's healthy for a person to unburden herself at times, and who better than a close friend? Of course, I have Giselle, and she knows my entire life. But, you've become nearly as close to me as a second sister."

"I'm a bit confused. What shouldn't you tell me? You're the sort of girl who's never had a secret in her life."

"Oh, I wish that were true. And it would have been, not so long ago. But all of that changed in May 1940. Before I say anything more, please promise you won't think badly of me."

"Elise, I can't imagine anything you could ever tell me that would make me think badly of you. Don't worry for a tick about that. Now tell me this great secret," she smiled.

"Anne, Chloe was born out of wedlock. I know that's probably a shock. It was a shock to me. I didn't know I was pregnant until I arrived in England."

"Oh, you dear girl! I don't think badly of you – only sorry. The same thing must have happened to hundreds – probably thousands of women. Honestly,' there but for the grace of God go I,'" she smiled. "If Sloan had asked on the night before he left, I suspect I would have given myself to him. Who knows what could have resulted?"

"But no, Anne, it wasn't like that. I feel defiled – dirty – just speaking about it. You see, on the afternoon of Dunkirk, three drunk Nazi soldiers pushed their way into my house, and – well – they – they..."

"They raped you! Oh my God! Oh my God! How did you live through such an attack?"

"I really don't know. I think I went into sort of a daze. Of course, I had to be in shock. They were monsters. They lined up and took turns, all the while cheering and saying obscene things. It went on and on."

"Oh, Elise. My heart aches for you. And, are you saying that Chloe was the result of this attack?"

"Yes. Of course, she'll never know, if I can help it. Imagine what it would be like for her to find out she was conceived due to such disgusting, evil behavior?"

"Don't worry. I'd never say anything to her. I hope she never finds out. It would be the vilest thing a girl could learn. So then, you're telling me you don't even know who her father is?"

"No, of course not. How could I? And what does it matter? One was as bad as the other. I hope they're all dead and rotting in hell."

"That's a strong statement, coming from you. It sounds more like something I'd say," Anne smiled sadly. "I couldn't agree with you more. They should all have been hanged. So, is that why you left France?"

"Yes. I was terrified they might return. I had to get away. My neighbor told me of a friend who lived in Brighton. I was fortunate enough to be picked up by a fishing boat, and deposited on English soil at Dover. I took the train to Brighton. Finally, I found the boarding house." Elise poured another glass of wine for both of them. "Actually, it wasn't a boarding house." Elise giggled. "You won't believe this, but it was a brothel! Can you imagine? I was so naïve, I had no idea. The owner had to explain what it was to me. It's hard to believe I was such a fool."

"I think that's better than knowing right off. Obviously you'd led a sheltered life. So that was two shocks in a short time frame."

"Yes. But, the lady who owned the establishment was absolutely wonderful to me. I don't know what I'd have done without her. She took me under her wing and was so kind. When I learned I was expecting a baby, she was such a comfort. She helped me sort it all out. I had nine months to think. At first, I didn't want the baby. You can imagine. But as time passed, I began to have tender feelings toward the little one and realized nothing that happened had been the poor infant's fault. The baby deserved a good life and a mother who loved it. Now, I believe God gave Chloe to me as a reward for what I'd had to endure."

"What an incredible way to think of such horror. You truly are a wonder. How were you received by the other girls who – um – worked there?"

"Very well, actually. I learned a lot while I lived there. I always thought such women should be shunned. But the vast majority weren't evil. Life's circumstances had brought them to that environment. I felt dreadfully sorry for most. There were only two I didn't care for. Adele and Lana. That's only because they weren't nice to me, which I suspect was jealously because Madame Violette treated me so well – gave me the nicest room, with a private loo and expected nothing from me."

"I can see where that might cause some envy."

"But Anne, the others were very loving. I only left because I realized it wasn't a place to raise an innocent child."

"Wise thinking," Anne murmured.

"So you see, I'm not the angel a lot of people think I am. I'm not an angel at all."

"Elise, none of it was your fault. Surely you know that. It's one of the saddest stories I've ever heard. But you mustn't let it ruin your life. I'm so proud of you for having risen above it, and made something good come of such foul behavior. I think a lot of girls would have been done in."

"I might have been too, but I was fortunate to find people who helped me."

"Is that when you met Giselle? In Brighton?"

"Yes. Um... but not at the brothel. She'd just escaped from France, too. We were naturally drawn to one another. She had a bed-sit, and her landlady introduced us, knowing we had a lot in common." Elise crossed her fingers behind her back. She detested lying, but Giselle's story wasn't hers to tell.

The day ended when Giselle returned with Chloe. It was time for Elise to bathe, feed and tuck her daughter into the cot. When Anne left for the day, she whispered into Elise's ear. "Your secret is safe with me. I admire your courage." Anne gave her a warm hug and thanked her. Then, she nearly skipped down the pathway. Why hadn't she thought of wine before? However, she doubted the outcome would have been the same, if it had been earlier in their relationship. It had taken time to convince Elise she could trust Anne. There was no way Elise would have spilled all of that information when they'd first met. Anne *did* feel sorry for her. It was a very sad tale. But, with a bit of maneuvering it could be used to Anne's advantage. If she told Sloan a slightly different version, Anne believed she knew him well enough to be certain he'd never want to be a part of Elise's life. His perfect angel was tarnished. The mere thought of her having been touched by those disgusting beasts would be enough to turn him away from her. She was sure of it. There'd be no difficulty enhancing the story. That was Anne's intention.

When Giselle returned, Elise didn't mention what she'd told Anne. She was well aware that Giselle wouldn't have been pleased. Elise was angry at herself for being so honest. It was due to the wine. She berated herself for her foolishness. Elise knew she had a tendency to speak her deepest feelings when she drank, which was why she usually stopped at one glass. She believed she could trust Anne, but it was embarrassing to have her know the truth.

As days passed, Elise decided there was nothing she could do about her reckless disclosure. Thankfully, she didn't see any evidence that anything had changed between she and Anne. Actually, they seemed closer than ever. When the day for the visit to *Meadowlands* arrived, Anne had Giselle and Elise collected in the family Daimler. Elise had rung a girl who lived a few cottages down from them, and asked her to tend Chloe while she was out. Elise had used her before, with good results.

She and Giselle felt like princesses, riding through the cobblestoned streets of Thornton-on-Sea. They crossed the old bridge to Whitfield Cove, the small hamlet named for Anne's family. It was a separate, little village from Thornton-on-Sea, but everyone considered them one entity. The gorgeous auto cruised along the tiny hamlet's High Street. Then, they turned into the avenue that led to *Meadowlands*, and gasped. It consisted of tall Chestnut trees standing four deep on either side. The ground was a carpet of golden daffodils mixed with hyacinths and graceful bluebells. Ahead stood the old, red-brick mansion. The entire front of the house was covered with flowers, and Ivy grew thick and green. It was nothing short of an Eden-like paradise. *Highcroft Hall* was, of course, splendid, but in a different way. Its setting, and ancient ambiance, made *Meadowlands* one of a kind.

They left the car and were welcomed to the home by Anne, her mother, and her father. They couldn't have been nicer. As the girls entered the enormous drawing room, decorated in gold and white, with a Persian rug covering the fine, polished wood floor, both were nearly speechless. French doors ran from ceiling to floor, leading out to the terrace in front of the mansion. The sunlight, through the glass, made everything in the room sparkle. A silver tea service sat on a marble-topped table, between two down-filled sofas. Other seating arrangements were scattered about the large room.

Major Cabot was already there. He stood as the two young ladies entered. Introductions were made, and everyone found a cosy place to sit. It didn't take Giselle and Elise much time to figure out why they'd received the invitations. Major Ted Cabot didn't mince words. He made it abundantly clear that there'd been a prior conversation about fraternizing with social inferiors. It wasn't put so rudely, but that was the gist of his words.

Major Cabot couldn't believe how stunning the French women were. His breath was taken away by Elise's beauty. She looked like a storybook character. Cinderella perhaps, or an innocent Greek Goddess. But the longer they visited, his attention turned to Giselle. He'd always been drawn to her sort. Her shiny, raven hair set off the fair porcelain skin, and her eyes, green, with long lashes, sent his head spinning. Her hair was long and swirled about her shoulders. He thought she was very lovely. There was nothing at all about her that seemed common. Regardless of her social background, she was exquisite. The only thought that kept running through his mind was whether he'd be able to see her again – preferably alone. Was there a chance she might be the slightest bit interested in him? He didn't have a clue. Ted didn't fully understand English tradition. It never crossed his mind that a girl like Giselle wouldn't dream someone of his social class might be interested in *her*. She tried to concentrate upon the present – to make small talk – not to be overly impressed by Major Cabot. But it was very hard. How many times had she talked about her fantasy of meeting and falling in love with an American gentleman? Was this the man about whom she'd dreamed?

10

1942-1943

Sloan continued his correspondence with Anne, although the letters were devoid of any romantic overtones. It was apparent that, at least as far as he was concerned, the issue of their engagement had been dealt with. He obviously thought of Anne as only a longtime friend. Anne answered his letters and tried to sound equally un-romantic. Sloan seldom mentioned Elise. Anne wasn't about to tell him that the girl for whom he'd been willing to break his engagement was living in his home village. Now that she had information about Elise's past, she felt certain Sloan would eventually reconcile with her, begging forgiveness. But that would have to wait until the war ended, and he returned to England. In the meantime, she wrote friendly letters, certain someday he'd come to his senses.

She followed all RAF military deployments with worry and concern. Sloan was sent from one country to another, as war spread across the globe. Burma, Java, Sumatra, India. Places she'd only read about in books. Now, in spring 1942, she hoped he might be transferred back to England. It was very hard to understand what his letters said. Censors made certain nothing that might render aid to the enemy was written. Anne came away with the impression that he was definitely leaving the area where he'd been for a long time. By paying attention to what was happening in the war, she was able to see that the Allies were concentrating a lot of attention on bombing Germany. The Italian campaign was also in full force. Spitfires were being flown from aircraft carriers in the Mediterranean Sea to reinforce air defences in Malta. He might be anywhere. If Sloan had been sent back to England, she wasn't aware of it. It was her hope that he'd be able to come home, for even a short furlough. Nothing of the sort happened. She continued to receive letters, but all mention of his whereabouts was deleted.

In truth, he never came near his homeland. He was still with the Allied forces in Northwest Africa. Sloan was heavily involved in the desert battle of El Almein, during which he was one of hundreds of RAF pilots who flew over five thousand sorties, assisting in delaying the Nazi General Rommel's advance, allowing the British Eighth Army to take up positions at El Almein. That was July 1942.

Although over two years had passed since his brief meeting with Elise, he hadn't forgotten her. He prayed a lot, as did the majority of his chums, and Elise was always one of those he asked God to protect. His mind was occupied with the war the majority of the time, but late at night, in the quiet of the desert, he often took out her photograph. Sometimes it all seemed like a dream. When other soldiers spoke longingly of their wives and lovers, Sloan never mentioned Elise, because he would have been embarrassed to admit he scarcely knew her. Still, he was as convinced as ever that she was his ideal — his soulmate — and his plans to find her, when fighting ceased, were as firmly entrenched as before. Naturally he'd go home first. He missed his parents, and longed to see *Highcroft Hall,* but as soon as possible after that, he meant to find the incomparable Elise.

⁓

Giselle and Major Ted Cabot began corresponding. He'd asked for her address when they said goodbye, after tea at *Meadowlands.* Giselle was secretly delighted and found it hard to believe that the handsome American Officer was interested enough to want to keep in touch. Anne was clearly surprised that a French lady's maid had caught his eye. Her opinion of him deteriorated, and she decided that American men had strange ideas about class equality. It didn't really matter to her one way or the other, since her primary objective was to win back Sloan's love. She felt she'd come a long way toward that goal by learning the truth about Elise's background. However, she wasn't finished yet. Now that she knew about Elise's life in Brighton, she began to plan a trip to that seaside resort. Needless to say, she didn't tell either Elise or Giselle about the pending journey.

She told her parents that she intended a trip to London, for some badly needed shopping, requiring only a day's absence. They weren't entirely in favor of her plans, due to the on-going war. She firmly promised to take every possible precaution. They relented, allowing her to leave. Of course, instead of the fictitious trip to London, Anne boarded a train to Brighton. When she reached that charming seaside resort, she found the brothel Elise had told her about. She also remembered the names of the two women who hadn't been fond of Elise - Adele and Lana. So, after knocking on the door, she asked to speak to one or the other. She was invited inside and was led to a small receiving room by a smartly dressed maid, wearing a traditional black dress with frilled white apron and cap. Soon, two attractive girls entered the room. They were both quite heavily made-up and weren't nearly as young as Anne. She introduced herself and told them she was an acquaintance of Elise de Baier. The one with red hair, Adele, laughed.

"Er name ain't really de Baier, ya know. It's Lisak. A Russian name. 'Er parents was peasants. She went to France when she was little. She picked the name when she found out she were in the puddin club, and decided to lie about bein a widow."

"Yes, I knew about her misfortune in France, with the Nazis," answered Anne. "I didn't know she'd changed her name, but it isn't so surprising."

"Why are you 'ere, if you know everythin about 'er? Is her a friend o yours?" asked Lana.

"Not really. In fact, I only want to know the entire truth about her, because she's romantically involved with a dear friend of mine, from childhood. I don't want to see him hurt."

"I'd tell 'im to stay away from her, if I was you," Adele continued. "She's a scammer, that one. 'E shouldn't believe anythin her sez."

"Can you tell me what basis you have for those remarks?"

"Cause, she's a liar. I suppose her told you she lived 'ere, but weren't one of the workin girls," Lana chimed in.

"Well – yes – she did," answered Anne.

"Tha's what I'd of thought," said Adele. "Well, I can tell you, she lived next to me room, and till her popped out with the babe, she was as busy as all the rest of us. How do you think she saved enough money to move away from 'ere? We've 'eard her has a posh cottage at the seaside."

"Yes, she does. Not large, but quaint. I assume the girl she shares the cottage with pays her share too."

"You mean Giselle? Giselle were the most popular whore in this 'ouse. She come from a very hoity-toity 'ouse in Paris. She's very, very good at what she does."

Anne found this fascinating. Lady Celia's lady's maid was a whore. She would keel over. Actually, Anne had no reason to hate Giselle, and didn't plan on telling her about what she'd learned. The details were strictly for use in her campaign to turn Sloan against Elise. However, such information might come in handy in the future. One never knew.

"Why do the two of you have such bad feelings toward Elise? She seems like a nice girl to me," Anne continued.

"That's the problem. She tries to pretend she's a nice girl. Did you know her slept with Nazis?"

"Oh My! Wait a minute. That's an awfully serious charge. I can scarcely see Elise doing such a thing. She left France because of the Nazis, but it's my understanding she was assaulted," Anne answered.

"So she sez. We thinks she left because she was found out – sleepin with the enemy, if you please. Mind you, we don't 'ave facts, but tha's our take. She wasn't married. Who's the father of 'er little girl?"

"I don't want to spread tales. But what I've been led to believe is entirely different. I'll only say that she didn't willingly have any relationship with her daughter's father."

"Oh, yeah. We know tha story. She were raped by a bunch of drunk Germans. That's totally against the law. They woulda been 'ung. German soldiers wouldn't take chances like 'hat. All she'd of 'ad to do were report them."

"You have a point, ladies," Anne responded, as she gathered up her handbag, preparing to leave. She had to get back to the railway station to catch the last train to Thornton-on-Sea. "I've enjoyed chatting with you. I won't tell Elise I met you. I don't imagine you care, but rest assured, what you've told me will be kept confidential."

"The only reason we care is cause Madame Violette wouldn't be 'appy. She treated Elise like a daughter. Just tell your friend to steer clear. If 'e's interested. She's not fit to be a wife."

Anne walked back up the beach, past the old, chain pier and on to the railroad depot. She was glad she'd come to Brighton. While she didn't believe one smidgeon of Adele and Lana's nasty comments regarding Elise, they could be repeated to Sloan someday, if necessary. She wouldn't be lying if she told him she'd visited Brighton and spoken with two ladies who'd known Elise.

⁓

The summer of 1942 drifted by. The entrance of the Americans into the war had begun to turn the tide, but it was still a hard slog. The Germans were adamant they were going to establish a new world, dominated by white Aryans, with Jews, homosexuals, handicapped persons, and whomever else they considered inferior, eliminated. The 'inferiors' were deported by the thousands, not only from Germany, but from conquered nations, including other Axis powers, like Italy and France. It was truly a battle of good versus evil.

Sloan found himself in battle again at El Alamein, in North Africa. On October 23, 1942, the second fight began at that desert location. Sloan maintained constant air patrols over enemy airfields, after a four-day bombing campaign wiped out most of the opposing forces. There were few suitable airfields, and the going was rough. On December 4, Sloan was shot down, along with nine other Bisley bombers, while they were attempting to destroy an enemy airfield. It was another close brush with death, but although his arm and pelvis were broken, Sloan survived. He was laid up in a base hospital for nearly four months. In April 1943, the Americans linked up with the British RAF, and they finally defeated the Germans at Tunisia. Sloan had recuperated and was in the cockpit again during that battle.

In Thornton-on-Sea, Chloe Arabella de Baier celebrated her second birthday in February 1943. Giselle and Elise had a sweet party for her, even managing to gather enough rationing coupons to bake a little cake for the occasion. She was a precious little girl, with golden hair and big brown eyes. Many people said she looked like Elise, except for the colour of her eyes. She had a winning personality, with a sunny outlook on life. Elise wanted her to have all of the love she herself had missed out on, due to having lost her parents at such a young age. She showered Chloe with cuddles and kisses, but also made certain she was taught proper manners and respect for elders. Because Chloe was the sole focus of Elise's life, she put all of her time and attention into her. There was always concern in the back of her mind that someday Chloe would ask the questions all children ask; "Where did I come from? Who is my Daddy?" Elise wasn't at all certain how she'd handle such queries. She didn't believe in lying to a child, yet it would be a very difficult thing to explain. All she could really do was hope that the issue wouldn't present itself until Chloe was much older, better able to understand the details surrounding her conception. Thus far, she was a happy child, who didn't show signs of wonder about why she didn't have a father. A lot of that probably had to do with the war, since few children her age had a father in the house.

Giselle continued to exchange letters with Major Cabot and grew fonder of him. She began to worry about what she'd do if the relationship became serious. How could she ever explain events in her past? He'd be disgusted. She'd never see him again. Yet, living with lies was anathema to her. It was already very hard to keep the many things she and Elise had said about both of their lives straight in her head. The idea of marrying a man and spending the rest of her life not being able to share the truth didn't seem realistic. She was trapped between a rock and a hard place. If she told the truth, she'd undoubtedly lose him; if she lied, it would eat away at her conscience. She'd live in fear that someone, somewhere would learn of her background and tell him. She and Elise discussed the conundrum, because Elise had the same difficulty. She thought her dilemma was even worse, because she'd made up such an elabourate tale about a non-existent husband, his death and her subsequent widowhood. She'd even changed her name. While there was no one in her life at the moment, she did hope that someday she might find that she was able to trust again. She'd like Chloe to have a father. Then something happened to make her think even more seriously about how she'd deal with the truth.

On one of Anne's regular Monday appointments, the two sat down for a chat after the lesson was finished. Elise was astounded when Anne dropped a bombshell. She said that Sloan had mentioned Elise in a letter. He'd said he wanted to be released from their engagement, because he believed Elise to be his soulmate. Anne confessed she'd known this for some time, but had ignored it because she didn't believe he was truly serious. However, he'd continued to say that his feelings hadn't changed, so Anne felt it was time to tell Elise the truth. She said the only reason she'd withheld the information initially, was because she thought he'd been going through some strange phase and would surely come to his senses. But he hadn't.

The news stunned Elise. She had already admitted to having met Sloan and was glad she'd done so. She explained to Anne that she, too, believed it was a passing fancy. Elise mentioned nothing about what had occurred that long ago day at her French farmhouse. Nothing about the flirting, or the kiss. Certainly not the kiss. She truly was astounded that the soldier, who she'd scarcely known, had ended his engagement because of her! Apparently, his talk about soulmates hadn't just been a bit of frisky behavior.

Anne had thought at length before divulging the truth about the engagement. She knew Elise would be in Thornton-on-Sea when Sloan returned from the war. The more she thought about it, the clearer it became that she couldn't go on pretending, after Sloan returned. The situation would become untenable when he met his mother's lady's maid and eventually learned that Giselle lived with a Frenchwoman named Elise. It would be obvious to Sloan that Anne had known both Giselle and Elise for some time; known them very well. Sloan made it clear, in his letters, that he hadn't given up hope of finding Elise after the war. So, it would be impossible for Anne to omit telling him that the girl he was pining for, lived in his own home village. By telling him that she knew Elise, Anne would be in a good position to hear about everything that went on between them after his return. That was assuming, of course, that Sloan would contact Elise immediately upon his return to Thornton-on-Sea. Anne knew he would. Because he'd believe Anne was Elise's friend, he wouldn't question anything Anne told him about Elise. So, long before the war ended, Anne had her final plans in place.

"What are you going to do, Anne? Are you releasing him from the engagement?"

"I already have, Elise. Actually, quite some time ago. I've been living under the delusion that he'd change his mind, come to his senses and return to me, but that isn't what's happened. He's begun to speak of you more often in his letters. He treats me as a friend and confidante, spilling his belief that you're meant to be his. I have no choice but to give him up. I haven't said anything to my parents, or to his. I probably won't until I've had a chance to see him, but I no longer believe his feelings are only pipe dreams. Tell me, how do you feel about all of this?"

"Oh, Anne. It's very hard to believe he'd give you up in favor of me. He's known you all of his life. You're everything that a countess should be. That's a huge part of the equation. I don't believe he's thinking straight. He doesn't even know me. As to what I feel for him? Nothing, really. He was very kind and attractive when I met him, but it was a brief encounter. At no time did I think of him in a romantic way. He'd been wounded, and it was war. It shocks me to hear that he has such a fantasy."

"Well, I think you should prepare yourself for the certainty that he'll arrive on your doorstep, as soon as possible, after he comes home. I don't want your friendship with me to have a bearing on any decision you make. You've become a good friend, and Sloan has been in my life since we were children. I won't deny my feelings for him. But, I honestly love him enough to want him to be happy. If that can't be with me, and it *can* be with you, then I won't stand in the way. He's a wonderful man. I know that with certainty. I quite understand your wariness of men, but I can assure you, Sloan can be trusted in every way. He would never lie, or take advantage of you."

"But Anne, as you well know, there are things in my past he doesn't know – lies have been told to protect Chloe. People think I'm a widow. I don't even go by my proper surname. I've never been married. How in the world would I begin to explain all of that?"

"I'll see him after he returns. I'm fairly certain he'll want to talk to me before seeing you. I'll tell him you suffered greatly, after he saw you in 1940, and that you're still not able to talk about it. Sloan is kind. He'd never insist on speaking to you about things that are upsetting. I'll tell him everything that happened to you. He'll understand that you were so terribly traumatized that it's no wonder you don't want to speak of it. I don't think he'll probe for answers. Not after he realizes what you've been through."

"You make it all sound so easy," Elise smiled. "I feel as though I'm digging a deeper hole of lies."

"No, Elise. He'll know the truth. He'll understand that you had to tell some small lies. Only designed to protect your daughter from harm and allowing you to begin anew."

"Oh Anne, I can't imagine. I believe any man would be repulsed by the thought that a woman he believed virtuous and as pure as the driven snow, had been intimate with those beastly men."

"Oh, but Elise, it wasn't voluntary. 'Intimate' isn't the right word. Sloan is a compassionate man. He'd hate what was done to you. He certainly wouldn't blame you."

"Anne, I feel soiled and dirty. I've been fouled and sullied. How could he possibly want me?"

"He'd want you, because he loves you. He'll be appalled at what happened. If I know Sloan, he will never make you speak of it to him. He won't be repulsed. Well, perhaps by the Nazi soldiers, but never by you."

"But don't you understand? I'm the one who feels repulsed. I hate myself for what happened. I probably should have killed them, or myself, rather than allow my body to be used in that way."

"Elise, that's silly. It's easy to say now what you should or shouldn't have done. You did what you had to do to save your life. That was the correct thing to do. Now, no more talk of this. Let's wait and see what Sloan has to say when he returns. Let's see how you feel when you see him. It's been a long time. Much has happened. Perhaps you'll only want his friendship, in which case all of this conversation is for naught. I only wanted you to know the truth. I've already told him you live here, so when this bloody war is over – sorry about the language, but, I'm so fed up with all of it - you two can see one another."

"I think it highly improbably that Sloan Thornton and I will ever be anything to one another. This is all some silly misunderstanding."

Anne left the cottage feeling extremely positive. Elise's reaction had been exactly what she'd envisioned. The stage was set for Sloan's return.

11

Of course, Elise told Giselle about her conversation with Anne. Giselle was pleased that everything seemed to be out in the open. She wasn't upset that Elise had long ago shared facts about Chloe's conception. She was also glad Elise hadn't said anything about Giselle's own past. There was no question in her mind that she was very much in love with Ted Cabot. She suspected that when the war ended, he was likely to propose. She'd practically made herself sick with worry. He was all she'd ever dreamed of in a husband. If she were lucky enough to marry him, she could leave Europe and start a new life in America. It was said that people over there weren't so judgmental about the class from which a person came. Most everyone she knew said Americans were potty over English people. Giselle had no doubt that she'd adore the United States. But, one, big question loomed. Should she tell Ted the truth? Or should she lie?

Ted was still based at RAF Ashford. From the little Giselle knew about his missions, many sorties were flown over the Continent. She suspected that he was heavily involved in the multitude of raids conducted over Berlin and other parts of Germany. Letters were a Godsend. Since Giselle worked during the week, it would have been hard for them to see one another, even if Ted had free days between weekends. She considered their correspondence a lifeline. The letters provided a wonderful means for learning more about each other. Sometimes it was easier to say things in writing than in person. Giselle considered telling him everything about her past in a carefully worded letter. But upon further reflection, it was clear she owed it to Ted to look him in the eye when she told the truth. Any man would be shocked upon learning that the woman he loved had a sordid past. She vacillated back and forth about whether or not to tell him. Whatever her faults, Giselle had an intense sense of honesty. Her conscience wouldn't permit her to live the rest of her life with such a lie. For an extended period, she procrastinated, telling herself there was no rush. She could wait until the war was over. The timing had to be right. However, she knew, in her heart that she was only stalling. Finally, she decided the time had come.

It was February 1943, the beginning of around-the-clock strategic bombing in Europe. In two days, more than two thousand sorties were flown against enemy targets. Giselle strongly suspected that Ted was among those who were a part of the mission. She followed the events in the *London Times*. *If Ted were involved, he* would likely be granted a weekend furlough. That wasn't uncommon procedure in the RAF. Often, after a particularly strenuous campaign, the airmen were given a rest. Giselle decided to seize the moment. She had no idea when she'd see him again. She needed to get the matter off her mind. Either he'd accept her confession, and they'd continue on together, or he would tell her it was over. Either way, she'd finally know.

She wrote and asked Ted if he could come to Thornton-on-Sea, if he got a furlough. Normally he stayed with the Whitfield family at *Meadowlands*, but because Giselle knew they'd be discussing sensitive issues, she asked if he'd consider staying at the *Dove's Cote Inn*, a small hotel, not far from *'No Regrets'*. He responded in the affirmative. Giselle made reservations for him, and they met at the railway station on a Friday. She waited while he checked into the pretty brick establishment, covered with climbing roses. It had been a warmer than usual winter, and some of the buds were already opened. After he was settled, they walked to her cottage. Elise had prepared a nice luncheon. Following that, Ted and Giselle decided to cycle to a spot they loved near the shoreline, where the woods came down to meet the water. It was a nice day – not at all cold - with a very blue sky. When they reached their destination, they sat together on an old pier, watching the waves and listening to the sounds of birds singing in the trees. Giselle searched her mind for the proper way to begin the conversation. However, before she had a chance, Ted began to speak.

"Giselle, I'm so glad we have this weekend together. I've been hoping for just this sort of break. If it were a different time – not war – I'd have so many wonderful choices – romantic choices – about where to do this. This isn't how I planned it would be. But there isn't any stylish restaurant, where two people can drink champagne, dance to romantic band music, and enjoy elegant surroundings. So, this will have to do. Perhaps it's fitting."

"I haven't the slightest notion of what you're talking about," she replied.

"I know. I'm not doing this very well. The thing is, Giselle, I have something important I want to ask. Please think before you answer, because what you say will mean everything to me. I'm asking you to marry me. After this damned war has ended, I want to take you to America. You'll love Boston, I'm sure of it. It's also on the sea, you know. My parents will adore you. I love you and feel certain you love me. Let's pledge to spend the rest of our lives together." Ted fumbled around in his uniform pocket, producing a jeweler's box. Handing it to her he said, "Please accept this as a token of my love for you, and wear it until we can marry."

Giselle looked down at the ring. It was a lovely centre diamond, surrounded by smaller stones of the same sort, set in platinum. It was exquisite. She wanted it more than she'd ever wanted anything in her life. This hadn't been what she'd expected. His proposal threw her off kilter. Should she continue with her planned confession, or simply accept the ring and tell him she loved him madly? There was silence while she sat staring at the beautiful piece of jewelry. Finally, she took a deep breath and spoke.

"Ted. I can't tell you what this means to me. From the first time I saw you, I believed you could be the man I'd always dreamed of marrying. As I've grown to know you better, that belief has become certain. I'd give everything I own to put this ring on my finger and to wear it forever as your wife."

Ted started to say something, but she put her hand up, telling him he had to let her finish. "Ted, the truth is, you don't know me well enough to be proposing to me. I understand that you think you do. I admit you should by now. But I haven't been completely truthful with you, and before I could ever agree to be your wife, I have to be honest. I can't let you go through life thinking one thing, when the truth is much less appealing."

"What are you saying? I can't imagine what I don't know about you. We've shared so many thoughts and feelings. You've told me all about your childhood and about how you escaped from France. What do you mean when you say you haven't been honest?"

Giselle put her head in her hands. She was trying hard not to weep. "I'm not the person you think I am. In order to make you understand, I'm going to have to start at the beginning and tell you everything. Please don't interrupt until I'm finished. Then you can say anything you wish. I'll understand completely if you decide you've made a horrible mistake. I won't blame you. The fault is all mine. Will you listen to me until I'm through with my story?"

"Yes, of course, if that's what you want," he replied, looking confused.

"All right. As you know, I was born in a small village in France – Beau Ville. I was only a few months old when both of my parents died in the flu epidemic of 1918. From that time, I was shuttled from relative to relative. No one really wanted me. The war had just ended, and money was scarce. I was just another mouth to feed. I had no brothers or sisters and no aunt or uncle who loved me. The relatives I was placed with were far removed cousins and the like. They didn't know me, and I didn't know them. I doubt my parents even knew them. I went to many, many schools and lived in over a dozen houses before I was in my early teens. I was a very unhappy girl. In 1934, when I was sixteen, I ran away to Paris. Nobody cared enough about what happened to me to even search. I was glad of that. It was a bad time in the world, economically. America was in the midst of your Great Depression. It wasn't so bad in France, but it wasn't good. Especially for a sixteen year old girl, with no education and no skills of any kind. I had one thing, and one thing only. I was pretty. I was also terribly naïve and innocent. I met another girl in a place where young people went to find food. It was a sort of soup kitchen, where I could get a hot meal once a day. The girl I met was older. She was very pretty, and seemed quite sophisticated to me. She said she was going to a place called The Pleasure Club, where they were hiring young girls to do hairstyling and make-up for working women. I had no idea what 'working women' meant, but the idea of a job was very enticing."

"I liked to do hair and play with make-up. I think all girls do. It sounded fun, and she told me they gave you room and board, so I wouldn't have to worry about those necessities. Plus, they paid a wage. So I followed her, and we wound up at a large, three-story mansion – really very lovely. We were interviewed by an older woman, who seemed nice, and we were hired. My friend's name was Colette. We shared a room. At first, it was everything Colette said it would be. I enjoyed the work, and we had good meals. Then, Colette came to me one night and told me we could make a lot more money. We would have to perform the same work as the women whose hair we styled and make-up we applied. I had no idea what sort of work they did. I know I don't have to tell you. Of course, it was an escort service. We lived there, and men rang the house, making appointments for assignations. We were taken to nice places – restaurants, the opera, theatre, galleries – and the men were of the highest caliber, at least as far as wealth, manners, and the like. Many were businessmen on trips to Paris, or young University chaps, travelling the Continent. Naturally, at the end of the evening it was clear what was expected. Because everyone around me did the same thing, I truly didn't see what was wrong with it. I made very good money and was treated well. I'd never been taught about religion or morals, so didn't think I was hurting anyone. Then, the war came. Many of the girls stayed and were excited because they knew business would soar if the Germans invaded. But I wanted no part of that. I was a very patriotic French girl. So, I left and escaped to England. I went to Brighton, where I met Elise. Of course, she too had escaped from France. When Chloe was born, we decided to leave Brighton together, to begin a new life. I'd become very spiritual and religious and understood how I'd sinned. I'm horribly ashamed of what I did. I would never do it now. I was stupid and young – stupid and frightened. So, here I am. In love with you, but unable to accept your proposal because of past behavior."

Ted leaned back against a post on the pier. His face had lost most of its colour. "Whew," he said. Then there was more silence, as the waves crashed against the wood. "I need to think, Giselle. I understand what you've told me. I can honestly say I'm not angry. It's a sad story. I just need time to absorb everything. Will you give me a day? Let me go back to my room. I need some time to myself? I admit, this is quite a shock."

"Yes, of course I'll give you time. All of the time you want. I don't blame you if you never want to see me again. If I repulse you. Most men would feel that way. But I had to be honest. I do love you – more than anything, and I could crawl at your feet, begging you to forgive me. But I don't want your pity. What I did was sinful and wrong. I should have known better. Perhaps deep in my heart I did. I really don't know. All I know is that I'm sorry now. Whether I'd met you or not, I'd already walked away from that life. I much prefer working as a lady's maid than dressing in fancy gowns and being wined and dined. Whether I lose you or not, it won't matter in terms of my lifestyle. But of course, it will matter very much to my heart, because I've never given it to anyone before. Now, go. Go and take the time you need. Whatever you decide, I'll still love you."

Ted stood, looking down at Giselle, who still sat on the pier, her dark hair shining in the sunlight.

"You're such a beautiful creature," he murmured.

Then he turned and walked alone up the beach. He didn't even remember to take the ring, which still lay in its velvet box next to Giselle. She wiped away tears and tucked the ring box into her pocket. She'd thought she'd feel better for having told him the truth, but she didn't. Perhaps later, when her heart had healed. Right then, she only knew she'd been very foolish to believe, for a moment, that any decent man would want to take a whore home to his parents.

12

Giselle returned to *No Regrets*. She kicked the small sign, at the entrance to the cottage, when she walked by and laughed aloud.

"We should change the name of the cottage to '*Nothing but Regrets*," she murmured to herself. Upon entering, she found Elise sitting in the parlour knitting, while Chloe played nearby on the rug. Giselle sat down and began telling her friend what had taken place. Elise saw the pain on Giselle's face. Putting her knitting aside, she moved to over her and offered comfort.

"Oh, my poor, dear Giselle. Obviously you made the decision to be honest with Ted. I think it was the right choice, but I know how hard it had to have been. What exactly was his reaction?"

"He was shocked. Appallingly so. His face lost all colour. He didn't say much of anything – just asked me to give him time to think it through. The last thing he said was that I was a beautiful creature."

"Well, I'd say that's encouraging. He didn't go into a rage and verbally attack you for what you'd divulged. Obviously, he didn't say it was all over. So perhaps there's still hope."

"I really don't think so, Elise. He doesn't want to be cruel, and he's probably thinking of the best way to tell me that our relationship has come to an end. I don't blame him. It's my fault. What sends me into the depths of depression is the realization of how hopeless my future is. What am I supposed to do? Go on trusting that I'll meet another nice chap, fall in love with him, tell the truth and be rejected again? Or should I spend the rest of my life lying? Everything seems so futile."

"I know, Giselle. But give Ted time. What you told him is an awful lot to take in. Anyone would want time to think. If you end up losing him, then he wasn't the understanding chap you thought he was. That doesn't mean someone else won't be. But, let's give Ted a chance. Wait and see."

"I suppose you're right," answered Giselle. "I just feel like crawling under the covers and never coming out again. I'm going to my room. Please don't bother me unless it's terribly important." Giselle walked up the stairway, with her head hung low.

"All right, Giselle. Perhaps that's the best thing for now. I'm going to take Chloe to the park for a bit. Do have a lie-down, and try to rest. You may still be surprised at the outcome."

An entire day and night went by, and there was no word from Ted. Giselle couldn't stand the silence anymore, and she rang the Inn where he was staying. She wanted to confirm whether or not he was still there, or if he'd returned to RAF Ashford. As she'd expected, he was no longer registered. He'd checked out that morning. Giselle lay back down on the bed and sobbed until she thought she would die. So, she'd been right. He'd probably write a letter. It would be easier for him that way. She already knew what it would say. Giselle walked to her dressing table, picked up the ring box, and threw it across the room. She would have to give it back to him, but would ask Elise to do it. She wasn't about to trek to the post office with swollen eyes, so everyone could see her heartbreak.

Finally, she bathed and dressed. She decided to take a long walk. She had a need for fresh air and thought it might help to clear her mind. Giselle ambled toward the High Street. It was chilly outside, so she'd worn a coat and a snug scarf. She'd left the cottage without even saying goodbye to Elise. It was Sunday, and she hadn't attended church. She was so downhearted, that she didn't even feel guilt about that. She walked over the cobblestoned streets and dusty lanes of Thornton-on-Sea, thinking about how much she loved Ted. Men like him didn't pop up every day. Giselle had never met anyone like him. She wished with all of her heart that she'd continued to lie. He never would have known. All of her dreams of a new life in America would have become reality. She had certainly learned the value of truth. There was none — absolutely none. After more than two hours of walking, she found herself back at the old pier, where she and Ted had said their last goodbyes. She hadn't meant to end up there, but that's where Giselle's heart led her. Once again, she began to weep. Sitting in the same spot where she and Ted had so recently been, Giselle fell apart. The pain was unbearable. If this was what love did to a person, she never wanted any part of it again.

She heard footsteps. Glancing around to see who it was, Giselle could scarcely believe her eyes. It was Ted. What in the world was he doing here? What did he want? Did she even care what he had to say? Giselle wasn't certain she could listen to his words. Ted slowly walked toward her and, without saying anything, he sat down in the same spot he'd been before. She raised her head and looked at him cautiously. At last, she spoke.

"If you've come to tell me everything is over, don't bother. I expected that. I told you before, I don't blame you. I don't want to go over everything again. I was stupid. I made terrible mistakes. I'm paying for them now. I'll pay for the rest of my life. Please, just leave me. I'm sorry for everything."

"Giselle, that isn't why I've come. I told you I needed time to think. That's all I've done since I last saw you. I want you to listen carefully to what I have to say. I probably should have contacted you sooner, but you have to admit that what you told me was a bit overwhelming. I've thought everything through carefully. You know how I am. I think deeply about important matters. Nothing in my life has ever been more important than this. Will you listen?"

"Yes, of course," she sighed.

"Giselle, at first I thought there was no way I could accept what you'd told me. It appalled me. But, then I began to think about myself — about society in general — about men in general. You know, from the time boys aren't even men, a lot of them have 'sown their wild oats', as is commonly said. In fact, it's expected. Men are supposed to be experienced when they marry. At university, it's a wonderful joke. If a fellow is innocent, and not yet initiated into love-making, all of his friends set to work trying to remedy that. You told me yourself that a large number of your clients in Paris were young men doing the Grand Tour. As the English say, it's the 'done thing'."

"Society doesn't address that sort of behavior. No woman would ever think of asking her fiancé if he'd had experience before marriage. Nor would she be upset if he had. After all, men are supposed to know how to perform on the wedding night. But god help a woman who has experience. That's an entirely different thing. Yet for centuries that's the way it's been. To tell the truth, Giselle, I would bet I've had more experience than you've ever thought about. I'm being honest. So, I think that would justify *you* being repulsed by me. Additionally, I've never been in a position where I needed to engage in that sort of behavior because I needed money, or because no one taught me properly. I have no excuse, except that it was expected of me. At least there were reasons behind your actions. So, I'm asking *you* to forgive *me*. I've learned from this incident. If I ever have a son, I'll teach him right from wrong. If he wants to behave as his father did, then he needs to accept that the woman he chooses to marry has the same rights. I see us as equals — perhaps I'm even more wicked than you, from a 'sin' standpoint. I never want us to speak of this again. I want you to put my ring on your finger, and wear it until the end of this war. Then we'll decide whether we want to marry here, or in America. I'll leave that to you. I love you, Giselle, and I've been wrong. Tell me you'll marry me and that you still love me."

Giselle was dumbfounded. Never. Never in a thousand years had she expected such clear, sensible, fair thinking. The idea of men versus women, in terms of intimate experience, hadn't crossed her mind. But it *did* make sense. She sat on the pier, stunned beyond words. Finally she gathered herself together.

"Ted, I love you so much. You're the kindest, most understanding, man I've ever known. There aren't ten men in the world who'd see this from your perspective. I'm so fortunate. But — and please, listen to what I have to say. I've been thinking too, during our time apart. I had no idea you'd be this understanding. I was prepared to lose you. In the midst of thinking about that, I came to realize that it would probably be for the best. Not because the idea of losing you doesn't break my heart. It does. But, in the long run, I suspect we'd be unhappy together. When I think beyond the present dilemma, and look into the future, I can see that it wouldn't work. You come from a wealthy background. You've attended the finest schools and have everything in the world to offer me. I, on the other hand, have nothing to offer you."

"That's not true, Giselle. You have love to offer me."

"Perhaps, Ted. But, you see, I don't feel like that's enough. A hundred other women could offer you love. I think I'd always feel as though you were doing all of the giving, and I was doing all of the taking. We aren't equals. I know, I know. You just said a minute ago that we *are* equals. And, yes, on the subject of experience with the opposite sex, perhaps you're correct. I'm talking about broader issues. I don't think I'd ever feel worthy of you. My self-esteem has always been good, in spite of the bad choices I've made. I'm afraid I'll lose my self-confidence. You see, I simply can't believe you *really* need me. How could you? In the end, we'd tear each other apart, Ted. Go back to America, and find a girl who shares your background. This is the hardest thing I've ever said or done. But, I know I'm right."

"Giselle, you can't be serious. You can't be. How can you say you love me and, in the same breath, want to end everything?"

"It isn't that I *want* to end everything. I'll probably kick myself a thousand times for what I'm doing. But, a voice inside of me says that it's the wisest thing to do. I'd end up being unhappy, because I'd feel unfit. It would eat away at me. I should have realized that before now."

"Will you please think about it? Don't make such an impulsive decision, without serious thought. I won't harangue you. I'll give you time. The war isn't over, and I'll be here for quite a while yet. Take some time to be alone. We won't see each other. But, don't say it's all over. Not yet."

Giselle sighed. "All right, Ted. I'll do as you ask. But, I don't think I'll change my mind. I hope time apart doesn't make me so lonely for you that I will change my mind, and decide to marry you, when, in my heart, I know it would be a mistake. Love doesn't really conquer all, Ted."

"I believe it can and will. But, as I said, I won't press you. I won't even write to you. Go ahead. See other men. Do whatever you want. Just remember, I'm still going to be in England, and, before I leave, we'll see each other again."

Tears were streaming down her face. "Thank you, Ted. Thank you for understanding. I truly believe that someday you'll realize I was right."

"I don't agree. I'll never agree. We'll wait to see who's right and who's wrong.

He stood, and put his hand out. She grabbed hold of it, and together they walked back to the shoreline. "Thank you for telling me the truth about your past. You wouldn't have needed to, you know. No one would ever have known, he said.

"I would have known, Ted."

Sloan continued operations from India, Egypt, and Burma. He longed for the green fields of home and wondered if he'd ever see England again. The Allies suffered some setbacks, but overall there was optimism that the fight would finally be won. He continued corresponding with Anne and, in one letter, asked openly if she'd told her family of their broken engagement. He'd never asked that question before.

Anne wrote back with news that sent him over-the-moon. She said she'd not told anyone of their broken engagement, other than a friend. Then she went on to tell him about a French girl named Elise, who had been living at Thornton-on-Sea for nearly two years. She explained that Elise's friend, Giselle Dupris, worked as a lady's maid for his mother at *Highcroft Hall.* Apparently, through Giselle, Anne had become well acquainted with Elise. She'd learned that Elise was the farm girl whose home he'd visited in May, 1940. Sloan couldn't believe it when Anne wrote that she'd told Elise about her lifetime friendship with Sloan, as well as their engagement and its subsequent ending. As to whether Elise seemed at all attracted to him, she couldn't tell. Another bit of shocking news was that Elise was a widow and had a child, born in England in 1941. There was no mention in Anne's letter of the talk she and Elise had shared, when Anne had learned the truth about so much of Elise's background. Anne was holding that information close to the vest, for use in her campaign to destroy Sloan's fascination with the French girl.

Sloan was perplexed. Elise had made no mention of a husband, or fiancé, when they'd met. In fact, the only person she'd mentioned was her brother, Josef. He thought back and couldn't figure how she might have married, become pregnant, escaped from Dunkirk and delivered a baby, all in such short order. Unless she was already married and pregnant at the time they met, it didn't add up. Perhaps she *had* been married and even pregnant. There was no reason she'd have told him everything about herself. She probably didn't trust him, and why should she have? It didn't lower his estimation of her. In fact his admiration grew, as he thought about the courage it must have taken for a pregnant girl to take a chance on fleeing France. It was truly miraculous that she was now in Thornton-on-Sea, and that her friend worked for his parents. Anne also said that she took French lessons from Elise and that Elise didn't like to talk about her past. All of this information only served to make Sloan believe that his first inclination had been spot-on. God had placed her in a location where they were bound to see one another again! He was somewhat surprised that Anne had been so open about everything. He supposed she'd felt it necessary, because sooner or later, God willing, he'd come home and learn the truth. He was pleased that Anne had met Elise. It was wonderful that they liked each other. It made him all the more anxious to get back to Thornton-on-Sea. He answered Anne's letter, thanking her for telling him everything. He said he didn't care whether she hadn't told his, or her, parents about the engagement having ended. He understood why it was his responsibility. Sloan also promised never to speak to Elise about her past.

Anne was relieved when she received his response. Everything was moving according to plan. While it looked, on the surface, like she was heartily in favor of Sloan's happiness with Elise, and was even acting as a go-between to further the romance, that wasn't at all the case. She didn't care if Sloan and Elise both hated her when the truth was revealed. Sloan deserved to be hurt, and while she felt less animosity toward Elise, the girl was a liar.

13

1943 - 1945

Giselle missed Ted terribly. She told Elise what had happened, and it was apparent that her friend wasn't wholly in agreement with what Giselle had done. However, it was Giselle's decision, and Elise didn't intervene. It had taken tremendous bravery for Giselle to do what she had, and all Elise could do was be supportive. In her heart, she couldn't imagine that the romance was truly over.

Then, in June, 1943, Major Ted Cabot was transferred to Ridgewell, in northwest Essex, to join the 381st Bomb group with its B-17 Flying Fortresses. The outfit, newly arrived from the United States, was particularly noted for its ability to fly formations. His first target mission was an airfield at Antwerp, Belgium. The contingent was composed of twenty-one aircraft. Two Fortresses were lost, and two returned to the base severely damaged with casualties aboard. Ted returned safely.

Giselle was very disturbed when Ted left Ashford. She knew nothing about his whereabouts – simply that he'd been reassigned to a new airbase. She only had that information because Anne's father had relayed the news. Had she known the size and scope of the missions he was flying, she would have been beyond disturbed. He no longer wrote letters, nor did Giselle. She knew that he was still alive, because of Ted's communication with Lord Whitfield, but that was all. She knelt each morning, in the village church, praying for his safe return.

On August 21, Ted was in the cockpit of a plane that flew on an important mission, targeting the great ball-bearing factories at Schweinfurt. They fought their way to the target, through swarming enemy fighters and thick flak, to hit the objective and then fought their way out again. Of the twenty-two aircraft contingent, there were eleven aeroplanes and ten crews lost. Ted's craft returned safely to base after a successful ditching in the Channel. The 381st accounted for twenty-two of the German fighters shot down that day. They returned to Schweinfurt on October 14. That time, while Eighth Air Force losses were at least as large as they were on August 17, the 381st lost only one Fortress. Ted was awarded the Military Cross for his action. Giselle read and heard snippets about the flying Fortress, but had no idea that Ted was connected to them.

So, life went on, as rationing became more stringent, and Englanders grew war weary. Little Chloe de Baier grew sturdy and strong. Both Elise and Giselle doted on her something fierce. She called Giselle "Aunt Gissy", pronounced 'Jissy'. Giselle's fondest hope was for Elise to fall in love with a fine man, someone who'd become a true father to Chloe. That was Elise's hope too. However, she still maintained her distrust of men and made no effort to meet any of the vast number of soldiers who roamed the streets of Thornton-on-Sea on weekends. She was content with the life she led, loved the sweet cottage that had become home, and only wished the war would end, so life could finally be peaceful and free from worry. She seldom thought about Sloan Thornton's return to *Highcroft Hall*.

Anne had a way, though, of reminding her that Sloan would someday return. She got little reaction from Elise when she did so. Although Anne seemed eager to see Elise fall in love with Sloan, nothing could have been further from the truth. Anne was a wise, sly young lady. However, she hadn't reckoned on the fact that Elise would be stubborn about a romance with Sloan. Not because Elise was obstinate by nature, but because, in her heart, she had a difficult time believing that Anne, who supposedly loved Sloan with all of her heart, was adamant that he forget his childhood sweetheart forever, and establish a relationship with Elise. Supposedly Anne loved him enough to let him go. She maintained that it was more important for him to be happy. While the notion was very noble, Elise thought it a bit far-fetched. Never, at any time, had Anne said she didn't still love Sloan. If she'd done so, Elise would have better understood how she could so calmly encourage him to marry someone else.

Elise harboured the hope that a message from her brother would appear, but none did. She even considered placing a personal ad, in the event that it might be seen by Josef, but when she read through the columns, she was disheartened by the multitude of people who were searching for loved ones. Perhaps when peace came, they'd find each other, if Josef were still alive.

At the beginning of 1944, there came a brutal series of Luftwaffe attacks on London and other English cities. Mosquito night flyers, equipped with radar, accounted for 129 of the 329 aircraft shot down during what was called the five month 'Little Blitz.' Greater London and southeast England were singled out for attacks, in retaliation of British saturation bombing of major German cities. Londoners accepted the resumption of the air raids stoically, but people were so very war weary. Three years of the sheer slog of wartime life, since the first Blitz, had inevitably taken a toll. During the 'Little Blitz' the noise was truly appalling. Most of it was caused by England's own much more formidable defences. Even a quiet night brought little rest. Many thousands of men and women, after their day's work, went home to do their bit as Air Raid Wardens and Firewatchers. Westminster was no more immune than other parts of London. On the night of February 20, 1944, Downing Street and Whitehall once again suffered bomb damage. All along the southeastern coastline, which included Thornton-on-Sea, citizens again spent a lot of time in Anderson shelters. The quaint village, where Elise and Giselle had found love and acceptance, escaped damage. But fear was evident on everybody's faces, and though there was strong belief that the finale was drawing near, the never-ending wail of sirens and roar of aircraft gave pause.

Sloan was still in Burma. After consistently receiving letters from him, in March, 1944, all correspondence had come to a halt. Anne had no idea what to think. What in blazes was going on? She read everything she could get her hands on, but there was no information. She had no way of knowing that a Japanese advance through Burma had isolated the British garrison at a place called Imphal. A three-month siege began, and 150,000 men had to rely entirely on air supply for their survival. More than four hundred tons of stores were flown daily into a heavily guarded valley, with only three squadrons of Spitfires available for air defence and six squadrons of Hurricanes for attack purposes. Major Sloan Thornton was one of those men, and it was a dire time. When the ordeal ended, with undisputed air supremacy enjoyed by the British, it was midsummer, and the largest battle of the war was upon them.

Sloan was finally transferred back to England to lead a squadron that would take part in the infamous invasion later known as D-Day. It was code-named Operation Overlord and was the largest amphibious invasion ever known. Sloan wasn't the only airman, known to the residents of Thornton-on-Sea, who would be participating in that heroic effort. Ted Cabot was there too.

On June 5, 1944, the day preceding D-Day, Bomber Command simulated an Allied air invasion by dropping dummy paratroops. Lancaster's and Stirlings also flew at fixed intervals over the Channel, to mimic the approach of an invading fleet. During the night, aircraft dropped the British 6th Airborne Division in the Caen area of France. On that same day, Rome was liberated by Allied forces. Although Ted and Sloan had never met one another, both took part in the D-Day operation. The invasion of June 6, went very well. Casualties were heavy and American forces on Omaha Beach suffered many losses. Ted was shot down and seriously wounded at Port-en-Bessin. He was rescued and sent to Number Fifty Mobile Field Hospital near a landing strip. There, he was stabilized and flown to a hospital in England. Sloan was successful in linking up with other Allied Forces and took part in cutting the rail links between Carentan and Cherbourg. With the successful toe-hold established under the air umbrella along the Normandy coast, emphasis was then shifted to ground operations.

Giselle didn't know Ted had been wounded. None of the civilian population knew about the operation until it was over. Thankfully, Ted had placed Giselle's name on the list of persons he wished to have notified in case of emergency. Thus, on June 8, 1944, she received a wire telling her that Major Cabot was confined to the Prince of Wales Hospital in London. There was no hint as to how badly injured he might be. She was frantic with worry. Elise helped her friend throw a few items into a travelling case, and catch the first train to London. From there, Giselle made her way to the hospital. When she arrived at Ted's room, she was horrified. He lay unconscious, swathed in bandages from head to toe. There were only small slits for his eyes and mouth, and from what she could ascertain, he was missing a leg. Giselle was a strong person, and though she felt like falling apart, she didn't allow herself to do so. Her words of months past were entirely forgotten. She certainly had something to offer Ted now.

Searching out a physician, she enquired about his injuries. 'Yes', she was told, Ted had lost a leg. He'd also been badly burned over a large portion of his body. His condition was critical. For nine days and nights, Giselle never left his side, except to grab a bite to eat. She held his hand, wiped his brow, and even assisted nurses when they changed bandages. Very, very slowly, he was removed from the critical list, but his condition was anything but good. When he finally regained consciousness, he said he wanted her to leave. He was extremely despondent and wouldn't consider letting Giselle stay with him. Nor would he speak of the future. Ted felt he no longer had anything to offer her and didn't want Giselle to spend the rest of her life caring for an invalid. The tables had turned. Giselle refused to listen. She stated clearly that she loved him and would always love him. His injuries had nothing to do with that love. She said she wouldn't even consider not spending the rest of her life with him. In the end, he gave up the fight, weeping over the love she showed to him.

He spent six months in hospital healing from burns. It wouldn't have mattered one way or the other to Giselle, but Ted was relieved that his face had escaped the worst scarring. Giselle took a small bed-sit close to the hospital, so she could be with him every day. Lady Celia and Lord Rowan understood completely, and even continued to pay her wages. Ted's family in America was notified, but he made it abundantly clear that he didn't want them to find their way to London. It was the end of the war for Ted. When he was able to write his family a letter, he told them of his plans to marry Giselle. The decision was made to wed in England before travelling to the United States. That couldn't be considered until a peace treaty was signed. In spite of the resounding victory on D-Day, and the liberation of France, the Germans still refused to admit defeat, and it was another year before all hostilities came to an end. In the meantime, Ted was transferred to a second rehabilitation hospital, where he learned to negotiate an artificial leg.

By the time happy day arrived, May 8, 1945, Ted was back in Thornton-on-Sea, ensconced in a guest suite at *Highcroft Hall.* There was pandemonium throughout England. Huge crowds, many dressed in red, white and blue, gathered outside Buckingham Palace in London, and cheered as the King, Queen, and two Princesses came out onto the balcony. Earlier, tens of thousands of people listened as the King's speech was relayed by loudspeaker to those who'd gathered in Trafalgar and Parliament Squares. Winston Churchill made a broadcast to the nation. In his wonderful and dramatic way, he told the people of Great Britain and her Dominions that the war was over. In it, he paid tribute to the men and women who had laid down their lives for victory, as well as to all those "who had fought valiantly on land, sea and in the air." Citizens of Thornton —on-Sea and Whitfield Cove rose up and celebrated with the rest of England. Ted could hear the cheers from his room.

━━━∾∾∾━━━

As a burst of hail swept the road outside of the train depot in the village of Thornton-on-Sea, Sloan found himself in the centre of a crowd seeking shelter. It was unusual to encounter a crowd in the tiny hamlet, but it was teatime, and shop owners on the High street were out and about. The rain reminded him of the day he'd met Elise. *Everything* reminded him of that day. He'd tried and tried to remove her from his thoughts, to no avail. It had been over five years, and her face still lingered in the recesses of his mind. He still treasured her photo, wrinkled and badly worn. He was home, the war was over, and it was imperative that he get on with the rest of his life. He had a clear-cut agenda and was anxious to follow it.

After seeing his parents, his first task was to see Anne. That was only proper. Although she'd been understanding in her letters, he suspected that she still harboured feelings for him. He hoped he was wrong, but it was hard to believe that the girl who'd said 'yes' when proposed to, could casually brush off his sudden and shocking rejection. Anne had undoubtedly been crushed by his letter saying she wasn't the one for him. He was terribly anxious to see Elise again, but knew it would be the height of rudeness to ignore Anne. It was, after all, still important that he keep close ties with his childhood friend.

She'd told him long ago, after he'd written and admitted he didn't love her as he should, that she didn't intend to tell her parents about the end of their engagement in case Sloan changed his mind before the war ended. In her opinion, there was no reason to put them through the anguish they'd surely endure, unless it was absolutely necessary. Obviously, at that time, Anne had been holding on to the hope that the comfort of familiar surroundings would bring Sloan back to his senses. 'Yes', she'd assured him over and over; she understood what had happened; she wasn't angry. But, he still had doubts. Now that he'd returned to Thornton-on-Sea, he'd have to face her, and make certain she really *did* understand. Sloan was well-aware that the story he'd told sounded odd, and it wasn't hard to understand why she might be holding on to false hopes. He was also concerned because Anne was, without question, the most beloved girl in their small village. She'd always been good, kind and lovely. Nevertheless, he'd had to be honest with her. It was clear that doing so was going to cause despair to a great many people, including his parents. Anne's mother and father would be livid.

He wouldn't have argued that the entire conundrum was irrational. Every bit of his indecision and pain was due to a chance encounter with someone he hadn't been certain he'd ever see again. But her memory was so fresh in his mind. After having met her, there was no possibility of his marrying Anne, or anyone else. Yet, Lord Rowan and Lady Celia adored her. Her parents were close friends with his family. Lord and Lady Thornton thought of her as a daughter. Anne was of the aristocracy. From what little he knew about Elise, she was descended from Russians. Lord only knew what her lineage was. Both sets of parents would probably consider her a foreigner of dubious stature. Lord and Lady Thornton wouldn't be pleased at the prospect of their son bringing Elise to *Highcroft Hall* as a future countess. But the fact remained that he didn't love Anne. As much as it would pain everybody, they would have to face reality.

It seemed like another lifetime when he'd asked Anne to marry him. He wasn't the same young, naïve boy who'd left on that bright September morning, in 1939. From Dunkirk to D-Day and countless battles in between, he'd evolved into a mature man, whose outlook on life had altered dramatically. There'd been several close brushes with death. Such frightening moments had caused Sloan to ponder life's most profound and mysterious questions. Why was he here? What did it all mean? What was love? The only question he felt equipped to answer was the one concerning love. As soon as practical, he intended to see Elise. Although he scarcely knew her, she was the sun and the moon to him, and he wholeheartedly believed that once they had time to be together, she'd realize they were meant for one another.

Sloan hadn't told his parents when he'd be arriving, since he hadn't been certain himself. Trains were notoriously difficult to predict in the post-war frenzy. Thousands of soldiers were returning to their homes, and extra carriages had been added to accommodate them. His train wasn't even listed on the regular departures and arrivals board. When he reached Thornton-on-Sea, he left his gear at the depot, to be looked after by the stationmaster, and walked the three miles to his home. There'd been a brief, heavy shower, but when it ended it was a beautiful summer day. Tall trees shaded his way with thick foliage, and the fields were green, dotted with white sheep and spotted cattle. Flowers bloomed in the front yards of small cottages and spilled from flower boxes. While he'd seen the scars of war, when his train travelled through London, the peaceful countryside appeared untouched and as pristine as it had always been. Thornton-on-Sea sat high above the ocean, and he could see the blue of the water on that bright, sunny afternoon. It was just as he'd remembered. The breeze rustled his light brown hair, and it was heaven to smell the fresh salt air.

Finally he could see the roof of *Highcroft Hall,* rising stately and grand in the distance. There'd been many times during the war when he'd wondered if he'd ever see his home again. Beautiful, elegant *Highcroft,* where his ancestors had dwelled since the 1600s. It was one of the country's finest examples of a seventeenth century, Jacobean country house, with an impressive great hall, magnificent reception rooms, libraries and a Gothic-style chapel. Capability Brown had designed the formal gardens, which were spectacular. It was as unchanged as the ancient Lime trees at the entrance. He quickened his pace, soon finding himself standing at the imposing entrance, where wisteria and Ivy climbed the red brick façade, and roses meandered to the second level.

While Sloan made his way toward the house, his parents were sitting in the drawing room, wondering when their son would appear. They'd had a wire from him when he was mustered out, but no news since. Lord Rowan paced the room, jingling money in his pocket.

"Why should it be taking so long?" he complained to his wife, Lady Celia. "It's been nearly a week since we received the wire. You don't suppose something has happened to him, do you?"

Lady Celia was sitting on the striped, satin-upholstered sofa, calmly knitting.

"Rowan, you should know enough about the military to understand that one has to be patient when dealing with them. You used to tell me that everything connected with service to one's country involves waiting. He'll be along just as soon as he can be," she responded. "We must remember to ring Anne the moment he arrives. You don't suppose he'd stop to see her first? After all, she is his intended bride."

"I rather think not. Of course he'll be anxious to see her, but knowing Sloan, he'll be wanting to set foot in *Highcroft Hall* before anything else. He'll probably ring Anne, and ask her to pop over. After all, it's really no distance at all."

There was silence between the two, and the only sound was Lady Celia's knitting needles, clicking and clacking as they finished another row of stitches.

"Won't it be lovely to have him home? And a hero, too. They don't give the Victoria Cross to everyone. The Mayor told me they've planned a celebration in his honour. As soon as they know he's arrived, preparations will get underway," Lord Rowan stated proudly.

"I know, Rowan. It's all too magnificent. I've made certain his room is ready. There are fresh flowers, and everything is just as he left it."

"Yes, I expect... Wait, Celia. I believe I heard footsteps on the gravel."

Just as he spoke, the front door opened, and Sloan was there, standing in the flagstone great hall. Both parents rushed to greet him.

14

S loan," they cried out simultaneously.

Their handsome son stood alone in the wide, expansive entry. He was taller and a bit thinner. On the other hand, he was no longer a boy. His arms and chest had filled out, and he wore his uniform with great dignity. His dark, blue eyes were as intense as they'd always been, and he hadn't lost his winning smile. There were small lines etched beside his mouth and next to his penetrating eyes, from years of flying aeroplanes into sunrises and sunsets. His father shook his hand, and his mother stood on tiptoe to kiss his cheek. Strangely, there was a feeling of unease – as if the two older people weren't familiar with the younger man. His mother began to fuss nervously.

"Sloan, your room is just as you left it. I thought you would like that. Of course, if you'd prefer, you may have your choice of rooms. I – that is – we thought you would want to sleep in your boyhood chamber. But if that isn't acceptable..."

"Mother, do calm down. Of course it's acceptable. I've thought of that room for the entire duration. In fact, let me go up there now and change into something more comfortable. I wouldn't care if I never put this uniform on again."

"Oh, but Son. Anne will want to see how splendid you look in your uniform, with your coveted medals and your silver wings. Do wait until she's had that chance."

"Anne? But I had no plans to see her this evening. I thought we could enjoy a quiet time together on my first night home."

"Of course we can do that, if it's what you want," said Lady Celia. "Your father and I just thought you would want to see your lovely bride-to-be as soon as possible."

"Yes – well – of course I'm anxious to see her, but I have things I want to speak to you about. Don't you suppose we might keep my homecoming a secret until tomorrow?"

Lord Rowan was a bit perplexed, but it was pleasing to think that Sloan wanted to be alone with his parents after their long separation.

"We shall do whatever you wish, Son. I don't see any harm in a tiny, white lie. I don't think it's necessary to say that you didn't come in tonight – perhaps that you arrived later than expected."

"Yes, that will do," Sloan smiled. "So, let me put on other clothing and wash up. I'll be back in a tick."

He took the staircase two steps at a time, and his parents stood at the bottom, with worshipping looks on their faces. Lady Celia turned to Lord Rowan.

"Thank goodness I never moved his clothing. Do you think any of it will still fit?"

"I strongly doubt it. But let him prowl through his cupboard and see. He'll be needing to outfit himself with a new wardrobe. I should think a trip to London will be in order."

Lady Celia put her arms around her husband. "Oh Rowan. It's so good to have him home. After so many fretful years. He looks very dashing, don't you think?"

"Yes. Quite. A bit thin perhaps, but a few of Ruth's excellent meals and he'll be right as rain."

Lady Celia rang the bell for Mrs. Littleton, knowing of her keen desire to see Sloan - to welcome him home from the war. She came quickly, straightening her apron and patting her hastily pinned-up, white hair.

"Has he come home?" she enquired, nearly breathless with anticipation.

"Yes. He's gone to his room to freshen up. He'll be anxious to see you. Could you bring a tea tray? By the time you return, he'll be back down," Lady Celia requested.

Mrs. Littleton smiled broadly and scurried off to prepare a tray. He'd always held a special place in her heart. She'd tended to him almost as much as his Nanny had. Grace had watched him grow from a tot with dark-blonde, tousled hair to a strikingly handsome young man. She'd seen him off to Eton, Oxford and the RAF. Now, he was home for good. Back to Thornton-on-Sea, where he would marry the enchanting Anne Whitfield and take his place in the long line of nobility who'd overseen the magnificent estate she'd grown to love as if it were her own.

Mrs. Littleton spread the news to other members of the staff. By the time Sloan descended the staircase, they were lined up, waiting to shake his hand and warmly welcome him home. Sloan was delighted to see all of them. He gave cuddles to Grace and Ruth and shook the hands with the gentlemen on the staff. He also made certain to acknowledge those who were new to *Highcroft Hall,* since his departure in 1939. Giselle Dupris was one of those. He'd been on the alert for her name, since he knew she lived with Elise. When he reached her, he paused.

"If I'm correct, you're my mother's new lady's maid? Anne Whitfield wrote to say that you'd become friends."

"Yes, Milord. Anne, Elise, and I are friends. Elise is the lady I share a cottage with."

"I'm aware of that. I believe I've met her before."

"Yes, Milord. I believe you have," she smiled.

"I would imagine I'll see you again," he answered.

Sloan moved on, speaking a word to everyone. Giselle couldn't wait to tell Elise that he was home and that he was very handsome.

The tea was brought into the drawing room. Sloan sat in a winged back chair by the sofa, while Mrs. Littleton poured him a generous cup. He still wore his uniform, having discovered he'd outgrown all of his clothing. Someone pulled the large bell at the entrance to *Highcroft Hall.* Then, Anne's voice could be heard.

"Has Major Thornton arrived?" Sloan heard her enquire of Richmond.

"Ah - there she is Sloan," said Lord Rowan. "I'm not surprised she came. She's been checking with us daily. Sorry our private evening will have to be relinquished. Rush out to her, Son."

But Sloan only rose to his feet. His face turned quite ashen. He couldn't help the fact that he wore a grave expression. Anne quickly entered the room.

"I popped round to see if you'd arrived," she said, somewhat nervously. Then, looking him up and down with her eyes, she said, "Well, Sloan." She stopped talking and smiled. A blush highlighted her lovely cheek bones, and her long, dark lashes glistened with happiness. He thought for a moment that she was going to burst into tears. There was no question Anne was gorgeous, but his heart didn't speed up like it had when he'd met Elise. Anne was still the beautiful, high-spirited girl he'd known as a youngster. Her vivaciousness and animation had always amused him.

"Aren't you going to kiss her, Sloan?" asked his father. "You needn't be shy in front of your mother and me."

Sloan stepped forward. He took her hands in his, kissing the cheek she offered. He couldn't force himself to act against his feelings, and knew Anne understood why. He'd essentially told her that it had all been a giant mistake. Now, he dreaded a face-to-face conversation more than he'd loathed flying into a formation of Luftwaffe planes. Why couldn't he love her? Most of his mates in the RAF would think him daft. But they'd never met Elise. He felt treacherous. Now the war was over, he was home, and they were face-to-face. He tried to be considerate of her feelings and said that he'd see her the next evening. They'd dine at a restaurant by the sea, where they could chat at length. She nodded in agreement, understanding his desire to spend time with his parents. She stayed for a bit and drank a cup of tea. Then, she left, saying she looked forward to the next evening.

⌘

The moment Sloan dreaded finally arrived. He looked across the table at Anne. Knowing he'd broken her heart, he wished he could have avoided doing so. They were seated at an outdoor restaurant, next to a seawall, and waves could be heard crashing against the stones. Occasionally, a fine spray of mist drifted through the air. He'd ordered a bottle of wine. After it was poured, he began to speak.

"Anne, it's good to be able to talk to one another. From the moment I arrived, I've wanted to be alone with you. There are so many things we need to discuss."

"You've already made it clear that you've changed your feelings," she exclaimed. "I don't think there's much to discuss. I know you think you're in love with Elise - that she's your soulmate. I wrote to you a hundred times saying that I understood."

Sloan was somewhat startled. "I know that, Anne. You've been unbelievable. But since I'm back home, we finally have the chance to talk this through. I don't think that my feelings changed so much. It's more that I came to a realization about them. I nearly died several times while fighting. When one comes so close to death, it causes a re-evaluation of everything. I realized what a simple, pre-ordained existence I've led. Everything was mapped out for me. I'm not sure I want that anymore."

"Sloan, there isn't a lot you can do about altering plans for your future. You're the heir to *Highcroft Hall.* You'll have to assume that responsibility someday. Until then, you'll have to train for the many duties you'll undertake."

"Yes. That much is true. But hopefully it will be many years in the future. Anne, I never wanted to hurt you. You were incredibly faithful and loyal to me. I hate what I did to you. But it's so important to me that you understand why it was what I had to do."

"Sloan. If you're trying to tell me that you broke our engagement because you began to re-evaluate your life after many dangerous missions, that's rubbish. You met Elise before there'd been so many risky times. It was solely because of Elise." Tears began to flow down Anne's lovely face. "The only thing I've never understood is how you could change your feelings so quickly, when you scarcely even knew Elise. Is there something I could change about myself to make you want to marry me, like you did before you left for the war?"

"No, Anne. What would I ask you to change? You're a beautiful, intelligent lady. You have everything a man could ask for. You're like my sister. I've had the opportunity to chat with so many of my fellow RAF chums. I've heard their feelings for the girls they left behind. I now know that the word love shouldn't be used lightly. It's a terribly serious subject. There's such a thing as passion, which you and I have never shared. The truth is, as much as it may hurt, I don't believe I ever really wanted to marry you.

"Then, why did you propose? I don't understand."

"That's what I meant when I said everything had been mapped out for me. You and I were childhood friends. It was expected of me. But, I never felt the spark that should have been there."

But Sloan, that's because we've always known one another. We grew up together. It would have been unusual to feel the passion you're speaking of, when we'd seen each other during every phase of our lives. There was no mystery. But there was a deeper feeling. Like that of a husband and wife, who've spent many years together and cannot imagine a future without the other."

"But don't you see that what you're describing is the kind of love one feels for a sibling, more than for a spouse? It's important to have the magic. The spark. I can't describe it. I only know it's not there between us."

"Sloan, don't you think I know what love is?" She was openly weeping now. "Maybe you don't feel passion for me, but I know I feel it for you. I don't see you as the small boy I played with as a child. I see you as a handsome man, and for nearly six years I've longed to feel your arms round me. I've felt the spark you refer to. Don't describe love to me."

"I'm sorry, Anne. I'm sorry. What can I say? There are different sorts of love. Perhaps what you feel is the real thing. How can I know?"

Anne truly was delightful to spend time with - a wonderful companion — but he really couldn't imagine facing all of life's challenges with her by his side. Try as he may, there was no way he was going to change his mind. He felt abysmal, like the worst sort of scoundrel. He'd taken precious years of her life – had broken her heart. It was plain to see that however much his feelings had changed, hers had only grown stronger with time. He hung his head in shame.

"Would you rather I'd lied?" he asked.

"No. No, of course not. I would have known the truth anyway. I'm not a fool, Sloan. You know that. I'll survive. I won't lie either. This has been an awful disappointment. But I'll move on with my life. You can't help the way you feel. I understand that. And I can't help the way I feel either." She broke into sobs again.

There was silence between them for several minutes. She quietly wept into her handkerchief, while Sloan waited awkwardly, wishing there was more he could do and knowing there wasn't. Finally, she spoke.

"What are your plans now?" she sniffled.

"I want to see Elise. You know that. I'm aware that I don't know very much about her. I know her name, and that she's Russian by birth, brought to France as a tiny child. Beyond that, I know very little. You probably know more than I do. You've certainly had more time to get to know her. But there's absolutely no doubt in my mind – none whatsoever. She's the person meant to be my partner forever. Whatever the circumstances, I've firmly made up my mind. I have to see her again. It's my hope to persuade Elise she's meant to be my wife. It sounds insane, even to my ears. But she's the girl I've dreamt of, since I was old enough to have such thoughts. Anne, if I don't win her love, I'll live alone for the rest of my days."

"Do you suppose if Elise doesn't feel the same way, you might decide we were meant to be together after all?"

"Oh, Anne. I surely don't want you hoping for that, wasting more of your life. I beg you to think of me as your dear friend. Go find your own soulmate. If I believe so strongly that there's someone God meant for me, then I equally believe that there's someone waiting for you. Please find him. Don't be bitter and angry with me. You have to believe there's a reason for everything in the world. Someday you'll find the reason for the pain you're feeling now."

"I won't be bitter. I'm not angry. As I said before. It isn't your fault. You can't help your feelings. You'll always mean the world to me. I want you to be my special friend for the rest of our lives. I'm glad I know Elise. She's a special person. If you love her, I'll love her, too."

Sloan's heart soared. That was what he'd hoped to hear. Finally, Anne understood. He truly wanted them to be friends, although it would have been perfectly understandable if she'd turned on him with vengeance. Many women would have. He reached across the table and took her hand.

"Thank you for accepting this so graciously. We'll always be the dearest of friends. I look forward to someday seeing you filled with happiness, because you've discovered I wasn't wrong. I know life holds great joy for you."

"I'll be all right, Sloan. Go and do what you have to do. Don't worry about me." She smiled. A truly lovely smile. All appeared to be right with the world.

When they parted that night, Sloan's heart was much lighter than it had been at the beginning of the evening. He still had to face his parents and dreaded that scene, but at least he could tell them that Anne had accepted what he'd had to say, and that they'd vowed to always be friends.

As he entered the house, his parents were still seated in the drawing room. As usual, Lady Celia was knitting, and Lord Rowan was smoking his pipe, reading the *London Times*. Both looked up expectantly when he came into the room.

"Hello there, Son. Did you have a good evening? Did you and Anne set a date? Your mother is anxious to speak with Caroline about wedding plans."

Caroline was Anne's mother. Both women had been waiting anxiously for the happy news that would set into motion a flurry of exciting preparations. Sloan sat down in a chair across from his parents.

"No, Dad. We didn't set a date. She's released me from the engagement. There will be no wedding plans. I'm sorry to disappoint you this way. I know how fond you are of Anne. I understand how much you've both counted on our marriage, but I can't make such a commitment. I simply don't love Anne in that way. I think of her as a sister. That's the simple truth. I wish I could love her enough to marry her, but I can't make that happen."

Lord Rowan sat up straighter, and Lady Celia put down her knitting.

"Please say you're not serious," his mother said. "We love Anne like our own. I've always thought the two of you would marry."

"Perhaps that's one of the problems, Mother. You and Caroline Whitfield got it into your heads, when Anne and I were just toddlers, that someday we'd marry. You used to talk about it to both of us when I was still in short pants. It was always assumed. If there hadn't been a war, I probably would have married her by now. But there *was* a war, and it gave me time to think. I don't love her in the proper way for marriage. It's as simple as that."

"But Son, shouldn't you spend some time with her, now that you're home again? Of course the war has brought about confusing feelings. I remember when I served. It seemed like everything in my life was different. But you'll settle in again. The old routine will be re-established. You need to give it time."

"No, Dad. I don't want the old routine. I now understand how contrived it was. I *am* happy to be home again. Of course I'm pleased to be with you and Mother. But I have no intention of marrying Anne."

Lady Celia threw her hand to her breast. "Sloan, why are you talking this way?"

"I want time to think. To decide how I want to live my life."

"Son, you haven't much choice about how you live your life. Do you mean to say you would refuse your inheritance and leave *Highcroft Hall*?"

"No. No. Of course not. Nothing like that. But since I'm certain I have no intention of marrying Anne, I need to rearrange my thinking. I believe I've found someone who's meant to be with me."

"What the devil do you mean?"

"Father, I mean that I believe I've found my soulmate. That's something I've never said out loud before. But I've thought about it for years. I believe god meant for me to find the one special person he wants me to spend the rest of my life with. It isn't Anne."

"Sloan, you're talking foolishness. Something has happened to your thinking. Perhaps you should talk to Father Powers. After all, he *is* an Anglican Priest. He's trained to counsel on these matters."

"Mother, I don't need Father Powers, and there's nothing wrong with my mind," Sloan laughed. "Have the two of you never thought that you're soulmates? Can either of you imagine being married to someone else? Was there anyone in either of your lives whom you considered marrying, before you met each other?"

"Well - no. We made the decision very quickly. When we met, we were certain about how we felt. Our parents weren't happy about our rush to the altar. But we were right, weren't we Rowan?"

"Yes, of course, dear. I'm not quite sure what to say to you, Sloan. I suppose if that's what you believe, there's no point in trying to convince you differently. It just seems quite cruel to have kept Anne waiting for so long, only to break her heart."

"We've had a long talk. Anne is hurt, naturally. But she understands. She was wonderful about it. I *did* write to her midway through the war, releasing her from the engagement. She chose not to tell her parents or you. I *do* feel very badly. But as she says, I can't help my feelings. We've vowed to always be the best of friends. I couldn't ask for her to be more harmonious about the entire thing. I made clear what I believe. I explained that I've been through a lot of trauma and need time to adjust. But she understands completely that there's no future for us, other than as friends."

"Well, you definitely couldn't have married her feeling as you do. If you don't love her, we'll have to accept it. You do understand that the entire village will be indignant about this. Everyone loves Anne. There will be few people who'll be able to see why you wouldn't want to marry her."

"I know that, Mother. To make matters worse, I have to tell you something else. The girl, who I'm certain is my soulmate, lives here in Thornton-on-Sea."

"She lives here? Who? How? I don't understand a whit of what you're telling us."

"You know her. Her name is Elise. I believe she makes her home with your lady's maid."

"Giselle? Yes, Giselle does live with Elise. Elise is a widow. She has a child, Chloe. How can this be? Elise and Giselle didn't even live here until after you'd left for the war." She was silent for a moment, and then a light came into her eyes, as reality dawned upon her. "Oh my goodness! I nearly forgot. Elise is the girl who bandaged your wound, and saved your leg. But, that was a brief encounter, Sloan. You don't really know her."

"I know. It's a long story. I met her in France at Dunkirk. The moment I laid eyes on her, I knew — I just knew. I can't explain it. She makes me whole. I'm sure of it. She and Anne have become friends. You probably know that. It's all very strange, isn't it? That convinces me all the more that it's god's work. I have to see her. She knows I'm returning from the war. Anne tells me that Elise has no feelings for me, but I won't believe that until I've had the chance to prove to her I'm not a madman. I'm afraid I got rather carried away when I met her in France. I scarcely knew her, yet I blurted out that I believed she was my soulmate."

"Well, this is truly astonishing," said Lord Rowan. "What can I say? You seem to know your mind. There's no point in arguing with you. You've earned the right to be happy. We shall stand by you, no matter what others say. We'll support your wishes. We do know Elise. I personally think she's a fine girl. So does your mother." Lord Rowan placed his pipe in its rack and reached out his hand to Lady Celia. "Come along, dear. Life has a way of leading us where we need to go. Sloan will be all right. He has a good head on his shoulders."

Together, the two middle-aged people walked toward the stairs. Sloan heaved another sigh of relief.

⸺ ⁓ ⸺

Anne, on the other hand, climbed the stairway to her room and threw herself upon the bed. She was filled with rage and indignation. She wished that she could rant and rave at the top of her lungs.

"How dare he treat me like this? How *dare* he? *Soulmate!* What daft foolishness. He's suffering from some sort of mania." She was incensed. She'd never felt such fury. "He won't get away with this. Let him dare to bring his wretched soulmate to *Highcroft Hall* as a countess. Just let him dare. I'll make certain Sloan erases these idiotic ideas from his head. Oh, he'll pay. *He will pay.*"

No matter that Anne had led Sloan to believe she'd accepted his change of feelings. She was every bit as angry as she'd been when she'd received his letter in 1942. She still wanted to hurt him as much as he'd hurt her. And she would. She vowed with all of her heart that she would. Anne wasn't a fool. Sloan wouldn't know of her wrath. She wouldn't blow her top, or erupt into a frenzy. She'd remain calm. He'd think she was sweetness personified. But God help him. He would regret what he had done.

15

After a week with his parents, Sloan left Thornton-on-Sea bound for London, where he planned on refurbishing his wardrobe. He was sick to death of wearing his uniform. He had an appointment with his tailor and reservations at the *Grosvenor House Hotel*. Then, he would return to his home village and, at long last, contact Elise. The week he'd spent at *Highcroft Hall*, after seeing Anne and confessing his feelings to his parents, were fraught with turmoil. The celebration that had been planned for his return, with a band and parade, was abruptly cancelled when word reached the Mayor that his engagement to Anne had been broken. Anne strolled about town, acting as though she was perfectly all right, but all of the villagers rightly assumed she was hiding her heartbreak behind a façade of pride. Sloan, when venturing out of *Highcroft Hall*, was actually spat upon by a number of women, and heads were turned as he walked along the cobblestoned streets. He took to cocooning himself inside the walls of the great estate. Even his parents were looked upon with disdain. Anne's parents were outraged. He had a visit from her father, Lord Adrian, who threatened to horsewhip Sloan for his abysmal conduct.

Thus, Sloan was glad for the trip to London. For a man who'd only recently returned from the one of the worst wars the world had ever seen, what he was experiencing in his beloved home village was almost as disturbing. He'd never dreamed people he'd known from childhood would turn upon him. He intellectually understood the feelings of villagers, but their actions were emotionally devastating. Sloan prayed Anne would move on with her life. He wondered how long it would take for her to find the partner who'd make her understand that he was right. He could only stay focused on one goal – that of seeing Elise again. As he stood on the station platform, his heart ached for his mother and father. They stood with bowed heads, trying not to show disappointment in him, nor to reveal the pain and heartbreak he had caused. They were at a loss to understand any of it.

"Sloan, darling, please don't be gone long. It shouldn't take but a few days to buy the items you need. The tailor will send whatever you order. We've been apart for so long. I hate seeing you leave again."

Lady Celia looked as though she might weep.

"Of course I won't be gone long, Mother."

He bent down and kissed her. She seemed to have grown frailer during the short time he'd been home. She was such a kind lady, and he'd never heard her speak a harsh word about another human being. Perhaps he'd modeled his soulmate upon Lady Celia. A striking beauty as a girl, she was still uncommonly attractive. In her fifties now, her golden hair streaked with silver, and lines showing the anxiety she'd experienced through two world wars, her eyes were still as blue as a young maiden's. She was the epitome of a genteel lady.

Sloan turned to his father – the man whom he idolized beyond all others. He was the height of gentility, and Sloan could think of nothing the man had ever done, in his lifetime, that might have brought shame upon the family. He was the same height as his son, and there wasn't an inch of excess weight anywhere on his body. Anyone who had ever met Rowan Thornton knew he was a man of honour. Sloan was chagrined at the disgrace he'd brought upon the family name and the way he'd let his parents down.

"Dad, I'm sorry. I know I've caused you and Mother distress. I'd do just about anything not to have done so. But I cannot marry a woman I don't love, simply to please others. The mistake lies with the fact that I ever asked Anne to marry me. I was too young and naïve. None of us had any idea how many years the war would last, or of the changes I'd undergo. Surely you understand the impossibility of going through such a deplorable experience without coming away changed. I'm not the same person."

"I know that, Son. I wasn't the same when I returned from France in the Great War. Fortunately, I hadn't stopped loving Celia. But, we were already married, and there was never a question as to whether I loved her. I don't blame you for feelings you can't change. The world is a strange place. People like a cause. This village is no different. There are probably many men living here who wish they hadn't acted hastily and wed women whom they later realized weren't meant for them. Society's attitude seems to be that if *they* can do such a thing, so can *you*. I've had time to sort this through. You're entitled to a good life. Go and find it. Your mother and I love you. It's not for others to tell you what they think you should do."

"Thank you. Thank you from the bottom of my heart, Dad. I absolutely promise that what I'm doing isn't a whim, nor a fruitless effort to make fantasy into reality. I'm very certain about my feelings. I know what I'm doing, and your support means the world me."

He shook his father's hand and clasped him to his chest. It was unusual behavior for both of them, since they were generally rather reserved when it came to a show of affection.

"You and Mother have met Elise. You've told me you think she's lovely. Can it be surprising that I'd be in love with her?"

"No, not at all. It's just the way it seems to have happened, and the fact that you don't really know her."

"That will be rectified," Sloan smiled.

The train chugged into the station, and he gathered his belongings. He had one bag with uniforms and another empty one. It was meant to accommodate purchases he'd make in London. Kissing his mother one last time, he boarded and readied himself for the journey.

Upon arrival in London, Sloan settled into his hotel room. Then, he decided to pay a visit to his club, which he hadn't seen in years. He had no idea whether there would be even one soul whom he might know. No matter. It was a quiet place to escape the crowds of the city, enjoy a drink, and do some reading.

He didn't recognise anybody. Sloan ordered a neat Scotch and found a quiet corner next to the bookshelves. Sorting through the extensive collection of leather bound tomes, he extracted a volume of Dostoevsky. It was heavy reading. But, he'd made a firm resolve, during the war, to plough his way through all of the classic literature he'd only skimmed while at university. It was hard going in the beginning, but before long he found himself engrossed in the writing. Thus, he was startled when someone tapped his shoulder. He glanced up, and to his great surprise, saw a close friend from Oxford, who'd also recently returned from duties as an officer in the war.

"Sloan Thornton! Great to see you, old boy. What are you doing in London? I figured you'd be luxuriating back at your family's estate," Elliott Woodbridge exclaimed.

"Elliott! I can't believe it's really you. When did we last speak? Surely, it was before the war. I've been to Thornton on-Sea already. I'm in London to order new clothing. Nothing in my cupboard at home fits. How about you?"

"London is home now. I've joined my father's firm of solicitors. It was always the plan. I understand about the wardrobe. I went through the same thing. I wish I could join you for a drink, but I'm just on the way back to my office. It's wonderful to see an old friend. Where were you during the war?"

"I was in North Africa for quite a spell after Dunkirk. Did you know I was RAF? Then, later I was in Italy. I didn't get home for the entire duration."

"I was BEF. I was all over the place. The last was the Battle of the Bulge. Bloody awful situation wasn't it? The whole muddle, I mean."

"Quite. I had some narrow scrapes. I imagine you did too. I feel fortunate to be in one piece. I'm appalled at the condition of London, especially the East End."

"I've spoken to some of the boys who fought during the Blitz. God, what a job they did."

"Yes," Sloan replied. "I knew fellows who were in that fight. I almost wish I had been. They were the real heroes."

"As well as those who fought on D-day," answered Elliott."

"I was one of those," answered Sloan. "That was my last stand. Bloody horrible. Thank God for the Americans."

"Absolutely," Elliott replied. "Weren't you supposed to be getting married when the war ended? That's the last news I had of you."

"Ah yes - well, that's a long tale. I'm no longer engaged, and the wrath of God has befallen me. The girl's father has threatened to horsewhip me."

"'E Gads! Is that why you've escaped to London?"

"Partly, to be honest. People who pass me on the street have actually spat upon me. I'm the world's most despicable scoundrel for releasing her from the engagement. But I couldn't do it, Elliott. The war made an enormous difference in my thinking. I realized I wasn't in love with her in the proper way. I think of her as a sister – she was a childhood playmate, after all."

"I haven't been to the altar yet, either. But I've never even made it as far as a proposal. From what you're saying, it's a damned good thing I didn't. So, we're both free. Why don't we make the rounds in London and see what we've been missing?"

Elliott was a very good-looking chap. He'd always been able to nab any girl he set his sights on. Yet, he was a decent sort. To Sloan's knowledge, Elliott had never taken advantage of his outstanding appearance. The two hadn't been extremely close friends at Oxford, but were more than simple passing acquaintances, too. Everyone had known who Elliott was.

"Thanks for the invitation to do the town, but I don't feel in the mood. I'd love to get-together again though – perhaps for dinner. I'll be here a week. I'm at the *Grosvenor House*. Ring me, and we can set a time."

"I'll do that, Sloan. I have to rush back to my office now. I just popped round for lunch. I can't tell you how terrific it was to run into you. I'll surely give you a ring and see you soon."

They said their goodbyes, and Elliott left. Sloan went back to reading his book, looking forward to a lengthy conversation with an old chum. He wasn't sure whether he would tell Elliott the full story of his quest for Elise, but he suspected it might be good to talk it over with someone his own age.

Sloan and Elliott did meet a few nights later, at a pub they'd both enjoyed as far back as undergraduate days. Sloan did go through his entire story, from the moment he'd met Elise to the present.

Elliott didn't react as though he thought Sloan had lost his mind. In fact, his response was the complete opposite. He told Sloan that he shared his beliefs about soulmates.

"That's one reason I've never come close to marrying. It has to be right, and it never has been. I've met some wonderful, charming girls. Pretty, nice and bright. But something has always been missing. It's interesting to be having this conversation. I wonder how many other chaps feel this way, but never say it aloud? Probably more than anyone suspects."

"I've never thought of that, but I'd bet you're right. People seem to grow uncomfortable with the subject. I don't know why. Perhaps men aren't supposed to fantasize. It seems to me all women dream of soulmates. But, those I've known seem to believe that every man they meet is their soulmate. I think that's the way Anne felt. I'm positive I wasn't the right man for her. But, until she finds someone else, she'll never believe that."

"What a shame. She's wasting her life. The correct man could be right in front of her eyes."

"What sort of girl are you searching for Elliott? Do you have a picture in your mind of what she'd be like?"

"Certainly. Of course, she'll be attractive. At least to me. I prefer brunettes – sultry, spunky, and sexy – you know the type. I'm not so worried about whether she's aristocratic. But, I do want a lady. Do you understand?"

"Of course. Many ladies aren't aristocrats. Elise isn't an aristocrat, but she's certainly a lady."

"Exactly," Elliott responded. "But I like a woman with gumption. You know, someone who can match me in an intelligent conversation. I can't abide a simpering fool." He laughed aloud.

"I'm not as keen on the intelligence aspect," Sloan replied. "Not that I want a dunce," he smiled. "But sometimes very intelligent women cause me discomfort. You were always more confrontational, if I remember. Weren't you on the debate team at Oxford?"

"Yes. I like a good give-and-take of ideas. So much the better if it could be with my life's partner. But I also look for kindness and empathy. Loyalty, of course. Charm, wit, grace – I'm looking for a lot, aren't I?"

"Aren't we both? I guess the only difference between us, aside from the descriptions we give of our imagined soulmates, is that I firmly believe I've found mine."

"Tell me about her. You've given me details about how you came upon each other, but what's so extraordinary about her to convince you of her certain place in your life?"

Sloan rummaged around in his breast pocket, and produced the pitifully worn photo of Elise. He laid it on the table in front of them. "Naturally, her appearance plays a part. All of my life, I had a notion of what the lady, who God intended for me to fall in love with, would be like. I've *seen* her in my dreams. When I first set eyes on Elise, I thought I *was* dreaming. She so perfectly matches the woman I've seen in my imaginings. She's breathtaking. Absolutely breathtaking. Lovely masses of golden curls spill down to her shoulders and beyond; she has picture-perfect features, and a face like an angel. One almost expects a halo. She has eyes that defy description. Bluer than the bluest sea, yet fringed with the longest, darkest lashes I've ever seen. Lips that are the colour of a beautiful baby's mouth, or the softest, pink rosebud. Well, you can see from the photo."

"My God, Sloan, are you certain she's real. She really is magnificent. How long have you had this picture? It looks like you need a new one." Elliott laughed.

"Yes. It's been through five years of war. She gave it to me the day I met her. We only spoke for a short while. Her voice is soft and gentle, with a magical, feminine tone. She's very articulate, but also meek – not given to use of words that overwhelm or try to impress. There's an incredibly demure quality about her. One only has to be in her presence to recognize her innocence. There's not one feature that isn't graceful and charming. There aren't words, Elliott – refinement, poise, elegance. None really tell the complete story. From the moment I saw her, she's been lodged in my heart. I cannot forget her. Call it an obsession if you will. I think there are some people who would. I suspect my parents might use that word. Frankly, I wouldn't argue. I *am* obsessed with her. If I don't win her, I can't imagine ever finding another woman who would satisfy me."

"Whew, Sloan. You have it bad. But, I envy you. How incredible it must be to feel that way about someone. I've longed for such love. That, to me, is true love. Have you ever studied the history of the soulmate notion?"

"Not really. But, because my life has been so transformed by meeting Elise, I do mean to study whether great minds of the past actually believed such things are possible," answered Sloan.

"You'll discover a lot of historical figures who wrote about, and discussed, the concept. As far back as Plato. I'm sure you're familiar with Edgar Cayce, the fascinating man from Kentucky in America, who went into trances and performed miraculous feats. He believed we're meant to find our other half in order to be complete. Jewish people have a word – *Bashert*. It refers to one's divinely ordained spouse. The Bible, in Genesis, refers to the belief that forty days before a child is born, its mate is determined. It's a remarkable subject when you honestly study it in depth."

"My God. I had no idea. I have a lot of studying to do. What you're saying only solidifies my own beliefs. I'm glad we ran into one another and that I opened up to you about what I'm going through."

"I'm glad too, Sloan. I sincerely hope the reunion with Elise turns out to fulfill your destiny. You've whetted my own appetite. After listening to you, I feel I should be doing more to find my own other half. But truthfully, I don't think that's the way it works. I think fate brings your soulmate to you, and when she appears, you know it. There doesn't seem to be any question in your mind, based on the way you've described your certainty about Elise. One can't go gallivanting around the world searching for one person among the masses."

"Precisely, Elliott. You'll know, I promise. But, I do think you have to be keenly aware at all times. From my own experience, I can tell you that I felt like I'd been hit over the head. There won't be any question in your mind, when it happens to you."

"Let's drink to your future, old friend. Promise you'll let me meet her when I visit Thornton-on-Sea."

16

As soon as he returned to Thornton-on-Sea, Sloan made a beeline to the small, stone cottage near the water. He knew he should have rung Elise to give her warning, but he was afraid she'd put him off. It seemed more promising to simply show up at her door. He was familiar with the whereabouts of her home, since he'd lived in Thornton-on-Sea all of his life, and the cottage had been there as long as he could remember. It was a pretty, early autumn day, and he decided to walk. He'd met Giselle, his mother's lady's maid, on that first evening home, and it was likely she'd be at the cottage with Elise, since it was a Monday. Sloan was aware that Monday was a day-off for her. Giselle had only recently returned to her employment, since she'd been caring for her fiancé, a Major in the American Air Force. Sloan knew all about their love story and looked forward to knowing her better. Her fiancé, Major Cabot, was actually living at *Highcroft Hall,* still recovering from ghastly wounds suffered on D-Day. Sloan had briefly met him, and liked him a lot.

When he approached the cottage, Sloan could see an abundance of blooms in the front garden. Amidst them was a tall, fair-haired figure, bent over a thicket of roses, lilies, delphiniums, and blue hydrangeas. He stopped and studied her, without her knowledge. He could have stood there for the entire day. She was compulsively charming. The oval contour of her face was perfect, just as he'd remembered. She surely hadn't been a dream, nor had he made her into more than she was. The same crown of pale, golden hair fell around her smooth brow. He could imagine seeing her in the dim aisle of a country church, as an angel or Madonna. As he walked closer, she looked up with a startled glance – shy, sweet, hesitating. He unlatched the front gate and went to her. A beautiful blush spread across her face, as pretty as the colour of a pale, pink rose. She smiled.

"Lord Thornton," she exclaimed.

"Yes, Elise. I'm pleased you remember me after all of these years."

"Yes, I do. Of course. Anne speaks of you often. Your name is a household word here."

"I hope you're not tired of it."

"No, of course not." Then she drew back, with what seemed like hesitation. It was clear she had doubts about him.

"Elise, I want you to think of me as a friend, just as you do Anne. I know I frightened you, and was perhaps a bit too aggressive, when we met in France in 1940. I didn't mean to. There was so little time. But, now I'd like to begin anew. I'd like to get to know you, and for you to know me. Can we be friends?"

"A friend of mine?" she questioned. "Surely you know I'm not one of the aristocracy, from which you choose your friends."

"That's rubbish, Elise. Anne has a title, and she's your friend. Why not me as well?"

She looked up at him and murmured, "I don't think you understand."

"Yes I do, Elise. Anne has told me your entire story." It was impossible for Sloan not to notice that she visibly shrank from pain at his words.

"Did she? I wish she hadn't. That was rather cruel of her. She knows my story isn't meant to be shared with others."

"Yes, she does know it. She wouldn't tell just anyone. I'm certain of that. It wasn't simple curiosity on my part. I needed to know. Anne and I have been friends for a long time. She's like my sister, and we don't keep secrets. It was natural that she'd tell me about you. After all, I'm no longer engaged to her, because I met you."

"I know. That seems so utterly unbelievable. You don't even know me. After hearing my story, I'm surprised you still want to be my friend?"

"Why in blazes wouldn't I? Just answer one question. Is that sad story any fault of yours? Are you to blame for it?"

"No. But, while I don't share the fault, I share the shame."

"There's no shame in what happened to you. I consider you courageous and brave. I told you when we first met that I'd see you again in England. I had no idea what both of us would endure before that became reality. I know you don't like to speak about what you've been through, and I understand completely. There's no reason to speak of it. You've turned a page and started a new life. That's what's important to me."

"You have quite a different point of view than I think most men would. It's nice to know that. I'm still not certain you totally understand, but if you say so, then I'll accept your word."

"I understand you have a lovely, little girl. Chloe, is it?"

"Yes. Chloe. I adore her. She's my world."

"How old is she now?"

"She turned four years last February. She's just started school. I'm very proud of her. Because I read to her from the time she could understand words, she can already read herself. She loves her books. I suppose she takes after me in that regard."

"I'm anxious to meet her. I've also heard a lot about Giselle. She may have told you that I briefly met her. My parents adore her. I understand she'll be marrying her American airman before too long. I've met him, as well. Will you stay here in the cottage after she goes to America?"

"Yes. Now that Chloe is in school, I have more free time. I'll extend my French teaching. I have a class of eight little girls now. I'll add another class - perhaps two. I've fast become the person from whom everyone wants their child to learn French. That's how I met Anne. She took lessons from me, too. Now she's so fluent, she doesn't need me anymore. But we became friends during that time. She visits just to see me, not to learn."

They were still standing in the beautiful garden. Elise suddenly realized she hadn't invited him inside, nor offered any refreshment.

"I'm so sorry, Lord Thornton. I should have invited you in." She removed her gardening gloves and moved to open the door. "I wasn't expecting a guest, so forgive me if everything isn't as tidy as it should be."

Sloan laughed. "I didn't pop over here to examine your housecleaning abilities. Thank you for inviting me in, and please call me Sloan."

He followed her into the charming cottage and on into the parlour. Of course everything was neat as a pin, which he'd suspected would be the case. She asked if he would like a cup of tea, and he answered in the affirmative. So, she bustled into the small kitchen, and put the kettle on. He watched as she walked from the parlour to prepare the tea. She was every bit as lovely as she'd been that first day in France. Perhaps even more so. There'd been so much fear and anxiety that day, and now Elise looked relaxed and fulfilled. Her mass of curls was pinned on top of her head, with tendrils falling about her pretty face. She wore a floral sundress and a white cardigan. The dress showed off her waistline, which was very small. There was nothing self-centered about her, but she had a proud, graceful demeanour.

When she returned to the parlour, she brought a tea tray. Placing it on the table in front of the chintz sofa, she said, "I remember you wanting cream and sugar when I offered you coffee in France. Is it the same for tea?" she asked, as she filled a cup.

"No. Just plain, thank you. I'm surprised you remember such a small detail. It's strange how certain things remain in our minds, isn't it?"

Elise nodded her head. "Yes. For some reason, that's clear as a bell." She smiled as she handed him the cup.

"Although I was injured, and in a rush to reach the beaches at Dunkirk, I think I remember everything about that day. It was quite extraordinary for me."

"Extraordinary in what way?" she asked.

"I promised myself I wouldn't go into all of that again," Sloan laughed. "I was struck with the fact that you so resembled the lady I'd dreamed of for such a long time."

"Sloan, you can't still be obsessed with the fantasy you spoke of then?"

"Yes – I'm afraid so." He stopped talking and reached into his trouser pocket. When he removed his hand, there was the crumpled-up photograph.

Elise was amazed. "Do you mean to say you still have that picture? How incredible. It looks quite worn."

"It should. I carried it on every mission. Sometimes, at night, in the desert, I'd take out my torch and flash the light upon this picture. When I felt particularly despondent, it helped me get through the loneliness." He put it back into his pocket. "But, I came here to ask for your friendship, so I won't go into a dissertation about my belief in soulmates."

"You're the first person I'd ever heard use that term. Since then, I've heard it many times. Giselle, my housemate and dear friend, is a firm believer. She's convinced that Ted Cabot, the man she's going to marry, is *her* soulmate."

"Ah — so perhaps I've been redeemed. You see, there are others who think as I do."

"Yes, but Sloan, didn't you think Anne was your soulmate too?" she asked, with a gentle smile.

"You'll probably be surprised to learn that I didn't. I know. I know. I asked her to marry me. Yet, she wasn't at all my ideal. I was leaving for the war. I'd known Anne since childhood, and as you're aware, she's a beautiful woman. I loved her, but not in the way I should have. She'd always been like a sister to me. I was wrong to propose to her. It was what could be called a weak moment on the eve of war. It didn't take long for me to regret my actions."

"I know. She told me the entire story. She's a very brave lady, but I suspect you broke her heart."

"I suspect I did. But we've seen each other and talked it out. She completely accepts everything. Now I want to see her move on with her life and find the right man."

"I hope that happens too." Elise got up from her chair, and refilled his teacup. When she was settled again, Sloan changed the subject.

"What of your brother? Wasn't his name Josef? Have you heard from him?"

"No. Not a word since Dunkirk. I don't know how to go about searching for him. I continually look at advertisements in the *London Times*, but he seems to have disappeared."

"Perhaps I might help you. Have you any idea what sort of fighting he would have done, assuming he reached England and joined with the British Forces?"

"Not really. I suppose it might have been anything. He was trained as a civilian pilot, so my first guess would be aeroplanes, in some capacity."

"Let me do some checking. There were entire squadrons comprised of French Resistance."

"I didn't know that. I'd give anything to find him. I pray he wasn't killed. Somehow, I have an inkling that he's safe, but I can't say why."

As they sat in the parlour chatting, the front door opened and beautiful, dark-haired Giselle entered, holding the hand of an adorable, little girl. Elise jumped up and ran to the child.

"My precious Chloe. How was school today? Did you and Aunt Gissy go for a treat afterwards? Come along, darling. I have someone for you to meet."

Elise's face was flushed, and it was obvious that she was immensely proud of the child. Taking her by the hand, she led Chloe to Sloan.

"Lord Sloan Thornton, this is Miss Chloe Arabella de Baier". Chloe looked up at him with expressive brown eyes and dropped a small curtsy. She had Elise's blonde curls and an exquisite face. There was no question about whether she would grow up to be a beauty.

"How do you do, Lord Thornton," she murmured, a bit shyly.

"And how do you do, Miss Chloe. You look a lot like your Mummy. I think you must have many people tell you how pretty you are."

"Yes," she answered, looking at the floor. "But Mummy says that's not important. I must be beautiful on the inside."

"Mummy is right," Sloan laughed. "But I suspect you are both."

"Sometimes I'm naughty."

There was more laughter. "Not very often, *Mon Cherie*," said Elise.

Giselle walked into the room and joined the conversation. "So, I suspected the renowned Sloan Thornton would pay a visit to our cottage before too much longer. We met at your parent's home on your first evening home." She reached out her hand to shake his.

"Yes, of course I remember. How fortunate for my mother to have you.. But I understand you'll be leaving now that peace has come. I've met Ted. It's off to America, is it?"

"Right. I'm looking forward to my new adventure. I have a lot to thank your parents for. If it hadn't been for them, I'd never have met Ted."

"I didn't know that," Sloan responded. "How did it come about?"

Giselle poured herself a cup of tea, while Elise took Chloe up the stairway to change her clothing.

"It's a convoluted tale. I met Anne Whitfield through your parents. Lord and Lady Thornton were good friends of Ted's parents, in Boston. John Cabot, Ted's father, went to Oxford. John and Lord Whitfield have kept in touch, and when Ted was sent to England in the Air Corps, John Cabot wrote to his old friend, asking him to keep an eye on Ted. They invited him to dinner at *Meadowlands*, where Anne met him. After that, the next time he was in Thornton-on-Sea, she invited your parents, Elise, and me to a tea, where we met him. So, that was that. It wasn't too long before Ted and I knew we were meant for each other."

"What a nice story. I liked him. We have a lot in common. Was he based in England throughout the war?"

"Yes, First in Ashford, and later in Ridgewell. He flew the flying Fortress."

"Impressive. When are you planning your wedding?"

"Soon. We haven't chosen a date, but it will be here in Thornton-on-Sea. The Whitfield's would like for it to be at *Meadowlands*, and your parents have offered the chapel at *Highcroft Hall*, but I think we're going to opt for *St. Martin's-by-the- Sea*. That's where I've attended church since my arrival in this village. Ted likes it too."

"And then you'll be going to America?" Sloan asked.

"Yes. Boston. I'm a tad frightened, but I'd go to the moon with Ted. He says it's a lovely place. I'm sure I'll like it."

"Right. I've never been there, but I've heard a lot about it. It's one of the oldest cities in America. I'm sure you'll have a good life."

Giselle smiled. "I am too."

Elise returned to the room, having put Chloe down for a nap. Sloan was finding it difficult not to tell her how often he still dreamed of her and how certain he was that she was meant for him. But he'd made that mistake before, and the last thing he wanted was to frighten Elise by acting impulsively. This time he meant to take it slow and easy. She had to grow to trust him.

Elise sat back down in her chair by the fireplace. "So, have you and Sloan had a good chat?" she asked.

"Yes, we have," Giselle replied. "I'd say we've made another friend, Elise. Of course, I've heard about you, Sloan, ever since I started working for your parents. They worship you, which I'm sure you know."

"They're wonderful parents. I'm a very lucky chap. No matter what my choices in life, they've always been supportive."

"You're referring to the broken engagement with Anne?"

"That's the latest topic in the village, I understand." He smiled ruefully.

"It has been. But I think Anne has managed to calm things down. The word has gone out that the end of the engagement was *her* idea. Of course that's the way it should be. People accept that much more readily."

"Absolutely. I'd say it turned out to be mutual, anyway. We agreed. We've pledged to be lifelong friends. She's like a sister to me."

"And do you hope that Elise will be like a sister, too?" Giselle asked.

Elise put her hand over her mouth, astonished at Giselle's cheekiness. Sloan, however, didn't look in the least discomfited

"That's a good question, Giselle. One I wish I could answer. That's the very least I'd hope, I suppose."

Giselle grinned. It was a rather cat-like smile. "I think you can wish for quite a bit more, Lord Thornton."

17

The wedding was planned for September 10, 1945. It wouldn't be large. Neither Ted nor Giselle was in favor of a big spectacle, and they didn't have a large number of friends and acquaintances for an invitation list. Many of his friends from the military had already shipped out for the States, and only a handful of special people were close to Giselle. Of course, Elise would be her Maid of Honour, although she was referred to as Matron of Honour, since everyone assumed she was a widow. Chloe would also be a bridesmaid. Ted chose Sloan as Best Man.

That was quite a surprise, since they'd only known one another a month before the big day. But the moment they met, it seemed they'd been friends forever. Giselle wasn't surprised. The moment she met Sloan, she suspected he and Ted would hit it off. They were the same sort of men in many ways. Both came from aristocratic families, even though one was English and one American; they were tall, rugged, yet genteel; kind, with good senses of humour, and thoughtful natures. Then there was the fact that both had flown aircraft during the entire war. They could talk for hours about sorties and bombing raids. Because of their newly formed friendship, Giselle, Ted, Elise, and Sloan spent more time together than might normally have been the case. The four met at least one night a week to play Bridge, and another evening was spent at the local pub. Lady Celia and Lord Rowan watched over Chloe on those occasions. They never said a word to Sloan, but their dream was to have a grandchild of their own. Because they knew of Sloan's fascination with Elise, they didn't interfere, but hoped the relationship would lead to another wedding. They weren't the least put off because she wasn't of the aristocracy, which had been a relief to Sloan. He'd worried a bit that they might be. But Elise was so charming, those thoughts soon evaporated. Lord Rowan and Lady Celia had never been that sort. Sloan had been raised never to look down on people because of inferior social standing.

Anne was also taking part in Giselle and Ted's ceremony. She'd be another bridesmaid. Perhaps that should have made Sloan somewhat uncomfortable, but it didn't. It wasn't his wedding, and Giselle and Ted had every right to choose who they wanted to participate. Anne seemed fine with the fact that Sloan would also be playing a part. So, it wasn't even discussed. Giselle might have gone to London to choose a wedding gown, due to the generosity of Lady Celia, but she selected one from a shop on Thornton-on-Sea's High Street. It was ivory taffeta, tea-length, with long sleeves and a high neckline. The skirt was bell-shaped, with a scalloped hemline. Elise found a dress at the same shop, in a similar style. Hers was pale pink, also taffeta, with a tailored look. The wrists were French cuffed, and the collar stood up stiffly on her pretty neck. Giselle wore a wedding gift of pearls from Ted, and Elise wore a locket on a golden chain - the only item she had left from her mother. Anne also wore pink, but a shade darker. Again it was taffeta, with long-sleeves. Both Elise and Anne carried bouquets of pink roses and white lilies, surrounded by white violets. Giselle carried a larger one of mixed roses, interspersed with traditional English flowers, like larkspur and lily of the valley. She wore a crown of Lily of the Valley in her hair. Little Chloe wore an ivory frock, trimmed with pink ribbons at the wrists and neckline. A large pink sash encircled her waist. She carried a basket of rose petals. Lord Rowan Thornton gave the lovely Giselle to her new husband.

There were just enough guests to fill the small, weathered chapel by the sea. Lord and Lady Whitfield, Lord and Lady Thornton, and all of the staff from *Highcroft Hall* were present. In addition, as a great surprise to Giselle, Madame Violette travelled from Brighton. An invitation had been sent, but Giselle never imagined she'd actually attend. When she wrote back saying she would be there, both Giselle and Elise were giddy with joy. Violette arrived looking every bit a lady. She presented herself at the church dressed in a pale lilac dress, made from *peau de soie* and trimmed with the finest French lace. There was no way anyone would have guessed her occupation. In addition, there were several guests from the village with whom Giselle had become friendly during the four years she'd lived there. All of the parents of Elise's students came, as well as numerous shopkeepers from along the High Street. All in all, it was exactly the wedding Giselle had hoped for. It was as lovely and old-fashioned as a scene from Charlotte Bronte or Jane Austen. Afterwards, a reception was held at *Highcroft Hall*. No one would have guessed that the groom walked with the aide of an artificial limb. He was very handsome in his grey morning suit.

Giselle and Elise wept sadly, as they held each other and said goodbye. Giselle and Ted were sailing from Southampton the next morning and would be spending the night at an Inn in that seaport town. So, when the reception ended, it was the last the friends would see of one another. Promises were exchanged. Elise would visit Boston, and Giselle and Ted would return to England. But in truth, nobody had the slightest notion how long it would be before they were reunited. The two friends had gone through so much together, and it was hard to think they wouldn't still be sharing their quaint cottage, drawing on each other for strength and wisdom.

Still, Elise was delighted that Giselle had found happiness. She wished her godspeed and great good luck. Sloan walked Elise and Chloe back to the cottage after the reception. Elise was still trying to stop sniffling, but he managed to bring a smile to her face when he asked her to bring Chloe and come to dinner at *Highcroft Hall* the following evening. He was well aware of how lonely she was going to be without Giselle. It was his intention to do everything possible to make it easier for her. If it had been up to him, he and Elise would be exchanging their own vows soon, but their friendship hadn't progressed to that point. There was no question that they'd grown closer. Often he wondered what would happen if he spoke to her about his deep feelings. He talked with Anne about how to proceed, and she continued to tell him that he should wait – that Elise had been through so much sorrow and wasn't ready to think about marriage. Sloan continued with the assumption that Elise was a widow. She'd never told him differently. So, that's what he assumed Anne was referring to, when she spoke of everything Elise had endured. Elise, of course, thought Sloan *did* know everything about her, judging from what he'd said after returning from the war. He'd said he understood, and she went on believing he knew of the assault by the Nazi soldiers and all that had happened since. On the other hand, Sloan believed she'd suffered the awful trauma of marrying, losing her husband, learning she was pregnant and having to face life as a single mother. Anne was perfectly content for things to continue in that vein.

Sloan had invited Elise and Chloe to dinner for two reasons. First and foremost, he loved to spend time with them, and it was important to him that his parent's learn to know them well. Secondly, he had information that was going to make Elise very happy. He'd located the whereabouts of one Josef Lisak, who was a member of Number 347 Squadron at RAF Elvington. Prior to that, he'd been a member of the GB I/25 Tunisian airmen, who'd been based in the Middle East. Squadron 347 was formed on June 20, 1944, and was equipped with British Halifax Heavy Bombing aircraft. They'd taken part in night raids over Germany.

After the Armistice, officially removing France from the war in 1940, following Dunkirk, twelve entire French Squadrons were formed. They were comprised of civilian French pilots living overseas. Josef Lisak had escaped to England in May 1940, with the thousands of others who were rescued from the beaches at Dunkirk. After joining the RAF, he was sent to Tunisia, where he'd spent the majority of the war. After hostilities ceased, in October 1945, Josef was transferred from RAF to French control on November 15, 1945. Sloan found him in Bordeaux, in the southwest of France. He didn't contact Josef, because he felt that was Elise's prerogative.

When everyone gathered for dinner at *Highcroft Hall* the evening after Giselle and Ted's wedding, Sloan didn't keep Elise in suspense. He immediately shared what he'd been able to learn about her brother. She was overjoyed.

"Oh, but how absolutely wonderful to know he's alive. I can't believe you learned all of this so quickly. I'm so grateful. Now, how do I go about contacting him?" She had tears in her eyes.

"Write him a letter. I have the address for the French Squadron to which he's attached. It will probably be dismantled soon, if it hasn't been already.

Perhaps it would be better if you sent a cable. Just give him your name and address, so he knows where to reach you. I'm sure the moment he receives it, you'll hear from him. I'll wager he's been as anxious as you've been for news of your whereabouts."

"I'll do it immediately. I can't thank you enough. My brother is the only family I have, besides Chloe. He means so much to me. It's been such a long time."

"I'll go with you tomorrow to send a wire. I'm anxious for the two of you to reunite. It's nice to have happy stories, after so much sadness and loss during the past five years."

So a cable was sent the following morning. Elise spent two days biting her nails, waiting for an answer. Finally, on Tuesday, she received a call from *Western Union*, telling her she had a wire from Bordeaux. She asked that it be read over the telephone.

"Wonderful news dear sister. Arriving on 3:45 p.m. train to Thornton Saturday, Sept 18. So anxious to see you. Josef.

Elise was overcome with emotion. She immediately rang Sloan. He made a dash for her cottage, and they sat drinking tea in the parlour, discussing Josef's arrival. Elise wondered how much her brother had changed. Of course, Sloan had never even met the Frenchman, but he was wise enough to know that it was imperative that Josef like him. A brother's approval was necessary if Sloan's hopes for marriage to Elise could come to fruition. In any event, he knew if Josef was anything like his sister, he'd immediately feel comfortable around him.

Chloe danced a little jig when she returned from school and learned her Mummy's brother was coming to visit. She'd grown up hearing about her uncle, and now, at long last, she would meet him. Elise prepared Giselle's old room, now doing duty as a guest chamber. She made certain she had ingredients for many of the meals Josef had loved long ago. Elise intended to spoil him unmercifully. Actually, Josef was an excellent chef, having studied at the *Culinary Institute* in Paris. That had been his career before the war. Still, Elise would be the cook for the time being.

While Sloan wanted very much to be a part of the happy reunion, he also felt it would be rude to interfere. There was no question in his mind that Elise should have her brother all to herself, at least at the beginning of his stay. Elise appreciated his thoughtfulness, since she felt the same way. It had been such a long time. Her life with Josef was a separate niche. She had so much to tell him. Although she believed Sloan knew everything about her, she wanted time alone with Josef to explain everything in detail.

She met him at the station alone. Chloe was in school, and Elise chose not to interrupt her daughter's routine. In addition, some of the background she needed to share with her brother pertained to issues about which Chloe knew nothing. Elise waited impatiently, pacing up and down on the platform, peering down the tracks to see if she could spot an engine and listening for the sound of a train whistle. As usual, it was late, but finally it chugged into the depot. Elise was dressed in a pretty, woolen dress - blue, with a pin tucked bodice and a flared skirt. It was the first new dress she'd bought since the war, besides the frock she'd worn for Giselle's wedding. She looked breathtaking on that crisp autumn morning, her golden hair shining in the sun and her blue eyes filled with happy expectation. After a few minutes, Josef stepped from the carriage. She wasn't certain she'd have known him. He was so much more mature – larger than she'd remembered. His hair was cut very short, in the traditional military style, and that changed his appearance more than anything. He was tanned, probably from years in Tunisia and Italy. Still, it was definitely Josef. Dear, special, wonderful Josef. She ran to him. He picked her up in the air, swinging her about. Kisses were exchanged on both cheeks and numerous hugs. He held her away from him and said "Let me look at you. You've grown up, Elise. You were always pretty. Now you're exquisite. I knew you would be. There's so much I want to know. So much we need to talk about. *Mon Dieu*! Five years is a long time."

"I know, I know. I want to hear everything. Where you've been. What happened after you left me that morning in the farmhouse? Your plans for the future. Simply everything."

"Yes. I do, too. Let me get my bag. Ah – you even have an auto. How grand, Elise."

"Not so grand, Josef. But it gets me where I need to go. Come. Hop in. I'll take you to my cottage. I know you'll love it. It's by the sea. Of course, it isn't really mine. I lease it. Up until recently, I had a dear friend who shared it with me. She married and went to America. Now, it's just Chloe and me."

"And who is Chloe?" he asked.

"Oh, Josef. She's your little niece. She's four years old, and you've never even seen her. How sad. We'll make up for that."

"A niece? Are you married then? How could I not have been there?"

"It's a very long story, Josef. No, there's no husband at home. Chloe will be thrilled to have an uncle. She's had no man in her life. Well, yes, there are friends. But an uncle is something special."

"So is a niece," he smiled.

They reached the cottage, and Josef laughed heartily at the little sign that said '*No Regrets*'.

"Is that true?" he asked, pointing to it.

"For the most part," she answered. "There've been bad times, but they've always been followed by happiness. I'm much more fortunate than so many who lived through the war, let alone those who didn't."

"I know. I feel the same way. I'm very angry with the leaders of France, I can tell you that. There were many reasons for their actions, but I don't believe we should ever have laid down arms. To let those barbarians take over France. Really. It was unbelievable. I think I'm going to make my home in England. I've seen the bravery and courage this land displayed for five long years. I want to be one of them. I hope you plan on staying here. Together we can become British citizens."

"That's my plan too, Josef. I *feel* British. When I tell you everything, I think you'll understand why. I'm just so glad to hear that you want to stay, too. I wish you'd move to this village. I love it here. What do you intend to do in terms of employment?"

"Restaurant Management. It's what I did in Paris. I have the experience and the education." He laughed, "If need be, I'll return for more study. I'd like to eventually own a gourmet establishment. Does this village have many places of that sort?"

"None, Josef. That sounds excellent. If you stay in Thornton-on-Sea, there's a chance that people I've met could help you."

"Any help would be appreciated," he smiled.

Josef had an artistic touch with food preparation, and Elise knew he'd be successful. There was no French restaurant in Thornton-on-Sea, and there wasn't any question in Elise's mind that such a spot would be welcome. Stepping out of the car, they went into the cottage, making themselves comfortable in the parlour. Chloe was at school, so they had plenty of time to chat openly. Tea was ready in the kitchen, and after drinking a cup, they settled and began to speak about all that had happened since they'd parted in May 1940.

"So, Elise. You escaped France for England, just as I did. Did you go on the same day I last saw you? How did it all come about?"

"It's a long tale, Josef. After you left that morning, I was awfully afraid. I knew that the smart thing would be for me to follow you to the beaches and try to get to England myself. But that was a terrifying thought. I'd just about made up my mind to stay in the farmhouse and ride it out, hoping the Nazis didn't end up occupying France. Then, a young RAF Lieutenant came to my door. At first I was frightened to answer his knock, but I looked out of the window and could see it was an English soldier. He was in obvious distress. He was lying on the porch, clearly wounded. It was pouring rain. So I did open the door, and he asked for my help. Of course I didn't turn him away. I couldn't have."

"You must have been afraid you'd be seen, and reported for aiding an enemy of the Third Reich?"

"Oh, *Mon Dieu*! France wasn't yet occupied, so I didn't really think of that. But, I did know there were Germans swarming the area. However, he needed aide. What was I to do? I helped him over the threshold, and he explained about his aircraft being shot down. The same bullets had wounded him in the leg. I gathered every medical supply we had and set about splinting and bandaging the leg, after I removed the bullet."

"The nursing experience came in handy, eh?"

"Yes. I was glad I knew what to do. I only wish I'd had better instruments with which to work. Anyway, after I treated his injury, I gave him food — soup, cheese and bread. He was finally able to put weight on the leg, and we sat in the parlour for a short time, chatting. He was very nice, and I was confused a bit."

"How so, Elise?"

"Well, he began to speak about soulmates. He told me he'd always dreamed of an ideal woman and, when he saw me for the first time, after I opened the door, he was certain I was the person he'd waited for all of his life."

"Ooh la la." Josef laughed. "I can imagine your confusion. Did you think him daft, as the English say?"

"Yes, a bit. I thought perhaps his wound had left him with some difficulty thinking clearly. But he went on and on, and finally I realized he was serious. He was extremely well-spoken – obviously a gentleman – clearly well-educated. I didn't think he was saying those things as a means to seduce me. It would have been a strange time for a man to attempt seduction – Nazi aircraft flying overhead and Germans on the march very nearby, not to mention the queues of soldiers and refugees trying to reach the beaches and safety."

"So, how did it end?"

"He maintained that I was his soulmate until the end. He described me perfectly – on the inside – what I was like. It was eerie. He was adamant that if we had more time to spend together I'd realize that *he* was *my* soulmate, too."

"And so..."

"And so, I told him I thought he had a fantasy – an ideal, and that he didn't know me well enough to be saying such things. Shortly after that, he left. Before he did, he took my hands in his and said he knew he'd see me again in England."

"Haven't you ever been curious to learn more about him?"

"A little. But I didn't have to search for answers. When I moved here, to Thornton-on-Sea, I learned that my 'soulmate visitor' was none other than Lord Sloan Thornton, the Viscount who will eventually become the Earl of Wessex and oversee *Highcroft Hall*, the family seat."

"*Mon Dieu*! How ironic. Do you know him now?"

"On yes, indeed. But let me finish telling you what happened. Not very long after he left, there was another knock at my door. I thought perhaps it was him, returning for some reason. I was careful, but I opened the door slightly, and the next thing I knew it was forced inward. Three Nazi soldiers forced their way in."

"Oh, my dear sister. I'm not sure I want to know the rest of this story."

"Yes, well, it isn't pleasant. They'd seen me aiding Lord Thornton, although I think that was just an excuse to break into the house. They said they were going to punish me. All three assaulted me, repeatedly. I wished I were dead. I thought it would never end. Finally they left. I was terrified and, of course, in shock. My only thought was getting away. I was so frightened they'd return. I still believe they would have."

"I imagine you're right. The dirty swine. I wish I'd been there. I would have killed them."

"I'm glad you weren't there, Josef. You might have managed to kill one of them, but you would have been killed, too. They were large, brutish men. There's no way you would have been able to overpower all of them. Anyway, they did finally leave. I bathed, and made ready to escape. Actually, I put on some of your old clothing." She smiled and laughed ruefully. "I went over to the farm next door – you remember Brigitte, our neighbour? I told Brigitte that I was going to England if I could get on a boat. She told me to go to Brighton after I reached Dover. She had a friend from long ago who owned a boarding house there. She made me repeat the name so I wouldn't forget it. *Maison de Violette.* It's a long story, Josef. I did as she said, and Madame Violette took me in. I hate to admit this, but her so-called 'boarding house' was, in reality, a brothel. I was so naïve. But she was lovely to me, as were most of the girls who worked for her. I really don't know what would have become of me had it not been for her."

"But, Elise. Your reputation? Weren't you concerned that people would think you were one of her – eh – her girls?"

"At first, yes. But you know, Josef, I've learned that there are more important things in life than what others think. After I'd been there three months, it became obvious that I was pregnant."

"*Mon Dieu, Mon Dieu!* Oh, my sweet sister. How unimaginable. So this is how Chloe came to be?"

"Yes. Of course I don't ever want her to know. Madame Violette suggested that I change my surname, acting as if I were married, and wear a ring on my left hand." Elise held out her hand. "I still do." "So, then, that's what I did. I'm now Elise de Baier. That's the name on Chloe's birth certificate. Everyone in Thornton-on-Sea thinks I was married, and that my husband was killed at Dunkirk – that I was pregnant when I left France. Of course, I truly *was* pregnant when I left, although I didn't know it. So, that part is true enough."

"Poor Elise. Did you stay in Brighton until Chloe was born?"

"Yes. Madame Violette made arrangements for me to deliver in hospital. I had the best care. When I returned to *Maison de Violette* I realized, however, that no matter how kind everyone was, Chloe needed to be raised in a better environment. I had no idea what I'd do. Then, the best friend I'd made there, Giselle Dupris, presented an offer I couldn't refuse. She said she wanted to find a decent job and quit the life she'd been living. She wanted me to share a cottage with her, in a village somewhere far removed from Brighton. So we came here. She got a job as lady's maid to Lady Celia Thornton at *Highcroft Hall.* I packed up Chloe and moved here too. We were able to lease this cottage, and it's been wonderful. The people are gracious and kind. They've been very welcoming. Naturally, I was stunned when I learned that Giselle was working for the mother of Sloan Thornton, the man who'd visited our farmhouse on that fateful day. He wasn't here, obviously. He was RAF – based in North Africa. It's all so complex. I learned of his engagement to a girl named Anne Whitfield – a Duke's daughter. It infuriated me that he'd made such overt comments to me about soulmates and the like, when he had a lovely girl waiting at home for him. "

"This does get more and more complicated. Can we take a pause while I refill my tea, Elise?"

"Yes, certainly. I'm sorry. It *is* a long tale. But I want you to understand all that's happened, and where things stand now."

"I want to know every bit of it," her brother answered. "I'll just be a second." He went to the kitchen and refilled his cup. Returning, he settled back in, ready to hear the rest of the story. "All right, Elise, where were we? So, you found out that Lord Thornton was engaged to someone else, when he made overtures to you."

"Yes. That's the gist of it. I didn't care, except I thought him a terrible cad. Eventually I met his fiancé, Anne. She ended up taking French lessons from me. One day we drank wine, and I'm afraid it loosened my tongue. I told her the truth about my not being married, the Nazi brutes – all of it. She was very sympathetic. She knew I'd met Sloan, but only that I had bandaged his wound. I didn't say anything about the conversation about my supposedly being his soulmate. But, he'd actually written a letter telling her about me. I was stunned."

"But, he scarcely knew you. Also, Elise, was it wise to tell her your story? Do you trust her?"

"Yes, I do. She's a lovely person. She and Sloan broke off their engagement. Actually he asked her to release him from the commitment. He said he loves her like a sister, but should never have proposed. He'd proposed the night before he left for the war."

"Many men made that mistake. War is a dreadful thing, and it also makes people more impetuous. There's great romance associated with the idea of going off to fight and leaving someone you love behind."

"I know. It's not unusual. Anyway, to make a long story shorter, Anne and I are good friends now. She doesn't harbour resentment towards Sloan, and now he's home, they've pledged to be friends forever. She's actually very keen on getting Sloan and me together."

"She must be very special. He's a lucky man. If that had been me, the scorned woman would have had my head," he laughed.

"I know. But, she's been very nice about everything."

"Are you involved with Sloan, then? Don't tell me you believe in this soulmate business?"

"Not especially. But I do like him a lot. We're friends. Whether it goes further, I don't know. At first I thought he would be repulsed if he knew my story. But apparently Anne told him everything, and he says it doesn't matter – that it will never be spoken of again."

"Well, he certainly sounds like a compassionate sort. Of course, none of what happened was your fault Elise. Why do you think he, or anyone else, would be repulsed? Repulsed at the Nazis' behavior, but not at anything you've done."

"Yes, but I can see where a man might find me disgusting to be with. I feel soiled and unworthy of a decent man."

"Elise! None of it was your fault. You need to stop such thinking."

"That's what Sloan says, too. That's really the only thing he said about it. He asked if anything about my story was my fault, and I replied that it wasn't. That was all that mattered to him."

"Elise, are you in love with him?"

"I don't know, Josef. I'm afraid to give my heart to anyone. Men frighten me. And I have Chloe to think about. I'm confused, to be honest. I think I *could* love him, if it weren't for everything that's happened to me. I'm terribly afraid to trust."

"I'd like to meet Sloan Thornton. I could form a better opinion about whether I believe he's trustworthy."

"I fully intend for you to meet him. That's one reason I wanted to tell you all of this."

"So, that's settled. Now, it's your turn to hear about my five years away from you."

18

They chatted the entire morning. It was wonderful to be able to speak with someone who had known her since birth. Elise suddenly realized how stressful it had been having no one with whom she could be honest. So few people knew her entire story. Now that Giselle was gone, Anne was really the only person she could speak openly with, although Sloan, too, knew of the trauma she'd endured. She found the thought of discussing anything to do with her assault extremely uncomfortable. To talk openly to Sloan about it would be embarrassing. Although he supposedly knew the entire story, she was glad he understood her reluctance to discuss it. He didn't seem particularly eager to discuss it himself.

Elise and Josef moved on to talk about what had happened to him during their long separation. She was astounded to learn that he'd endured his own romantic heartache. After they'd parted, and he'd gone to England, Josef immediately joined a group of French Resistance émigrés. They were assembled and became a squadron in the RAF, ready to fight against the Axis Forces. Josef was delighted that he'd been allowed to participate in action directed at the enemy who'd taken over his homeland. He was in England for a short time before being sent to Sicily. There, he flew sorties into and out of Tunisia, bringing supplies and aiding the Allies who were fighting for control of Tunisia and Algeria. While in Sicily, Josef met an Italian woman. Her name was Daniela Carissa. He fell madly in love with her. They engaged in a torrid love affair and planned on marrying. She was beautiful, refined, well-educated and kind-hearted. He was absolutely certain she was the one with whom he wanted to spend the rest of his life. But during a terrible bombing raid, the old palace, in which she lived, was almost completely destroyed. Daniela was killed, along with all of her household. Josef's heart was broken. For the rest of the war, he never allowed himself to look at another woman. He still hadn't recovered from the loss.

Elise felt terribly sorry for her beloved brother. Josef had always been so level-headed and had never had a serious romantic interest. So, she was well-aware of how unusual his involvement with the Italian woman had been. She knew that only time would heal the wound. But it made her more adamant about persuading him to stay in Thornton-on-Sea, where he'd have her love and support. She also knew his presence would be a positive influence for Chloe, who needed a father figure in her life. While it wouldn't be a father, having an uncle would be very good for her.

Josef had been wounded twice during the war – once seriously enough to have been hospitalized for several months. But he'd recuperated fully and described himself as healthy and strong. He'd lost many friends during his time served and, like his sister, had learned to be somewhat guarded with his feelings. Elise hoped peace would bring back the old twinkle in his eyes and a desire to find someone who could fill the ache in his heart. Josef was a handsome man. Although he'd lived in France practically all of his life, he had the distinctly Russian appearance of his forefathers. There was a slight Slavic slant to his eyes, and they were a very light blue. His hair, on the other hand, was dark chestnut-brown, and his colouring was olive. He was a large man, unlike many of his French counterparts, who tended to be of smaller stature. Strong and muscular, he gave off a fine impression of masculinity. Yet he had a kind mouth, with lips that were soft and sensitive. Elise had always adored him. She knew Josef was attractive to women, but he was very choosy when it came to settling on just one. Having to care for his little sister, from the time they'd left Russia, had always been foremost in his mind, and he'd never let other thoughts interfere with that responsibility. Now Elise was grown, and she hoped she could repay the attention he'd given her by helping Josef along the road to his own happiness.

After chatting through the early afternoon, she showed her brother the bedroom she planned to make into his own. He was pleased with the charming cottage. Elise told him to have a lie-down, while she tidied-up and got ready to collect Chloe from school. He was sound asleep when she silently left for the school building, only two lanes over from 'No Regrets'. She arrived just as school was being dismissed. Chloe ran down the steps, into her arms.

"Mummy! Did my uncle come? Is he at home now? I want to meet him, she exclaimed.

"He did come, Chloe. He's just as anxious to meet you. He was very surprised when I told him about you. He's already seen your photo and thinks you look a lot like me."

"Everybody says that," Chloe giggled. "Is Uncle Josef going to stay with us forever?"

"I don't know about 'forever,' sweetheart. But for a long time, I hope. We'll have to persuade him not to leave."

"I can do that," she announced confidently. "Aunt Gissy used to say that I could make anyone do anything, if I talked with my eyes."

Elise laughed. "There's some truth to that. But you mustn't become dependent on that. Use your power only for good things."

"I would never do anything bad, Mummy. You know I've become better and better, as I've grown."

It was a typical conversation between Elise and her daughter, and it took all of Elise's self-control not to burst out laughing at Chloe's adult way of speaking. Her first four years had been spent almost exclusively in the company of adults, and it showed.

"You're a very sweet, good girl, Chloe. Mummy loves you so much and is so proud of you." She leaned down and cuddled her little girl, kissing her on the cheek.

When they got to the cottage, Josef was out in the front garden, examining the varieties of flowers. He was impressed with Elise's green thumb. Chloe acted somewhat uncharacteristic, running to him and shouting, "Are you my Uncle Josef?" Then, she hugged him round the legs.

He laughed and crouched down to her level. "Are you really my niece?" he asked. "You're so pretty. I'm a very fortunate fellow to have such a beautiful niece."

"I'm lucky to have you. I didn't even know I had an Uncle till Mummy told me. I don't have any brothers or sisters, and my Aunt Gissy just moved far away, so I'm really glad you're here."

"So am I, Chloe. I've missed your Mummy, but I'm so glad to know she had you. I'll be staying with you for a while, and perhaps I'll even move to this village. Would you like that?"

"I'd like it very much. Then we could play together and do fun things when Mummy is busy."

"We could do that, and we will. Now, let's go into the cottage. I want to hear all about the things you like to do. You have to tell me everything about yourself."

She took him by the hand. "Yes. And I need to learn about you, too. We'll be very special to each other."

<hr>

It was a busy autumn. Josef stayed on, and the threesome made a nice little family. Elise made certain he met all of her friends in Thornton-on-Sea, including Sloan. In fact, Sloan paid a visit the second day Josef was there, and they chatted easily. After he left, Josef told Elise he liked him very much. He believed Elise could trust him.

"He seems like a good man, Elise. I also have to say it's very apparent that he's quite taken with you."

"Well, I'm not sure. Of course, there was the talk about 'soulmates.' Since we've become friends, he's always kind and nice, but I think he feels about me like he does Anne – like I'm a sister."

"Then you must not notice the look he gets in his eyes when you enter a room. You're my sister, Elise, and I love you, but I know I've never looked at you like he does. I suspect he's waiting for a sign from you. He knows the hurt you've endured and definitely doesn't want to frighten you."

"Do you really think so? I wouldn't know how to give a man the sort of sign you're speaking about."

"Dear sister. You're a beautiful woman. You're also French. Surely you know how to flirt? All women know how to flirt."

"I don't really think I do. Maybe I'm too honest for that. I'd feel silly. Tell me what I should do."

"Just be very nice to him. Raise your eyes and look straight into his. Smile, and let him know you're happy to see him. Make plans to spend time alone together."

"But that's hard. I have Chloe."

"You also have me. I'll take care of Chloe anytime you want to spend time alone with Sloan. The weather is still warm. Why don't you suggest a picnic?"

"Where would we go?"

"*Mon Dieu*, Elise. Leave that up to him. He grew up here. The village is named for his family. I'm sure he knows a pretty place for a picnic."

Elise smiled at her brother. "Well, you're just full of good ideas. I just might try it. The next time I see him, I'll make the suggestion. Now pray that the weather stays warm."

Two days later, Sloan rang Elise and said he was going to pop over to the cottage. She seized the moment and, without missing a beat, asked him if he might like to go on a picnic. He sounded delighted at her suggestion and immediately said he would love it. He even told her not to bother with preparation of food. Instead, he said he'd have Ruth, at *Highcroft Hall*, prepare a nice basket for them. Elise promised to contribute a bottle of wine. The moment she hung up, she ran to tell Josef. He laughed and picked her up in his arms, twirling her around, as he used to do when she was a child.

"There, you see. I was right. I'll bet he's on cloud nine. He's been waiting for you to suggest this sort of outing. I'll take Chloe to the park and stop to get you a bottle of fine wine. You run upstairs and change into something very romantic. What time is he coming?"

"Half past twelve" she replied.

"Good, that allows plenty of time."

Josef called for Chloe, who came running from the garden. "Come on, little niece. We're going shopping, and afterwards, I'm taking you to the park."

Elise scampered up the stairs and pawed through her cupboard, searching for the perfect, picnic frock. It had been such a long time since she'd done something so young and carefree. Finally, she settled on a yellow cotton dress, with cap sleeves, in a fashionable style with a full skirt and a pretty white sash at the waist. It was very feminine. There was white ribbon laced throughout the bodice and hemline, which fell to mid-calf. She also found a darling hat which she'd bought on a summer day in Paris, years before. There was nothing passé about it. It, too, had a white ribbon band, and the ends trailed down her back. It was made of straw and looked like the sort of hat one would wear on a picnic. Pretty yellow slippers completed the outfit. She washed her hair and fluffed the curls with a towel, letting them dry naturally. Debating over how to wear it, she finally decided to pull it back on top, secure it with a clip and allow the curls to fall loosely around her shoulders. Elise was twenty-seven years old, but she resembled a bright, young thing, not past twenty.

Josef returned and whistled when he set eyes on her.

"You look radiant, Elise. If you aren't certain you're in love with Sloan, I can verify that you are. I've never seen such roses in your cheeks."

She laughed, but didn't deny his accusation. He presented her with two bottles of Pouilly-Fuisse.

"*Mon Dieu*! You went for the finest, Josef. If we drink two bottles, who knows what could happen? I think I'll only take one."

"All right. We'll save the other for the announcement of your engagement."

"Whoa," she exclaimed, as she put her hand in front of his face. "That's not going to happen," she said, shaking her head. "At least not now," she added, with a charming smile. She straightened her dress, and smoothed her curls when she heard Sloan's car stop in front of the cottage.

"Well, here he is, sweet sister. Now, remember to let him know you care for him. *Mon Dieu*, Elise. Remember, you're French!"

"I'll try, Josef. I'll try."

Sloan took her to a beautiful spot on the grounds of *Highcroft Hall*. It was near an orchard, and the peaches hung golden in the sunlight, ready to be picked. They spread out a picnic blanket on the lush green lawn, and sat on it, side by side. Sloan had a wicker hamper. He set it on the ground in front of them, unclasped it, and displayed a beautiful array of food; cucumber sandwiches cut into small rounds; chicken salad in small croissants; liver pate; brie cheese; water biscuits; French potato salad, with parsley and dill, and small lemon tarts. The top of the hamper contained plates, silverware and crystal wine glasses. The wine had been chilled and was a perfect temperature. Sloan uncorked it and poured them each a glass. Both said they'd like to enjoy a glass of wine before eating, so Sloan leaned back against the trunk of a large, old tree, and Elise spread her skirts round her, sitting comfortably on the blanket. It was so peaceful, and at first they simply enjoyed the lovely day, feeling no need to rush into conversation. Sloan looked especially handsome. He was dressed in casual, grey slacks and a crème-coloured, linen shirt. His light brown hair had grown longer since returning from the war, and it fell onto his forehead. Little wisps blew softly in the breeze. His stunning blue eyes nearly matched the intense blue of the sky. Elise's heart beat faster when she looked at him, fully aware that if she were honest with herself, she cared for him deeply. It was truly the first time in her life she'd felt this way. She couldn't help but wonder if his statement, in 1940, about soulmates, didn't have validity. The more time she'd spent with him over the past months, the more she'd come to realize that they seemed to complement each other in every way.

Finally, he spoke. "My God, Elise. It's been ages since I've felt so completely decadent. The past five years were so barren of anything resembling this. You can't imagine how nice it is to take time to enjoy a pretty day, with a beautiful woman, splendid wine, and peace of mind. Thank you for suggesting this picnic. It's such a treat for me."

"Oh Sloan, you're welcome. It's special for me, too. I can't remember the last time I did anything like this. I'm very content with my life, but it's nice, every now and then, to get away from routine, and remember how fortunate we are to finally have the war behind us — to still have the freedom to take time out for idyllic diversions like this."

He smiled at her, and she remembered what her brother had suggested. She looked down at the ground and then raised her head, smiling sweetly as she looked straight into his eyes.

"Elise, you're the picture of perfection. I'm not just saying that. You really are. Everything about you reminds me of a fine, old, Victorian portrait. I wonder if you truly know how special you are."

"I'm just me. There are hundreds of women more special than I am. Thank you for such a nice compliment, but I think you're a bit prejudiced."

"I've always been prejudiced about you. You know that. From the first time I saw you."

"Yes, I remember. Are you still such a believer in soulmates?" She sighed, and sipped her glass of wine.

"Absolutely. In fact, perhaps even more. I have an old friend from Oxford, whom I ran into in London, after I returned from the war. We met for a bite to eat and ended up discussing that very topic – soulmates. His name is Elliott Woodbridge. He's probably an even bigger believer in that concept than I am. He's actually studied about it."

"Studied about it? Where in the world does one study about soulmates?" Elise laughed.

"In a library for starters. He quoted bible passages and Plato. I was amazed. If the theory is only rubbish, a lot of very admirable sources beg to differ."

"The Bible?" Elise echoed.

"Yes. I'll show you the chapter and verse someday. In any event, it's a concept that's been around for centuries. So you see, I have some very good authority to back up my beliefs."

"That *is* very interesting. I have such a practical way of thinking. I've never been what one would call a dreamer. But perhaps it isn't only a notion for idealists."

"It isn't, Elise. I probably *am* somewhat more of a idealist than you – I've always tended toward romanticism – but when it comes to important beliefs and ways to conduct my life, I'm quite logical. When I say 'romanticism', I'm speaking more in terms of the type of art and literature I enjoy, and, yes, having a tendency to see the world through rose-coloured glasses. I wouldn't call myself a 'romantic' in the sense that I've spent my life bowling women over with poetry and music."

"I understand what you're saying." Elise reached for a little plate and asked if he'd like her to put some selections of food on it for him. He nodded and thanked her, but continued the conversation.

"Elise, I know I spoke of my feelings impulsively when we first met. I was honestly astonished when I saw you. You fit my ideal so perfectly, and it seemed fate had intervened in my life. But it was poor timing. There were things I didn't know about you then. I was too forward and too blunt. I'm sorry for blurting out things I should have kept to myself, but I can't apologize for the feelings I had."

Elise filled a plate for herself, after handing one to him.

"There's no need to apologize to me for anything. You didn't say or do anything wrong. You couldn't help what you felt, and then too, you'd been injured. It was war, and neither of us had any idea what was going to happen next. I wasn't offended. I just thought that you were a bit strange," she giggled.

"What a nice compliment," he replied, also laughing. "Well – so – I believe I'm fortunate to have had the chance to see you again and to test out whether my original thoughts were correct."

"I suppose I should ask if they were?" she answered.

"I hesitate to say. Not because I don't have an answer. But because I'm not certain that you're ready to hear."

She glanced at him again and smiled. "Well, I suppose you could try."

They'd finished eating, and he refilled their wine glasses. "All right, Elise. I'll tell you. Not only do I feel the way I did in 1940, but those sensations have grown a hundred-fold. When I first saw you, it was your outward beauty that knocked-me-for-six. Now feel that I've learned to know what you're like on the inside, and every facet of your exquisite loveliness is a reflection of your inner beauty. In short, I'm very certain I'm in love with you. Can I be more honest than that?"

Elise was silent. She hadn't expected such a proclamation of love – not in a thousand years. Her heart beat very rapidly. How should she respond? She felt as though her entire life might hinge on her next words. Finishing her glass of wine, she set the empty glass in the hamper. She thought very carefully before speaking.

"Sloan. 'Love' is a very important word. It implies so many things. Are you certain you know me well enough to use that word? I know you say you do. I know Anne told you my entire story. But, it's important to me that you really understand everything. I'm frightened to give my heart to you, only to learn later that you didn't know all of the facts. I'd feel so much better if you'd let me tell you myself."

"Elise, I don't want to ruin a perfect day by putting you through the sadness of having to recall painful memories. I do understand. I'm not the least interested in your past. Honestly. The future is what's important to me. Please, let's leave the past behind."

"All right. If that's what you prefer." There was silence again, and she sat looking at the ground, playing with a blade of grass.

"What are you thinking, Elise?" he asked.

She looked up at him. There were tears in her lovely eyes. This time it wasn't artifice, and Josef's advice was far from her mind.

"I'm thinking that I love you, too. It frightens me to say that. But it's true."

He leaned over and took her into his arms. "Elise, I don't ever want you to be frightened again in your life. I want to marry you, take care of you, and always protect you. The bad times are over for both of us. I want you to be the future Countess of Wexford – the beautiful lady who will oversee *Highcroft Hall* someday. Please tell me you want that, too."

His lips found hers, and the kiss was overwhelming. He was gentle and tender, yet the passion ran deep. She melted into his arms. Never in her life had she imagined feeling this way. She'd been kissed before, of course, but not like this. Never like this. She was acutely aware of everything around her – the soft breeze, the birds in the trees, the colour of the sky and the soft, green grass. It was a moment of perfection.

"Of course, I accept your offer," she murmured. "How could I not, when it's what I want more than anything in the world?"

His arms tightened about her, and he kissed her again – her eyes, her cheeks, her neck. Finally, they released one another. Her face was flushed and her eyes sparkled.

"I do love you so, Elise. I'll spend every moment for the rest of our lives making you happy."

"I love you, with all of my heart, Sloan. I'll try to be the best wife to you. There's only one other thing I think we need to discuss."

"What, darling? Surely there isn't any impediment to our loving and marrying?"

"No, no. Nothing of the sort. But there *is* Chloe. You know I adore her. I could never consider marrying any man who wouldn't love her as much as I do- who wouldn't think of her as his own daughter. If you don't feel you could do that, tell me now. She is so precious to me. She needs a father. I'll never marry unless the man can fill such a role."

"Elise, of course I'll make Chloe mine. I already love her. She reminds me of the way you must have been at her age – before the war and loss had done things to you. I would do anything to make certain she has a wonderful life. I'd like to adopt her, if that's what you want. I want her to be Chloe Thornton. I'll be her father in every sense of the word. I'd hope we have more children, but if not, then Chloe will be a radiant ray of sunshine in my life."

They kissed again. It was exactly what she'd hoped to hear. She prayed they'd have other children, too. She wanted a brother or sister for her daughter. Elise was well-aware that Sloan had a responsibility to produce an heir. Her next child would be born of love and would be planned. She couldn't imagine loving a son or daughter more than she loved Chloe, but if those circumstances were added, it would be unimaginably perfect.

When the afternoon ended, they walked hand-in-hand to the automobile, still a bit lightheaded from the wine and the love they'd confessed. They'd made the decision to tell Josef, Chloe, and his parents first. Then Sloan knew Lord and Lady Thornton would want to announce it to the world, with a splendid engagement party. If Elise had ever been happier in her life, she couldn't remember when.

19

To say everyone was happy about the news of their engagement would be an understatement. To begin with, Chloe was over-the-moon. She didn't know Sloan as well as she was about to, but the idea of having a Daddy was a dream come true for her. He'd always been exceptionally kind and loving towards her, and there was no doubt he would be a wonderful father. When Elise told her their happy news, Chloe jumped up and down and screamed. She had taken to dancing a little jig when filled with happiness. Sloan laughed and told her he would buy her a pony of her own, and allow her to name it whatever she pleased. At four years old, it was every child's dream. Chloe was no exception. He told her he would teach her to ride, and they'd explore the woods around her new home, *Highcroft Hall.* She had visited there before, with her Mummy and Aunt Gissy. It was unbelievable that she'd soon be living there.

For that matter, Elise felt the same way. She fretted a bit about whether she had the necessary skills to oversee such a large estate. Sloan assured her that she did, and also promised that his mother would be there to teach her anything she didn't know.

Josef was ecstatic when he heard they were engaged. He'd strongly suspected that would be the outcome eventually, and was glad it hadn't taken forever to come to fruition. He told Elise that if he could find employment in Thornton-on-Sea, he'd stay on and continue to lease *No Regrets,* which, he said, was certainly living up to its name. He and Sloan spoke at length about what Josef wanted to do regarding the restaurant business, and when they announced their decision to go into partnership in a new French Brasserie, Elise was bowled over. The idea of Josef no longer having to take orders from an employer was divine. He'd put away a substantial bit of money during the war years. The farmhouse in France was also for sale. In addition, Sloan was chipping in half of the investment. So, there was plenty of capital to lease a building with a smart address, renovate it, and employ necessary staff. They'd already settled on *Chez Chloe* as a name. Needless to say, the idea of having a restaurant named for her, practically took the child's breath away. Josef planned to have a life-sized portrait of Chloe, dressed in an old-fashioned Victorian frock, hung over a fireplace inside of his country-French restaurant.

Then there were Sloan's parents. Lady Celia was happy that she'd have full reign over planning the wedding, since Elise had no mother of her own to assume that task. She thought Elise was a lovely, sweet girl – perfect for Sloan. Although she still loved Anne, she wasn't the least disappointed that he'd settled on Elise. When she'd had time to think it over, the conclusion was reached that Elise was a better choice for her son. Lord Rowan had always thought her a grand girl. Her demure prettiness pleased the old gentleman. He knew she would be a perfect countess and, besides his son's happiness, that was a primary concern.

Sloan bought Elise a magnificent, emerald ring, and they set the wedding date for December 28, 1945 two days following Boxing Day. Since on Boxing Day, itself, servants were given time off to visit relatives, as a means of thanking them for their hard work over the holiday period, the chosen date, two days after that, allowed time for all plans to be finalised.

Preparations needed to be put into effect immediately. An engagement party was planned for the end of October. Elise and Lady Celia went to work on an invitation list. Elise also began to plan for the wedding itself. She wished more than anything to have Giselle present, to act as Matron of Honour. Whether such a thing was feasible was yet to be determined, but she planned on contacting her friend to find out. Chloe would, of course, be a bridesmaid again, just as she'd been at Ted and Giselle's ceremony. Elise also intended to ask three other girls who'd become her friends after she'd taught them French. Sloan was going to ask Elliott Woodbridge, from London, to be his Best Man, and there was no shortage of friends from Thornton-on-Sea to act as ushers. He hoped Giselle and Ted would make the trip. If so, he would ask Ted to be a part of the nuptials. Things were off to a wonderful start, when Sloan had lunch with Anne, and everything came to a grinding halt. It was like a bad thunderstorm after a sunny day.

He only rang Anne because it was the proper thing to do. After all, they'd once been engaged and were still close friends. She was also a friend to Elise. He didn't want her to learn of his engagement through word-of-mouth, or from an invitation to the party. Sloan wasn't in the least worried about breaking the news to her. Everything between them had been settled long before. He extracted a promise from his mother that she wouldn't say anything to Lady Caroline Whitfield, until he'd had the chance to tell Anne. He honestly believed Anne would be happy for them. She'd certainly not hesitated to let both of them know, often enough, that she was in favour of them as a couple. He made plans to meet Anne at a quaint restaurant off the High Street, where they used to go when they were still a very close to each other. He arrived first and requested a table in the small, private alcove. He wanted to be able to speak freely, without others over-hearing their conversation. Shortly after he was seated, Anne arrived. She looked pretty, in a red dress, with white gloves and matching hat. She smiled as she sat down, telling Sloan it was wonderful to see him.

"We haven't seen much of each other lately. I guess we've both been busy. But it's definitely time for a catch-up," she said.

"I agree. That's why I rang you. So much has happened. The summer has been busy and autumn even more so. Have we seen one other since Giselle and Ted's wedding?" Sloan asked.

"No. I don't think so. I went to London for a week in early September. I hadn't been shopping for so long. It was great fun, although depressing to see what the Nazis did to that wonderful city."

"I know. I had the same feeling when I was there right after the war."

"So, tell me what you've been up to?" Anne asked, tilting her head to one side.

"Well, I have very important news. Something I think you'll be happy to hear.'

"What? I can't imagine. Oh, do tell me."

"Elise and I have set a wedding date. It all happened rather quickly, after we'd seen a lot of each other and become good friends. We went on a picnic one day and it was wonderful. We confessed our love, and the rest is history. I'm terribly happy, Anne. I wanted to tell you personally, because we've been so close, and you've been a brick about everything."

Anne's face lost all colour. Her cheeks no longer matched the red in her dress. Sloan could see her hands begin to tremble.

"Anne, what is it? You look shocked. Surely this doesn't surprise you? I told you long ago how I felt about Elise. I'm just fortunate enough to have found out that she feels that same way about me. I thought this is what you wanted for me."

Anne tried to regain her composure. "Yes – yes – I knew you still had feelings about her. But she's always given the impression that she thought the whole matter rather silly. She never indicated she was in love with you."

"I don't think she was certain of her feelings for quite a while. Plus, she had doubts about being from a lower socio-economic class than mine. Finally she resolved all of those issues and gave over to her feelings. Aren't you happy for me, Anne?"

"Oh dear, Sloan. I wish I could say yes. I'd hoped it wouldn't come to this, to be honest with you. I really thought you'd realize, at some point, that Elise simply wasn't right for you. I thought you'd move on. I didn't think Elise would be foolish enough to believe a marriage to you would work."

"Why shouldn't it work? We love each other. Madly. I know she's not from the same background as you and me, but there isn't a thing about Elise that isn't charming and gracious. She's a beautiful, sweet, good person."

"No Sloan, she isn't. I so hate being the one to hurt you, but I can't sit back and watch you make such a horrific mistake. I'm your friend, and friends are supposed to be honest with one another. If this were something I could simply keep quiet about, and let you go on with your life, with no fear of harm, I would. Believe me. But it isn't that simple. There are things you don't know."

"What in blazes are you talking about? You, yourself, told me everything about Elise. There's no mystery. She was married. He died. She had his child. That happened to thousands of girls during the war."

"Oh, Sloan." Anne put her head in her hands and shook it back and forth. "I should have told you everything. I simply thought there was no need to hurt you unnecessarily. But, I see now that I was mistaken."

"What the devil do you mean? Please, Anne. Stop this. You're frightening me."

"Sloan. Elise wasn't married. Ever. She doesn't even know who Chloe's father is. She – she – she slept with Nazis. More than one. She doesn't even know which one made her pregnant."

"That's a bloody lie! Why would you say something like that? It isn't true. I don't believe you."

"It is true, Sloan. That's why she left France. She could have been in serious trouble for collabouration. Especially when she found out she was going to have a baby and wasn't married. She wasn't even engaged. There was no one in her life. Well, no one in her life she would have wanted to claim as the father. It's even worse than that. When she left France, she ran to Brighton. Do you know where she was living in Brighton?"

"No. I assumed a boarding house of some kind. I know she became very fond of a French émigré there, who took care of her when she was pregnant with Chloe."

"Sloan, it wasn't a boarding house, and the French émigré is a Madam. The name of the establishment is *Maison de Violette*. It's a brothel. I even went there myself, to be certain I wasn't mistaken. I spoke with two women – Lana and Adele. They both work there. Both knew Elise. They were there when Elise came, and when Chloe was born. That's when she made the decision to change her name to de Baier and put on a wedding ring, so people would think she was a widow. Her friend, Giselle, was a prostitute, too. She was very successful in Paris before moving to Brighton. They decided to leave the profession after Chloe was born, cooked up a pack of lies, and moved to Thornton-on-Sea, where they could begin a new life. It certainly worked for Giselle. She managed to capture Ted Cabot. A move to America ensured that no one would ever know about *her* previous life. Now, apparently, it's about to work for Elise."

"This can't be true. I know Elise. Nothing you're saying sounds like her. How is it that you know all of this?"

"One afternoon we drank some wine together. I suppose it loosened her tongue. Giselle wasn't home. It was just the two of us, and we chatted about many things. I'm sure it was hard for her to have to live with such secrets. It was probably a relief to unburden herself to me. Naturally, I promised never to tell a soul but, under the circumstances, I don't feel I can hold to such a promise. I can't stand by and watch her make a fool of you."

Sloan put his head in his hands. "Oh God, Anne. Oh God. If what you're telling me is true, Elise is not who I believed she was. She's a liar. Worse still, she's – she's – oh God – I can't even say the word."

"She's a whore, Sloan. A cunning, manipulative whore."

"Does her brother know? I've made an arrangement to go into business with him. He's a terrific chap. I can't believe he'd be complicit in something like this."

"I don't know, Sloan. All I can say is that I find it hard to believe, as close as they are, that he doesn't know the truth. Certainly he must know about Chloe – that Elise doesn't even know who her father is."

"Anne! She's asked me to adopt Chloe - told me how much she needs a father. I bought it all. What am I going to do?"

"I can't tell you what to do. I feel like part of this is my fault."

"Anne, why did you tell me I shouldn't try to talk to Elise about her past? You had to have known all of this."

"I did know. But I felt sorry for her. As I said, I never thought it would get to this point. I didn't want to expose her. It wasn't my business, if she was trying to begin anew. Why should I ruin her life? I wouldn't have said anything if she hadn't carried her interest in you this far. I never thought she would. I thought you'd return form the war, spend time with her and, after a bit, come to your senses. I thought you'd realise that she simply wasn't right for you. I couldn't imagine that she would ever agree to marriage without telling you everything."

"In fairness to Elise, she did try to convince me that we should discuss her past. But, I believed that you had told me her entire everything. So, I said that there was no need to go back over the pain she'd been through. I don't know what she would have told me. I thought I knew the whole truth. I've learned a valuable lesson. One should never become interested in a person whom they haven't known for a long time. Better still, one should know the other's family – everything. It's easy nowadays for people to lie about who they are. The war has disrupted and displaced so many people. It used to be that one grew up in one's own village and knew everybody. Strangers were viewed a bit cautiously. But the war caused so much movement. Decent people welcomed strangers and felt badly for what they'd been through. That made it easy for people like Giselle and Elise to invent new lives. I wonder if I ever would have known this, if you hadn't found it out."

"It's hard to know, isn't it? I only know that I couldn't be still in the face of wedding plans. I'm afraid you *would* have found out, after you were married. Perhaps, after she'd protected the marriage with a child or two of yours. Anyway, I couldn't picture you married to someone with that sort of gruesome past."

"Anne, I don't know how to thank you. I owe you a huge apology. It seems my judgment isn't as keen as I thought it was. I have to reconcile this muddle with Elise. I'm heartbroken, Anne. I loved her. Really loved her. You know, I can even understand how a young girl could make bad decisions – especially one without a mother to guide her. But, to sleep with Nazi's! And lie about everything to me. I can never forgive that. Never." He put his head back into his hands.

"I'm sorry, Sloan. I wouldn't have hurt you intentionally. I think, under the circumstances, we should forget about lunch. I doubt you feel much like eating. I know I've lost my appetite. My only advice is that you don't let her manipulate you with more lies. She knows you love her. I'm sure she'll use your love to try to convince you that none of this is true. Of course, she'll say that I'm lying, or try to clean it up, by giving some sort of false explanation. If you don't believe me, go to Brighton yourself. Talk to Lana and Adele."

"I believe you, Anne. You'd have no reason to make something like this up. No sane person could invent this. It's too incredible. But don't worry. I'll remember what you said. She'll not get another chance to hoodwink me. I'm going to see her right now, and get it over with. I suppose she'll ring you. I don't intend to use your name, but she'll undoubtedly know where I learned the truth. What are you going to say if she calls? I hate to put you in the middle of this."

"I'll just hang up, Sloan. She hasn't any right to be angry with me. All I've done is try to protect a friend."

"You're absolutely correct. Right, then. Thank you again, Anne. I'm off to her cottage. After that, I'll go back to *Highcroft Hall*. I feel like hell. I just want to have it out and go home."

"I understand. I won't bother you. Ring me when you feel up to it."

Sloan left the bistro and got into his auto. Looking at his watch, he checked to make certain Chloe wouldn't be home. Poor girl. He had no desire to hurt her any more than she already would be, when she learned she wasn't going to have a Daddy, or a pony.

20

He decided he'd drive to the cottage and tell her what he knew. He wasn't about to give any warning. She didn't deserve any. He thought about the quaint, little place where she and Giselle had chosen to live. *No Regrets.* He laughed aloud as he drove. That really said it all, didn't it? If they were at all ashamed of what they'd done in the past, they'd have torn that sign down. But to leave it up! It was like announcing to the entire village that Elise and Giselle weren't a bit ashamed of the degrading life they'd led. He imagined the two of them, sitting in their cottage, laughing at the way they were making fools of the good people who'd accepted their lies. Damn her soul, he thought.

He pulled up in front and got out of the car. She was in the garden. He was beyond furious, but controlled his anger so they didn't have a row outside in the open. He'd have to go inside with her, where they could have privacy. She glanced up when she heard the door slam. She was clipping the last of the summer roses. There was a large bouquet in her hand. His heart ached. She stood there in the sunlight, golden hair streaming down her back, dressed in a sweet, pink and lavender pinafore. She was the epitome of innocence and purity. How different reality was from the vision. She smiled a sweet smile and waved to him.

"Hello, Sloan. I didn't expect to see you today. What a happy surprise. I've just finished clipping the last rose of summer. I always feel a little sad when that's done. No more blooms until next spring. But, by then I'll be living at *Highcroft Hall.* I'll have to come back and teach Josef how to care for all of the flowers."

Sloan nodded his head. "Can we go into the house, Elise? I have something I need to speak with you about."

She looked curiously at him. "Of course, Sloan. Is something the matter? Is everything all right with your parents?"

"Everything is fine with them," he answered shortly.

He opened the front door for her, and they stepped inside. She stopped in the kitchen and filled a vase with water, so the roses wouldn't die. After she'd tended to that, they went into the parlour. Sitting down on the sofa, she motioned for him to make himself comfortable. He choose to stand. That confused her even more, and she sensed his anger.

"What is it, Sloan? You seem upset."

"Yes. You might say that," he answered. "I now know that you aren't the person I thought you were. To begin with, I've learned that you had intimate relations with not one, nor even two Nazi soldiers. One of them is Chloe's father. My God, Elise. You don't even know which of them that is. You were never married. You made it all up. Even your name is invented. Does *Maison de Violette* in Brighton sound familiar to you? I understand you were very popular there, you and your dear friend Giselle. She's certainly taken Ted for a ride. Who would think a seasoned prostitute could win a Boston banker's son? She must be very good at what she does. To think, I might have had you for a few pounds, instead of a wedding ring."

Elise was stunned. She felt nauseous, and her face turned ashen. "Where did you get these accusations? Did these come from Anne? You have to let me explain. You don't understand anything."

"Oh I understand only too well. Don't think you're going to persuade me to listen to more lies. You're a whore, Elise. A whore! I'm disgusted. I can't believe I ever considered marrying you. Your portrait would have hung in the gallery at *Highcroft Hall,* next to all of the lovely ladies who are my ancestors. You aren't fit to be in their company. How could you ever have thought you'd get away with this? When did you dream up this scheme? Probably the minute I left the farmhouse. You saw a good thing and went after it. You must have been thrilled when you moved here, only to discover that I was a bigger catch than you knew. You'd attracted a Viscount. That set up Giselle to get her hooks into Ted. Women like you are very good at knowing how to read men. You knew what I was looking for. I'd been stupid enough to spell it out for you. My God! I even broke my engagement to Anne because of you. Anne! One of the loveliest ladies in the land – all of the things you aren't. Well bred, honest, decent. You should be ashamed of yourself. Damn you. Damn you, Elise."

Tears were running down her cheeks. No one in her life had ever spoken to her in such a manner. She tried again to make him understand. "No. No. You're wrong about all of this. Please, please listen to me. Sloan. Our entire life hangs in the balance. Won't you at least give me a chance to be heard?"

"Answer this, Elise. Is it true that Chloe's father is a Nazi and that you don't know for certain who he is?"

"Yes.... But... Please... There's more... "

"I know there's more. Not just one Nazi, but many. You admit that's true. What more do I need to know? Was there more than one?"

"Yes... Yes... But... Sloan... You're not letting me speak..."

"No. I'm not. If you don't think that's all I need to know, you're daft. There's nothing I want to hear from your lying mouth. Why don't you get out of this town? Go to America with your friend Giselle. Perhaps you can accomplish more with a naïve American."

Suddenly Elise stood and began to shout. "I do not have to sit here and be abused in my own home. I was wrong to think that you were different. You're not. You haven't the slightest notion of what you're talking about, and you're being unbearably cruel. I don't have to justify myself to you. You know nothing about Ted and Giselle. Ted makes ten of you any day. Now get out of my house. This is the last time I'll ever let any man into my house who only has the intention of hurting me. Get out!"

Sloan was amazed that Elise had the nerve to act as if she were the one who'd been wronged. But, it was obvious the conversation was over. She took off her engagement ring and threw it at him. "Take your stupid ring and leave," she shouted.

He stooped and picked up the ring. "I might as well throw it in the rubbish. After it's been on your hand, it's not fit for any decent woman's finger."

She ran over and slapped him across the face. "Get out! Get out! I hate you!"

"Don't worry, Elise. I'm going," he replied. With that, he walked out of the door, slamming it behind him.

Elise slumped down on the sofa. For a moment she didn't even cry. The shock was overwhelming. Then she let out a howl, and tears fell for hours.

Josef returned home shortly after Sloan had left. He'd been out looking for a building to buy or lease, where he could establish the restaurant. When he came into the cottage, he found Elise lying on the sofa, still crying hysterically.

"What the devil has happened? Who did this to you?"

She could scarcely speak. Finally, she managed to say Sloan's name in between sobs.

"Sloan? What do you mean Sloan? Sloan loves you. He would never hurt you. Has something happened to him? Oh God no, Elise. Don't tell me that."

"No. No. Nothing has happened to Sloan," she hiccoughed. "He's hateful, disgusting, and a pig. I never want to see him again. Never!"

Josef laughed. "So you've had a lover's quarrel, eh? It was bound to happen. Too much stress, you know."

"No – you have no idea, Josef." Elise sat upright and tried to talk.

"Then explain to me, dear sister. I've never seen you so upset. Tell me everything."

He sat across from her. It took nearly an hour for her to tell him. She kept breaking into hysterical tears, and he had to wait until she pulled herself together before she could continue. When she finally finished, he was appalled. He was livid that Sloan hadn't let her tell her side of things. He also wanted to go to Anne, and have it out with her.

"No. I already know what Anne is up to. I've figured it out. I believe she had this planned from the time she met me. She made certain to become my friend and managed to get me to reveal confidential things to her. Then she sat back, like a giant spider waiting to pounce. It worked. She got what she wanted. But, she isn't the one I blame. Sloan had to listen to her. He had to believe what she said. Without even giving me the benefit of a doubt, he believed her. He isn't the man I thought he was. I'll never trust another man again."

"Elise, never say never. I don't believe you can have stopped loving Sloan so quickly. I understand your anger. I'm furious. I can't even begin to imagine how you feel. It's a good thing the English banned duels. I'd challenge him to one. Whether you like it or not, I'm going to speak to him. He's my partner in the restaurant agreement. I'll gladly negate that contract, but not without telling him what I think of him. Someone needs to stand up for you. You're my sister. I love you, and I've always protected you. I'll always feel guilt for not having been there when those evil Nazis assaulted you. I'm not going to stand by and have you hurt like this. Someone needs to speak on your behalf. But, when all is said and done, I don't believe you've stopped loving him. I'm just wondering what you'll do if, after he learns what an arse he's been, he comes to you and begs forgiveness?"

"Josef. He wouldn't give me a chance to speak. It's impossible to believe he accepted the horrible things Anne told him about me and never even questioned them. All he had to do was come to me, and ask for an explanation. I've been operating on the assumption that he already knew everything. He said he that he did – that Anne had told him all about my past, and he didn't need to know more. Obviously she hadn't told him much of anything – probably that my husband had been killed, and it was terribly painful – that I didn't want to talk about it. She can't have told him the truth, because it's pretty clear now that he's only just learned the truth – and still not the actual truth! She made it sound like I'd willingly been intimate with several – many – Nazis. In other words, that I was sleeping with them – having affairs, or whatever one would call such behavior. How could he believe such a thing? It would be impossible for me to forgive him. You didn't hear the things he said and the scornful tone in his voice. He looked like I disgusted him."

"I understand. I'm disgusted with *him*. I'm trying to put myself in his place, as another man. Naturally I'd be upset, if I heard such things about a woman I loved. But, I hope I'd be decent enough to listen to her side of the story."

"I hope you would too, Josef. In any event, I'm awfully confused and hurt at the moment. I was so happy such a short while ago. Now, it's all been smashed to bits. What am I going to tell Chloe? She was so excited about having a Daddy. My poor baby. Perhaps I was selfish in not letting her be adopted by two, kind, people who would have given her a proper home."

"Elise. Let's not even discuss that. You made a decision, and Chloe is a sweet, well-adjusted, little girl. I agree that this will be a huge disappointment to her. We'll need to think of a kind way to tell her, but I don't think it should be now, when you're so upset. Let it rest for a few days at least."

"You're probably right. I'm not in any condition to have a long, difficult chat with her. I need to get my emotions under control."

⁓

Sloan stood by the window in his sitting room. He could see the orchard from there. The exact spot where he'd first kissed Elise. In the privacy of his own rooms, he let his emotions take over. Tears streamed down his handsome face, and he ran his hands through his hair, over and over again. "God Almighty," he thought to himself. "How could this have happened? I loved her. I loved everything about her. How could I possibly have been so deceived? I was positive she was my soulmate. Can she really be so wicked? Such a tramp? How am I going to tell my parents? What am I going to tell them?" They were upset enough about having lost Giselle. His mother refused to even look for a replacement for her.

He walked into the bedchamber and threw himself down on the big four-poster. He hadn't the faintest idea what he was going to do. Everything was in ruins. It was amazing that a person could go from being extraordinarily happy one day and in the depths of despair the next. He couldn't imagine ever loving a woman again - not the way he'd loved her. He kept trying to remind himself that what he'd loved hadn't really existed. He'd loved a fantasy. Anne had been right. Even Elise had said that to him, when he'd first met her in France. He'd been a fool. He got back up, and paced back and forth in front of the fireplace. Perhaps he should leave Thornton-on-Sea. But that wasn't feasible. He was being groomed to take over *Highcroft Hall* someday. Perhaps she would leave. But where would she go? What about little Chloe? He'd shouted in anger that she should go to America, but he didn't really mean it. Or did he? He was miserably confused. He lit a cigarette, but put it out after holding it for a moment. Walking back to the window, he allowed his mind to wander. She was the most beautiful creature. He could see her hair shining in the sunlight, and her perfect skin, with those lovely, pink cheeks. The idea that any other man had held her drove him mad. Nazis! How could she have? She wasn't desperate for money. She had a home, and her brother took good care of her. What about Josef? Had he known of her behavior? He must have. Until the day Sloan showed up at her door, Josef had been living with her too. None of it made any sense. Josef was a fine chap. Upright, decent, honest. Wasn't he? Sloan didn't trust his judgment about anyone anymore.

Just as his mind turned to Josef, the telephone rang. He had a private line in his suite. He hoped it wasn't Anne. He didn't want to speak to her right then. But he felt he should answer it. Picking up the receiver, he heard Josef's voice.

"Sloan, have you lost your mind?" her brother demanded.

"Hello, Josef. At the moment I'm not sure. I think I may be losing it now. Why are you ringing me?"

"Why? I think you know why. I don't want to discuss this on the phone. Meet me at the pub in a quarter of an hour. Don't say you won't, because if you aren't there, I'll show up at *Highcroft Hall*. I don't think you'll want everyone there to hear what I have to say."

Sloan's mouth formed a firm, straight line. "I'll be there, Josef," he answered and rang off.

***

A half hour later they were seated in a secluded booth at the local pub. Each had a glass of ale in front of him, but neither was there to drink. Josef started the conversation. He had no intention of letting Sloan say a word until he'd said what he'd come to say.

"I intend to get a few things straight with you, my friend," he began. "First off, Elise is a good, decent, moral woman. Any information you have to the contrary is absolute rubbish."

Sloan opened his mouth to speak, but Josef held his hand up in the air. "If you say one word before I'm finished, I'll shut your mouth for you. Do you understand?"

"All right," Sloan answered, sullenly.

"Good. Now, I'm going to start at the beginning and tell you exactly what a fool you are. When I've finished telling you the true story, you can say anything you like. If you aren't appalled at your behavior, I'll be amazed."

Josef went on to tell Sloan the entire story. Sloan heard about how Elise had endured the rape of three disgusting, drunk Nazis; he learned about how she'd had the wherewithal to pull herself together after that hideous experience and devise a plan to escape France; he listened while Josef told him about how Elise had gone to her neighbour and was directed to a boarding house in Brighton, named *Maison de Violette*; he found out that she'd been fortunate enough to be picked up by a fishing trawler in the English Channel, and had gone to Brighton; he was made aware that she was so naïve and innocent, she hadn't even known *Maison de Violette* was a brothel, even after she was inside of the house; he listened to Josef tell of the agony she'd gone through when she learned she was expecting a baby – of how she'd debated whether or not to have the child adopted, or whether to keep it; he heard Joseph tell of the pain, and of Elise's strength and courage once she'd decided to have the baby and raise it alone; and he wept when he found out how Elise had decided to leave the place where she'd been treated kindly, to make certain Chloe had a decent, moral upbringing.

The rest was trivial. Of course she'd changed her name; of course she'd purchased a wedding ring. She had a little girl to consider, and she would have done anything to shield her from rumor, innuendo, gossip, and cruelty. Chloe was her life. She didn't trust anyone else. Later, she learned to trust Giselle, and, in time, she added Anne to that list. Wasn't that funny? Anne! Lastly, she'd made the mistake of trusting Sloan. And what had Sloan done? He'd stormed into her home, like the Nazis, and viciously robbed her of the last bit of self-esteem. He'd brutally punished her for something she hadn't done - for a merciless act, perpetuated by a gang of madmen.

Josef sat back against the wall. He was finished talking. There was complete disgust in his voice. He took a long drink of the ale. Sloan sat in front of him, with his head hung low. His hands went up to his temples. Josef could see tears.

"My God! What have I done? What have I done? How can I ever undo it?" He looked up at Josef with red-rimmed eyes. "Tell me what to do. I don't know what to do. I love her, Josef. I can't believe I hurt her like this, when I love her so. Is there any chance she might ever forgive me? I said ghastly things to her. I deserve to be horsewhipped."

"Yes, you do. I agree," Josef answered. "As to whether she could ever forgive you, I can't say. I've never seen her so crushed. Obviously, I wasn't there when the Nazis came, but I can't imagine that they hurt her soul as much as you did. They took away her dignity and violated her. But you wounded her to the core. She didn't have any emotional ties to them. She loved you. I don't think I could forgive you, but I'm not Elise. She's an incredible lady. If anyone on this earth has the capacity to forgive such rotten behavior, it would be Elise. Frankly, if I were you, I'd begin by speaking to Lady Anne Whitfield, in the same tone that you used with Elise. Anne is certainly a princess, isn't she?"

"Anne? What she's done is deplorable. I see it all so clearly now. What a fool I was to ever believe she'd accepted my love of Elise. But it doesn't matter. I'm the one who believed her. Oh yes, I'll speak to her all right. But that isn't going to help. Elise will eventually know that I'm terribly sorry - she'll probably hear that I had a go-round with Anne. But obviously what Elise is broken-hearted about is that I didn't love her enough to trust her. Nor to let her explain everything to me. I acted like a lout. I probably reminded her of those Nazi swine."

"Yes. I think you probably did. I suspect all of the rage she's held inside about the rape came pouring out. Twice someone has invaded her home and placed her in an untenable situation. She must have felt powerless toward you. She kept saying to me that you wouldn't let her talk – wouldn't listen to her. My God, Sloan, I would never have thought you could be so cruel."

"Josef, I've never acted like that in my life. The thought of those filthy Nazis and Elise made me daft. Unfortunately, I believed Anne. I thought Elise had played me for a fool. I should have known better. There isn't a mean, conniving bone in her body. But Anne was so convincing. She must have practiced for a long time. She had so many facts – so many details –she even provided the names of two women who worked with Elise in the brothel."

"Damn you, Sloan. Elise *did not* work in the brothel. Can't you get that through your head? She stayed there, under the care of that kind woman - Violette. She had nothing to do with the business."

"I know, I know. I was just repeating what Anne said. Anyway, she said if I didn't believe her, I should go to Brighton and talk with Lana or Adele. That they would tell me the truth."

"I suppose now you're considering a trip to Brighton. In other words, you *still* don't believe what I've told you. My God, Sloan. You don't deserve to win her back if, after all I've said, you still have doubts."

"No, of course I'm not going to Brighton, and yes, of course I believe you. I was simply telling you what Anne said, and why I was convinced."

"Anne is a liar and a treacherous woman. To have known what Elise had been though in her life and then, to use that information - twist it around and tell half-truths - in order to give the impression that Elise is some sort of loose woman who preys upon men – well, Anne is utterly despicable – and this is what a well-bred, refined daughter of a Duke is like? God help her if I ever meet her."

"Josef, I'm so shocked at her behavior, I can't begin to tell you. I've known her all of my life. We were childhood friends. You can ask anyone in the village. People here adore her. I didn't have the faintest notion that Anne had this side to her. I suppose that's why I trusted her and believed she was telling the truth. Do you suppose it would do any good if I forced Anne to go to Elise and admit what she did?"

"I sincerely doubt it. She doesn't have to admit what she did. Elise knows what she did. Elise had Anne figured out two minutes after you left the cottage. I go back to my main point. Elise isn't nearly as upset about Anne's betrayal of her confidence, and telling sickening lies about her, as she is about you believing those lies. She feels strongly you can't have loved her, and believed such filth."

"She's right. What can I say? She's absolutely right. After all of my talk about soulmates – my God – for over five years, I refused to let go of her memory. I was so certain we were meant for each other. I still am. But, then, one false word and I lost all trust for the lady whom I firmly believe God put here for me? I can't believe I was taken in so easily. I should have known there was another explanation. Unfortunately, when I asked if Chloe's father was a Nazi, she said 'yes', which lent credence to Anne's lie. So, I immediately jumped to the conclusion that Anne was telling the truth. If I'd just calmly approached her and said there had to be some mistake -given her the chance to explain, everything would still be fine. I love her all the more for her courage and strength. We'd still be making wedding plans." Sloan put his head back into his hands and began to sob. "Oh God, I've ruined my life. I've dreamed of her since I was a boy. There will never be another like her. I'll never marry. I can't imagine feeling like this about someone else. What a total fool I've been."

Josef felt stirrings of pity for the man he'd thought would be the perfect husband for his sister. He was still disgusted at Sloan's behaviour, but it was certainly clear that Sloan's heart was shattered. Josef could see how it had all come about. Sloan's behaviour was abominable, but it wasn't difficult to understand how Anne's story could have sent him over-the-top. Josef was certain that, in spite of his sister's broken heart and apparent disgust with Sloan, she still loved him. He'd already told her that he doubted she'd stopped loving him in the blink of an eye. After listening to Sloan's obvious pain, he decided he'd do anything possible to help the two lovers get through the terrible muddle. However, he wasn't at all certain what that would be.

21

Anne lay on the bed in her fancy boudoir. She wasn't weeping, but she didn't feel well. Surprisingly, she didn't feel like she'd thought she would after accomplishing her goal. She thought she'd be joyous, knowing she'd succeeded in tearing Elise and Sloan apart. Unfortunately, when she'd seen the look on his face, as she told her lies, it became clear that she'd broken his heart. For some reason, Anne had never really concentrated upon how Sloan would feel. It might even have been different if what she'd told him was true. Even then, however, if she were honest with herself, she'd have to admit it was none of her business. Didn't a person have the right to start their life anew – to turn over a new leaf? Anne had always considered herself a Christian, and the entire basis of that religion's teaching was forgiveness. Poor Elise didn't even have a reason to start anew. She wasn't at fault for what had happened to her. Everything that followed had been a result of the terrible assault she'd endured. It was clear she'd made decisions based upon love and concern for her little girl. Of course she had to pretend she'd been married and, naturally, she had to wear a wedding ring. The bottom line was, she'd done nothing wrong. The more Anne tossed and turned on her elegant, white, bed, the more she realized what an evil thing she'd done. What had she hoped to accomplish? Certainly, there was no way Sloan would suddenly decide he loved Anne and wanted to make her his wife. That would be daft.

He'd hate Anne forever, even if he did lose Elise. Sooner or later, the word would probably spread throughout the village about what she'd done. Perhaps not word for word, or even the vague details, but people would begin to understand that Anne was responsible for the end of what had been a glorious love story. Anne would be hated.

All of those thoughts overwhelmed her, but the primary one was that she had done something evil and wicked. It wasn't in character for her. She'd always been a nice person. If someone she knew had done such a thing, she would never have spoken to them again. The idea of her parents finding out was frightening. Yet, she didn't have any idea how to make things right. She couldn't gaily waltz into Elise's cottage, saying she was sorry. What she'd done went far beyond a simple "I'm sorry."

⁓

Sloan was back in his own rooms at *Highcroft Hall,* at the same time Anne was at *The Meadowlands,* ruminating about her actions. It was beginning to seem like half of Thornton-on-Sea had taken to their beds. Sloan was berating himself unmercifully for his actions. He hadn't known he had such cruelty in him. Now he knew what searing pain could do to a person. Words he'd never thought himself capable of, had come easily from his mouth. Finally, he decided he had to let the anger out. He rang Anne. At least he could make her understand the devastating harm she'd caused.

Anne sounded miserable on the telephone. He told her he would either come to *Meadowlands,* so they could speak, or meet her wherever she suggested. At first she tried to beg off, saying she had a headache. He told her he wasn't interested in any excuses, and that either she would tell him where and when to meet him, or he would be at the door of *Meadowlands* in half an hour. She didn't want him to come to her home. Her parents were both there, and they would ask questions.

"Can we meet at the park in the village? By the gazebo?" she asked.

"That's fine. I'll see you then. Don't be late. We have a lot to talk about."

"I won't be," she replied.

There was a click. He didn't even say goodbye.

Anne washed her face and tried to make herself presentable, but there wasn't much point. She knew he wasn't meeting her because he couldn't wait to see her lovely face. She changed clothing, putting on a simple frock. She paid scant attention to her hair. After all, this wasn't a social get-together. Half an hour later, the two were seated in the gazebo. Anne started by admitting at once that she knew she'd done a terrible thing.

"I don't know why I said the things I did, Sloan. You know I'm really not that sort of person. I've been hell-bent on winning you back, ever since you wrote to me while you were still in North Africa. When I read that letter, my heart broke into a million pieces. I couldn't believe you'd throw away everything we shared, for the mere memory of a girl you'd only seen once in a farmhouse in France. It sounded obtuse. I thought it was a passing fancy - that you would recover from it, and we'd go on as before. But instead, your feelings seemed to grow. I couldn't believe it when I learned Elise was living in Thornton-on-Sea. It seemed impossible. All I could think about was keeping you from her, but I knew if she was right here, the chances of that were impossible. I truly thought about the whole dilemma for a long time. Finally, I reached the conclusion that the best thing I could do would be to ingratiate myself with Elise — to become her friend. That way I'd be able to have an effect upon her thinking, and most importantly, I'd learn all I could about her. Hopefully, there would be something to make you think twice about whether she was truly your soulmate. Well, there was."

"That's where you're dead wrong, Anne. There wasn't. If you'd told the truth about Elise, it would only have made me love her more. Do you honestly believe I would have said that I wanted no more to do with her when I learned about the appalling attack she'd endured? What sort of man do you think I am?"

"No, I didn't think that. Which is why I twisted the facts. If you thought she'd willingly been intimate with Nazis, it would put a different light on the matter. Obviously it did. It probably would to anyone. I knew you well enough to be certain you wouldn't want anything more to do with her. Unfortunately, my lies had the desired effect."

"Yes. Only because I was fool enough to believe them, without giving Elise the benefit of the doubt. I should have known her well enough to know she would have died before willingly involving herself in something as sordid as a fling with a Nazi, let alone more than one. "

"I don't know what I was thinking, Sloan. I guess the old adage 'Hell hath no fury like a women scorned' is true. At least that's the way I felt. I wanted you to pay for the pain you'd caused me."

"And Elise? Why should she have paid?"

"I don't know. Just because she was the 'other woman,' I suppose. I don't think I thought of her one way or the other. She was in the way, and I wanted her out of your life. Oh God, Sloan – I'd do anything to take it all away. But, I know I can't. This is the worst thing I've ever done in my life."

"If you were a man, I'd beat you to a pulp. Since you're not, all I can do is make certain you understand what you've done to a kind, trusting, and decent woman. You've put me into a position where I accused her of the vilest behavior imaginable. I know Elise has a lot of trouble with trust – particularly with men. It isn't hard to figure out why. Well, you've increased that fear. I can't imagine she'll ever trust a man again. Damn you, Anne. Damn you."

"I don't know what to say. I'm ashamed of myself. It was horrid of me. I'm embarrassed and humiliated. Worse, I don't know what I can do to set it right. Do you love her so very much, Sloan?"

He raised his voice an octave." I told you from the beginning that she's my soulmate. I acted like a fool. I still believe that about her. But, she never believed in that concept as strongly as I do. Now, of course, she thinks it's all rubbish. If a person is your soulmate, he doesn't go off on a rant, calling you every filthy name in the book – disparaging and demeaning you. Do I love her so? Yes, Anne. I love her so. You've known that for a long time. You've known me long enough to know that I don't casually use that word. I never used it about you. Never. In a weak moment I proposed to you. Whether I'd found Elise or not, I knew I'd never marry you. I didn't love you the way a man should love a woman he wants to marry. I told you that. What a daft question to ask me. Do I really love her so? Like flowers love the sun; like birds love the trees. I don't just love her. I *need* her to feel completely alive. You don't know how that feels. You thought you were so in love with me. You haven't any idea what *love* really means. I was just someone who'd been in your life forever. You wanted me as your husband. You've always managed to get what you wanted. This was nothing but a competition for you."

"What can I say? How can I make amends? I truly am sorry. From the depths of my soul. I was wicked and hate myself. Would it help if I spoke to Elise?"

"I don't think there's a thing you could say to Elise that would make a whit of difference. Why would she care what you have to say? I'm sure she's figured you out by now. Knowing Elise, she'd probably forgive you. God bless her. She's that sort of lady. So if your aim in speaking to her would be to salve your own guilty conscience, you'd probably succeed. But, if it's because you honestly believe what you did was abominable, and feel immeasurable regret at having ruined two lives, it becomes a bit more sticky, doesn't it? You can't simply wave a magic wand, and undo the damage. This is one time in your life when you can't have things the way you want them. Frankly, Anne, I don't trust you at all. I never should have. I'm not at all certain your motives now are so pure. I suspect you're wanting to prove to me that you're filled with sorrow for what you did, and that you're willing to try to convince Elise of your shame at having done such a thing. You know full well she isn't likely to believe much of what you have to say. I'm not either. How do I know that this great show of regret is nothing more than another scheme to say you tried everything to make it right, hoping in the long run you might manipulate me into returning to your arms?"

Anne began to cry. "Do you truly think so poorly of me, Sloan? Isn't there a shred of the old faith we once had in one another?"

"You must be daft! You destroyed that when you destroyed Elise. Can't you get it through your head that I'm destroyed, too?"

"Yes. I can. I'm only searching for a way to rectify the harm I've caused."

"Quit searching, Anne. When you begin to concoct ideas, this is what comes of it. Leave me alone, and leave Elise alone. I haven't any idea how I'm going to make amends. I don't know if it's possible. I only know I have to try. This isn't just a simple little tiff that all lovers experience. I'm not optimistic about the outcome. God help me if she leaves Thornton-on-Sea. That's what I told her to do in my rage. I told her to 'get out of this village' — that I never wanted to set eyes on her again. Now I'm terrified she'll do it. If she leaves here, I'll have no way at all to ever win her back. I'll have lost her for good."

Anne sighed and wiped away tears.

"I won't interfere, Sloan. I would probably only make it worse. But I do promise that I'm being honest when I say I'm disgusted with myself for what I did. I'll pray for you, and for Elise. I'm going to pay a visit to the Vicar and confess everything I did. Elise goes to the same church. Perhaps he can speak with her. I don't know. I can only do my part in trying to understand why I acted as I did, and pray to God he'll not allow my behavior to destroy the lives of two people who don't deserve such heartache. I'm going to leave now, Sloan, unless you have anything more to say to me. If I can do anything to help – anything at all – please do ring me. I'm sorry, from the bottom of my heart," she exclaimed, as she collected her handbag and gloves, and walked slowly, with her head down, away from the pretty gazebo in the park at Thornton-on-Sea.

***

Elise didn't sleep a wink the night after her heartbreaking scene with Sloan. Josef returned after his conversation with her former fiancé and told everything. While she had to admit it made her feel a mite better to know Sloan was suffering too, and to learn that he knew everything he'd been told was a lie, she still was shattered to the depths of her soul. That the man she loved could, for one second, have believed she was a loose woman – a whore - was inconceivable.

Did she still love him? Yes, of course. Josef was right. One didn't stop loving someone they'd planned on spending their life with. Not overnight. Somewhere, deep inside, she knew that Sloan hadn't meant all of the cruel things he'd said. She was wise enough to understand that rage turned a person into quite another. Thankfully, she'd been born with a calm, consistent manner, not given to bursts of anger and unjustified emotions. She'd never even thrown tantrums as a child. Elise may have led a sheltered life, but she knew enough about human emotion to understand that anger could be a trigger for a lot of untoward behavior. She also understood that a lot of ire was the result of heart-wrenching hurt. Instead of being able to voice pain, many people lashed out at the person or event that was causing the pain. She knew that was what had happened to Sloan. But, how could they possibly find their way back from this? Was there the slightest possibility she could trust him again? How could she know he didn't harbour a smidgeon of doubt? What if she forgave him, and they married? At the first sign of a disagreement, was suspicion likely to rear its ugly head?

After a long and painful night, Elise reached a conclusion. She was going to take Sloan's advice. She would leave Thornton-on-Sea. She tried to think about where she could go. Naturally, her first thought was Giselle. They were such dear friends. She knew she'd be welcomed warmly. But Giselle was just settling into a new marriage, in a foreign country. It seemed highly selfish and inappropriate for Elise to show up, aching with pain and sorrow. She would also have Chloe in tow. That was asking a bit much of their friendship. So, where could she go? London was out of the question. She didn't know anyone. It was an expensive place to live, and she had no means of earning a living. She might be able to find a position as a French teacher, but who would watch Chloe? It was the same dilemma she'd faced when back in Brighton.

When Brighton entered her mind, she thought of Violette, who'd told her long ago to call if she was ever in need of help. Was that what she should do now? But, the only reason she'd left that safe cocoon had been because she wanted a healthy, decent environment for Chloe. Chloe was four years old. She was old enough to question her surroundings. If it had been a problem in 1941, it would be more so now. Was there anyone she could leave Chloe with for a short spell? Just long enough to get away and collect her thoughts?

Of course there was! She hadn't been thinking straight. Josef was here now. That made things entirely different. He would understand completely. He wasn't working yet, because the restaurant was still in the planning stages. So, he was home every day. He'd be able to make certain Chloe was at school on time and that she was cared for properly. Elise wouldn't be gone forever. She needed a friend. Someone she trusted – and there weren't many of those in her life. She knew Josef would agree with her plans. Once she'd had time to think – time alone – she'd make a decision about how to carry on. Violette had been the closest to a mother Elise had ever known. She'd be kind and caring. Elise trusted her advice.

When she rose the next morning, she fed Chloe breakfast and saw her off to school. Then, she approached Josef with the plan she'd devised. While he hated the thought of her leaving him, even for a short time, he had to agree that her idea made sense. He didn't know Violette, but it was enough for him that Elise truly seemed devoted to her. There was certainly no question about the woman having been wonderful to his sister. She'd helped with money to begin anew and had made certain that Elise had the best care when Chloe was born. She'd cared for her during what had been a long, emotionally difficult pregnancy. If it hadn't been for Violette, who knew if Chloe would ever have been born?

"Of course I'll tend to Chloe. You know I love her. You need have no worry about your daughter. I do believe it would be good for you to be with a female friend for a while. From what you've told me, she sounds ideal. Rather like a mother. You've had a terrible shock. I understand your need to sort it all out and, while I'm your brother and am here for you, I also understand that women need other women. So, go with my blessing. There's one other reason I think this would be wise. If you stay here in Thornton-on-Sea, while trying to work your way through this morass, there's an excellent chance you'll run into Sloan. I've already told you he still loves you – greatly. You know that I hope you two can work through all of this. But you're my sister, and I want what's best for you. So, I don't think it would be good for Sloan to be able to have access to you. I know you still care deeply for him. Feeling as you do, it would be hard to think straight if you're face-to-face. You'd think it would be easy, when both of you obviously still care for each other. But, I understand why it's not. Take the time you need. Look at the dilemma from every angle and listen to any advice your friend offers. When all is said and done, you'll know what to do. I feel certain of it. When do you plan on going?"

"As quickly as possible. It's only a short train trip. But I need to let Violette know I'm coming. I wouldn't want to just turn up on her doorstep, unannounced. I'll have to write to her."

"Why not send a wire? It would be much faster. You don't have to give a long explanation at this juncture. You'll have plenty of time to tell her every detail. Just tell her you want to come, and I'm sure she'll cable back and say whether it's a good time for a visit."

"Oh Josef, you're such a dear. Why didn't I think of that? Of course, it's the sensible thing to do. My mind is all muddled."

Elise ran to the centre hall, where she grabbed her purse and cardigan. It was still September. Summer lingered with pretty, warm days and comfortable nights. She hoped such weather would continue until she'd accomplished what she wanted with her journey to Brighton. It was much easier to pack light, summer apparel, than heavy woolens. She sent the wire from the *Western Union Office*. It was short and to the point:

"Violette. You once offered me refuge. I need that now. May I come at once?"

She signed her name and paid for it to be sent immediately. The man at the counter told her they would ring her when a reply came. She'd ridden her bicycle and, as she left the storefront to return to her cottage, who pulled up to the kerb but Sloan Thornton? This was exactly what she was trying to avoid by going to Brighton. He disengaged from his automobile and walked toward her.

"Elise, please wait a moment. Don't run. I won't ask you to stay long. I know how you feel, and don't blame you. I'm sure you know, by now, that I've spoken with Josef. I know what my behavior did to you, and I know that an apology isn't going to begin to undo the damage I've caused. But it's a beginning. I'm so dreadfully sorry. I would do anything to make it right. But I've no idea what that would be."

Elise stood there with her head bowed, holding on to the handles of her bicycle. She was glad she had it for support. Finally she spoke.

"Sloan. I appreciate your apology. Yes, it was called for. But you're right. This isn't a time when a simple 'I'm sorry' is going to change very much. Your cruel words echo in my ears. Worse still, they echo in my heart. You must understand that it isn't a matter of forgiveness. It's a matter of trust. You showed me, unequivocally, that you didn't have one iota of trust in me. The moment you were told one untrue thing about me, you believed it wholeheartedly. A person who loves another doesn't act that way. And you! You, who prattled on about 'soulmates' from the very beginning. I don't think you understand anything about true love. I have to go now. Chloe is at home with Josef. I don't like to leave her."

She considered mentioning that she was leaving Thornton-on-Sea, but then thought better of it. She didn't want the faintest possibility that he would try to follow her. Elise climbed atop her bicycle and didn't even glance behind her. He was wise enough not to utter another word.

She'd been home about three hours when the *Western Union Office* rang, saying there was a return wire from Brighton. She asked that it be read over the telephone.

"Always your home. No need to ask. Advise arrival time."

Dear, special Violette. Elise had known her response would be positive. Next, she rang the rail station and learned there was a train leaving Thornton-on-Sea at 3:05 p.m. She would definitely be on it. She found Josef in the parlour, reading the newspaper and told him her plans. He smiled and said he was glad. She also took time to tell him about her run-in with Sloan. Josef thought she'd handled it well. Elise ran up the stairway and pulled out her old luggage. The last time she'd packed had been when she was moving to Thornton-on-Sea. 'How strange the world is', she thought. 'I would never have dreamed that I'd be returning to Brighton with a broken heart.'

She packed carefully – mostly clothing appropriate for a warm autumn, but she also put in some jumpers and a black, woolen skirt she could wear with nearly anything. Mostly, there were daytime frocks, under garments, and nightwear. She also put in a photo album of Chloe, so Violette could see how the little girl had grown. When she was ready, she went back down the stairs, where Josef waited to take her to the station. Chloe wouldn't be home from school until after she'd left. She hated not being able to say goodbye to her little girl and voiced her concern to her brother.

"I'll explain to Chloe," he answered.

"Yes, but what will you say? I don't want her upset in any way. She's bound to think it odd that I'd simply run off and not even wait to tell her goodbye."

"I'll tell her a little white lie. I'll simply say that you have a friend who's being married and has asked for you to be there. I'll say you received a wire. That you didn't have time to wait until she came home from school, or you would have missed the train you needed to take in order to arrive in time for the wedding. Does that sound all right?"

"I suppose so, although I detest telling Chloe any sort of lie. Isn't there something better you could say? If I get into a story about a wedding, she'll want all of the details, and one lie will lead to another. Can't I stay with the truth as closely as possible?"

"She remembers meeting Violette at Giselle's wedding, doesn't she?"

"Oh, I'm sure she does. That was the highlight of Chloe's life."

"Well, what about saying something came up, and you needed to speak to Violette about it. Nothing serious, but the sort of thing one about which one would seek advice from a mother. She knows you've always thought of Violette in that way, doesn't she?"

"Yes. Both Giselle and I spoke of Violette often. She knows how thrilled we were when Violette came to Thornton-on-Sea. You don't think it would frighten and worry Chloe if I run off so unexpectedly?"

"Not if I treat it casually. I'll make certain Chloe knows this has nothing to do with her. Furthermore, I'll let her think I don't even know the full reason for the trip."

"I hope she doesn't think it has something to do with my plans to marry Sloan. What if she mentions that?"

"Elise, you're analyzing this far too much. If she mentions Sloan, I'll brush it off. I'm not about to give her an inkling of the problem between the two of you, nor let her think that's what this is about. Maybe she'll think you've gone to beg Violette to come to your engagement party and wedding."

"All right. I'm going to have to tell Chloe the truth about Sloan and me, but that's another thing I want Violette's advice about. I want to do it in a way that will cause Chloe the least amount of pain."

"I know that, Elise. Now come, I'll drive you to the station. Then, I'll stop and wire Violette your time of arrival. I'll be back home by the time Chloe returns from school. Everything will be fine. Just make sure to let me know when you're coming back."

22

They sat in Elise's old room at *Maison de Violette*. Elise had arrived just after five o'clock, and Violette had met her at the station. They stopped for a bite to eat at a small bistro and walked to the familiar, lavender house. Violette had prepared Elise's room with lovely fresh linens, and the bed was turned back. Most of the girls in the house were either out, or sleeping, so there was no great fuss about her return. Neither Elise nor Violette had brought up the reason for such a spur-of-the-moment visit, but now that they were in a private, comfortable setting, it was time for a long chat.

"So, Elise. Tell me what this is all about. Of course, you know I'm happy that you've visited. But I know you well enough and, from the tone of your wire, there is obviously something amiss. I'm fairly up-to-date on happenings in your life – your love for Sloan Thornton – the engagement – the wedding plans. Something has gone awry. Am I right, *Mon Cherie?*

"Yes. You're right. How perceptive you are."

"Elise, I'd have to be a nit-wit not to have figured this out. What has happened?"

Elise burst into tears. Violette let her sob for a bit, before asking any more questions. She put her arms around Elise, holding her as a mother would, patting her on the back and murmuring soothing words. Finally, when Elise seemed to have reached a place where no more tears were flowing, at least for the moment, Violette resumed the conversation.

"Whatever happened, it's come near to breaking your heart. I've never seen you in such distress. Please tell me, Elise, so I can know how to help you."

Elise started at the beginning and told the entire story. There were many breaks in between, when sobs began again. Violette was patient and didn't rush her. Occasionally she reached over and patted her hand, or cuddled her. Violette looked extremely angry when Elise reached the part about the words Sloan had spoken, but she made no comment. When Elise was finished, which included having seen Sloan outside of the *Western Union Office*, she hung her head. More tears streamed down her face. Violette took some time to answer.

"Elise. You have every right to feel the way you do. If you never wanted to see him again, no one could argue. But I'm going to ask you to think sensibly. It's so easy to let emotions take over at such a time. I don't want you to make a terrible mistake that you'll regret for the rest of your life. First, let me ask you this. Do you still love him?"

"I don't know, Violette. I don't know. I shouldn't. How can I love a man who would believe such things about me, without even letting me tell my side of the story?"

"Oh, you could, my dear, you could. And it wouldn't be unusual or wrong. Life isn't a fairytale. You know that. People love one another; hurt one another. It's much easier to be hurt by someone you love than by a stranger. You care what someone you love thinks of you. So, I'm not a bit surprised to hear that you very well may still love him. I think you probably do. I don't believe there would be so many tears, if he meant nothing to you."

"You're probably right. But how could I ever forgive him? He says he's dreadfully sorry. He knows the way he acted was disgusting. But, how could I ever trust him again?"

"The answer to that is easy. You could trust him again because he has told you that he loves you, and that he knows what he did was wrong. Are you telling me you don't believe people make terrible mistakes in life?"

"No. You know I'm not like that. But I can't imagine a man who supposedly loves a woman, saying such heartbreaking things, let alone believing such rubbish about his future wife."

"Elise, you know how much I love you. One of the reasons that's true is because you're still such an innocent. Love doesn't always bring out the best in people. Love can also bring out the worst. Emotions are sensitive things. They're also volatile. If one can feel incredible passion with their lover, one can also feel the opposite. Love wouldn't be love if emotions didn't rise and fall. That's why marriage isn't necessarily an easy thing. They, who think it is, aren't very clear about what it means to put your heart into another's hands. Elise, I'm going to tell you a story that I've never shared with another soul. But, I think it might help you to see this situation more clearly."

"All right. You know I'll keep it confidential. I can't imagine that there's anything I don't know about you. You've always been so open with me."

"I have been, but this is something I never thought would be important."

"Please tell me," Elise implored.

"After my husband and son died, remember I told you I went to London, and because of depression and lack of caring about anything in the world, I involved myself in this business?"

"Yes, I remember."

"Well, I left out one part of the story. I wasn't a full participant, yet. The person I worked for was the head of what would be known today as an escort service. Gentleman paid us to accompany them to upscale events. It was rather like the venture that Giselle was involved with in Paris. Only, because it was at an earlier time in our history, there truly wasn't any inappropriate behavior between clients and working girls. Remember, it was 1920. I was a beautiful girl in those days..."

"You're still a beautiful woman," Elise interrupted.

"Yes, well, I was only in my early twenties then. Our clients weren't men on the prowl, looking for sexual partners. The vast majority were aristocratic gentlemen. Or, widowers, who didn't want a woman to misinterpret their intentions and start pressuring them for marriage. Often, the men were homosexuals. You know, they're still treated badly today. Back then, it was fearsome. They often needed a woman to accompany them to fancy balls and the like, especially during the Season, and our service fit the bill perfectly. It was all understood upfront. There was no concern on their part about marriage-minded mothers. I actually enjoyed the work. There was nothing seedy about it. We dressed in lovely gowns and were taken to elegant places. Seldom did anyone know we weren't part of the crème de la crème.

Then, of all things, I fell in love. I'd never dreamed I could feel that way again, after the heartache I'd suffered when I lost my husband. The gentleman was extraordinarily decent and fine. A nobleman. He wasn't a client. He was visiting his cousin in London. His home was in the Midlands. His cousin was a friend of mine. She was in not connected with my work – had no idea what I did. She rang and asked if I might like to accompany him to a debut ball at a country house. I saw no reason to reject the offer. I knew the girl whose debut it was. His cousin told me that he hated attending that sort of event without an escort. In other words, it was what would be called a 'blind date' in today's world. I wasn't the least concerned about it. After all, I'd been in many similar situations, except that the person escorting me knew it was a business arrangement. His name was Alan Bryant - Lord Alan Bryant. He was a young earl, who'd just inherited his father's estate. When I met him, face-to-face, I was bowled over. He was extraordinarily handsome, sophisticated, and refined. Yet, he was also thoughtful and considerate – very down-to-earth. As much as I'd adored my husband, I have to admit that I was even more taken by Alan. Of course, he knew nothing of my employment status. He just assumed I was the dear friend of his cousin – which I was. We met, and it seemed like we'd known one another forever. We got on famously.

The ball we attended was like something out of a storybook. It was a gorgeous summer night, the house was filled with flowers of every colour and kind, and I wore a splendid gown. I could tell, as the night proceeded, that he liked me. Although I really didn't believe in such things, it was honestly love at first sight. Nothing inappropriate happened. We were just two young people, who were very attracted to each other. After that, he asked me to walk out with him many, many times. I was so in love. I couldn't believe my good fortune. I began to believe that all of the heartache I'd endured had been preparation for the lovely thing that was happening to me. He spoke of marriage, and of course, I would have walked down the aisle with him the next day. He knew I was a widow, and it didn't matter to him. We were very close to announcing our engagement.

During that period, I continued to act as an escort, since I had no other means of making a living, and it was important that I always dress beautifully and look the part of a lady who could become a countess. That part of my life never interfered with the other part. It was as though I lived two separate lives. I knew the places where I might be likely to run into him and avoided them like the plague. Never once did that happen. Nor did I ever see anyone who knew him. That is, until one night when my escort was a gentleman who was also from the Midlands. He was older and a very decent sort, but no one in whom I would have been interested in. He took me to dinner at a lovely restaurant, following a stage play. While dining, he mentioned Alan's country house – *Over Hill Manor.* Apparently he lived very near there. That worried me a bit. Of course, *he* knew I was an escort. While there was nothing unseemly about my behavior, you can imagine that it wasn't the 'done thing' among noble people. I certainly didn't want Alan to know. But what was I to do? Tell the man the truth and confess my fears? Tell Alan the truth? Hope that he didn't find out until after we'd married, or preferably never? All of those options ran through my head. I chose the last. I definitely swore that I'd never see Timothy again – the elderly gentleman - and prayed Alan wouldn't find out. I would have quit the escort business at once, but I had nowhere to go. Because of the excellent money I made, I lived in a smart flat in Belgravia and dressed in the finest Paris-designed clothing. If I left the business, I don't think I would have had enough money to pay for a lowly bed-sit in West Ham. More than half of my gowns were on loan from the service.

Well, to make a long story short, Alan *did* find out. He ran into Timothy at some event or other, and when they chatted about London, Alan told him he'd met a lovely lady in London. He told Timothy my name. Timothy hadn't intended saying anything about the fact that I was a hired escort, but once he learned that Alan was serious about me, he felt he owed it to him to be honest. Alan was flabbergasted. And so began a scene similar to that which you've described with Sloan Thornton. He felt he'd been duped. I suppose he had been, but I hadn't known how to cope with it. He said horrible, foul things to me. He had a right. Everything he said was true, except that I hadn't done anything so terribly wrong. He was under the impression that women who did such work were prostitutes. I tried to explain, to no avail. He left me with a broken heart."

"Was that the end of it, then?"

"No. I went to his cousin, my friend. I explained everything, and while she was horrified at my confession, she wasn't disgusted with me. She was a woman, after all, and women understand these things better than men - righteous prigs that they are. She went to him and told him my entire story. He understood, after listening at length. He was ready to forgive me. But, fool that I was, I wouldn't allow my pride to accept his forgiveness. I thought he should apologize for the things he'd said, and the way he'd behaved. So, instead of reconciliation, there was another row. That time, I said terrible things to him. I won't go into all of it. Suffice it to say that what I said was enough to kill whatever feelings he had for me. That was truly the end. I threw my life and happiness away for pride. After that, I did become a full-fledged prostitute. I didn't have to. But, I was angry and saw it as a way of throwing his words back in his face. I was a fool."

Elise was weeping by that time. It was a miserable tale, and it hit all too close to home. Instead of finding the solution to her problems, she was even more confused. Violette asked her one more question.

"Elise, are you trying to punish him for hurting you, and is your pride overriding common sense? If you truly don't believe you could ever trust him again, then I don't think there's a future for the two of you. But, if you aren't being honest with yourself —well — perhaps you need to re-evaluate."

Violette stood and kissed Elise on both cheeks.

"Sleep, *Mon Cherie*. A good night's sleep can do wonders. I want you to be happy. You know I'll be on your side, no matter what. But I don't want to see you throw away happiness with both hands, like I did."

⸙

Elise was still at *Maison de Violette* two weeks later. She'd thought and thought about what Violette had said. She had finally come to the conclusion that, if she were very honest with herself, pride was the primary obstacle to a reconciliation with Sloan. She was sitting at the writing desk in her private rooms. There was a knock on the door. Knowing it was undoubtedly Violette, she didn't even turn around. She just called softly, "Come in." The door opened and she continued to write.

Without glancing up, she said, "I'm writing a letter to my brother, Josef. I've just finished one to Chloe. I've told them both that I'll be retuning soon. I know Chloe is anxious about me, and I miss her. I miss Josef too. I've reached the conclusion that my pride has been standing in the way of listening to Sloan. What's more, when I really think about it, isn't what I accused Sloan of doing to me, the same thing that I'm doing to him? Not allowing him to explain. I've been wrong. I pray I haven't lost him. I know that my love for him was very real. It still is. I need to go home and speak to him. We can work this out. It was a horrible misunderstanding. Just like what happened to you. I love him, Violette. I don't want to lose him."

"Elise, you're a very wise lady. I prayed you'd come to the right decision, and you have. You will be the most beautiful bride that Thornton-on-Sea has ever seen."

It was Sloan's voice. Elise jumped and overturned a bottle of ink. It spilled all down the front of her rose-coloured dress. Wheeling around, she stood there, stunned. She and Sloan stared at each other for a moment.

"Who do you think should make the first move?" he smiled.

"You, of course," she answered. "But if you're adamant about not doing so, I shall." She smiled back.

He walked toward her. "I love you with all of my heart and soul. Forgive me for doubting you. It will never happen again. Never."

She met him half way. "Forgive me, Sloan. We were both wrong. I do believe you're my soulmate. Soulmates need to be together. One can't be whole without their other half."

They came together in each other's arms, and suddenly all was forgiven.

23

On the train back to Thornton-on-Sea, Sloan and Elise were seldom quiet. She wanted to know how he'd learned where she was, and why he'd decided to come to her. Sloan explained that it had actually been by accident. He'd run into Josef in the village and asked him to have an ale at the pub. Josef agreed. While chatting about details concerning the restaurant, an agreement was reached that no matter how things turned out between Sloan and Elise, they'd go forward with *Chez Chloe*. Josef was a bit worried that reaching such a decision would hurt Elise, but he had to consider his own future. The two had already put money into a building on the High Street and, if Josef backed out, he would lose his portion. Plus, opening his own, top-drawer restaurant was the epitome of a dream. He'd stood up for his sister, told Sloan the truth about everything, and had been very clear about his feelings. That was all he intended to do with regard to their dilemma. It was time for him to move forward with his own future. He and Sloan didn't need to be the best of friends, in order to be partners in a business arrangement.

While the two were chatting, Sloan asked when he thought they could realistically plan on a Grand Opening. Josef answered without thinking.

"When Elise returns from Brighton, I'll need to sit down and chat with her."

He could have shot himself for opening his mouth and telling Sloan where she was. Sloan overlooked the slip and simply continued discussing *Chez Chloe*. But he tucked the tidbit about Brighton into his memory. If she hadn't returned by the end of the week, he'd go to Brighton. He remembered Anne having told him of *Maison de Violette*, so he knew exactly where to look, once he reached the seaside resort. It shouldn't be very hard. Few people visited Brighton in the autumn and winter months, so the town wouldn't be crowded.

Sure enough, he'd found her almost immediately. All he'd had to do was ask at the railroad station. The porter knew who Elise was and spoke fondly of her. Sloan found his way to the lavender house on the beach and was welcomed warmly by Violette. She'd taken him to her office, where they'd chatted for a good hour. By the time she led him to Elise's room, his head was full of more accolades about Elise than even he had ever uttered. It was obvious that Violette loved her like a daughter. She pronounced, over and over, how sweet and innocent Elise was and told about how emotionally devastated she'd been when she'd arrived in Brighton. Violette made it clear that falling in love wasn't anywhere near Elise's horizon when they'd first met. Of course Violette knew what had happened between them. Instead of tearing into him, which she felt like doing, she took a different tactic. She impressed upon Sloan what a wonderful lady Elise was – that she was truly one-of-a-kind. The man who married her would be the most fortunate soul in the world. She enumerated Elise's good qualities, of which there were a multitude, and practically had him in tears again when he thought about how shabbily he'd treated her. At long last, he was shown to her room and left outside of the door. Elise knew the rest of the story. Thank God for Violette. Her wisdom had brought home, with full force, just how pride might have caused her to lose Sloan forever.

But they were together again and had already vowed never to allow anything to come between them. Sloan brought the ring with him. Not the one he'd originally presented to Elise. There were those nasty words spoken when she'd thrown the Emerald at him, and he didn't want her reminded of that horrid scene for the rest of her life. He'd purchased a new one – this time a magnificent canary diamond that he said matched her golden hair. Elise was thrilled. She would have been happy to accept the original ring, but his thoughtfulness meant so much. He slipped it on her finger, and she swore it would stay there forever.

Their conversation turned to talk of the engagement party and wedding. No one in the village knew of the rupture in their relationship, outside of Anne and Josef. They were both immensely glad that they hadn't shouted it to the world. Things could progress as if there'd been no interlude. Sloan had told his parents that Elise had gone to Brighton to visit Violette, who was more mother than friend. She wanted Violette to be at the wedding. Neither Lord Rowan nor Lady Celia had any reason to question what Sloan told them.

Sloan and Elise also discussed what to do about Anne. Should she be included in the plans that were being made? Neither particularly wanted her present, but if they shunned her, there were sure to be questions, not only from his parents, but Anne's as well. They reached the conclusion that they would send an invitation, and she could decide whether she wanted to attend. If she came, they'd both be decent to her, but certainly not overly warm.

Sloan had also brought a letter from Giselle. Naturally, it hadn't been opened. Elise tore the envelope, and read the contents. Giselle was happy – settled – liked America. Elise's eyes scanned the words. She and Ted were going to come over for the wedding! She would be Elise's Matron of Honour. Other than having Sloan sitting next to her on the train, she couldn't imagine anything that would have made her happier. Now that everything had worked out, and plans were going forward, Elise was elated. The date was still December 28. There was so much to accomplish. Elise knew she'd be incredibly busy. She began ticking things off in her mind; invitations needed to be ordered; a wedding gown selected; attendants' apparel; a time set for a chat with the Rector; decisions about the reception – flowers, music, and food. On and on. It was all so exciting. She would let Lady Celia handle arrangements for the engagement party. After all, that was truly her affair. Of course it was in honour of Sloan and Elise, but she would rather Lady Celia make the decisions. Elise would be happy to lend her thoughts, but she really wanted to concentrate her attention on the wedding itself.

She would invite Lady Celia to accompany her on a trip to London to search for a wedding gown. She knew very little about which shops would be the most appropriate. Everything had to be perfect. She'd never dreamed this day would come. It was going to be flawless. She would have Josef walk her down the aisle. She could imagine how touched he would be. He'd been as much her father as anyone, from the time she could remember. Everything was turning out so splendidly. She was going to marry Sloan and live in the wonderful village she'd come to love; he would adopt Chloe who would, at long last, have a Daddy; Violette would be there; Giselle would be there; could any woman ever have felt such fulfillment?

The guests danced the night away at Elise de Baier and Sloan Thornton's engagement party. Lady Celia had outdone herself. *Highcroft Hall* was a picture. The ballroom was filled with yellow roses and white lilies, with purple and white violets as accents. Elise stood in line with her future in-laws, receiving good wishes from everyone present. She held a sweet nosegay of yellow and white rosebuds, encircled with lavender violets. Her dress was enchanting. It was very pale yellow, with a wide sash of lilac satin encircling her tiny waistline. The designer in London had made it according to her specifications, so that it fit perfectly with the décor of the evening. Constructed of organza, it had an Alencon lace overlay, with long sleeves and a high, Victorian collar. Not since before the war, had anyone seen such an elegant event. Ruth outdid herself with food preparation. Regardless of the fact that rationing was still in effect on certain items, it was a marvelous feast. There was even a delightful cake, covered with yellow icing and topped with candied violets.

Anne accepted the invitation, but did not bring an escort. She looked lovely, but somewhat subdued. Wearing an amber gown, with the shoulders bared, and her dark hair spilling softly around them, no one could deny she was a beautiful woman. Elise had a kind heart and couldn't help but feel a bit sorry for the person she'd once thought was her friend. Sloan and Elise accepted Anne's best wishes when she moved through the receiving line, but otherwise kept their distance. Naturally she knew most everyone present, so she wasn't lacking in attention. Sloan couldn't help but notice that his friend from London, Elliott Woodbridge, who was going to be his Best Man, seemed somewhat intrigued with Anne. Sloan briefly remembered the talk he'd had with Elliott back in London, right after the war. The girl he'd described as his own soulmate could well have been Anne. Elliott had said that he preferred brunettes – sultry, sexy, and spunky. Elliott had also said she would have to be intelligent. Well, Anne was certainly all of those things, as well as sly and manipulative.

Even Violette had come to the party. Dressed, as always, in a lilac gown, she could have passed as a member of the peerage. She was definitely a very attractive women, in spite of being in her early fifties. There was nothing flashy or untoward about her. Elise was exceedingly proud of her, and made certain that everybody present met her. Both Sloan and Elise chuckled to themselves when they noticed that old Lord Tom Sterling, an acquaintance of Sloan's parents, hovered about the elegant Violette, bringing her punch and asking for dances. If he had known what Violette did for a living, he would probably have keeled over in a dead faint. The gentleman was a widower, perhaps in his late sixties. He was good-enough looking, if one liked the type. Clearly he enjoyed his rank in the aristocracy.

Elise wasn't sorry to see the party come to an end. Although it was the most incredible ball she'd ever attended, and she couldn't quite grasp that it had been held in her honour, she was counting down the days until her wedding. Now that the engagement had been announced to one and all, the distinguished, engraved invitations she and Lady Celia had selected could be addressed and posted. Elise was anxious to get on with preparations. She loved Sloan with all of her heart, and the wedding day couldn't come soon enough.

Guests departed, and after the last one left *Highcroft Hall*, Lady Celia, Lord Rowan, Sloan, Elise, Elliott, Giselle, Ted and Violette gathered together in the drawing room to talk over the night's success. That was always one of the most enjoyable parts of hosting a large party. It was such fun to discuss everything afterwards. Everyone agreed it had been unsurpassed in loveliness. Elise continued to receive accolades from the small, intimate group. She smiled and thanked them, but insisted they move on to other topics.

"You spent a good deal of time chatting with Anne Whitfield," Sloan remarked, looking at Elliott.

"Yes, I did. I was very drawn to her. Do you recall our discussing soulmates when we met in London after the war, Sloan? I have to admit, Anne touched a nerve with me. She meets my definition of the ideal woman."

"Oh no, said Giselle. "

"Why do you say that?" Elliott questioned.

Sloan and Elise looked at each other. "Elliott, be a bit careful with Anne. You know she and Sloan were once engaged. That's all behind them now, but we're not certain Anne is ready for another relationship," answered Elise.

"I'll watch my step. But, I'd like to see her again."

"Anne could use some attention from a handsome gentleman. Just go slowly," Elise continued."

"I'm glad I'll see Anne again at the wedding. I may even make arrangements to see her before then. Believe me, you'll be the first to know if it develops into something serious."

Sloan shook his head, but said nothing more.

"Violette, you were the 'Belle of the Ball'. Lord Sterling was charmed with you. How did he strike you?" asked Lady Celia.

"He's a very fine man. I felt honoured that someone of his stature would find me attractive. We got on very well. Of course, he was just being gallant. Can't you imagine me traipsing about with someone from the aristocracy?"

"And, why not? Personally, I think he'd be lucky to have you."

"Lady Celia, you're very kind. But he doesn't know me at all. I doubt he'd even speak to me if he did."

Lady Celia had no idea that Violette owned a brothel. If she had, she too would likely have keeled over. "That's nonsense. Just because you're not of the peerage, and are in business for yourself, I think he'd find that admirable. We've known Lord Sterling for eons. His deceased wife owned an interior decoration business. He's always admired women who aren't interested in leaning on their men."

"Well, that's lovely. But I think we'll leave it at that. I'm far too fixed in my ways to think about changing them now. I'm really quite happy with my life."

"Of course that's the important thing, isn't it?" answered Lord Rowan.

24

1945

December 28th arrived with a blue sky and sunshine. The wedding was to be held in the chapel adjoining *Highcroft Hall,* and the reception would follow in the beautiful ballroom where the engagement party had taken place. The chapel was adorned with red roses and white lilies, along with pine boughs draped along the railings. Red bows were tied on the end of each pew.

The chapel was filled to capacity, since every person who'd received an invitation was present. Elise, Violette, Giselle, Chloe, and the other three bridesmaids had spent the previous night at *Highcroft Hall,* so that they would be able to dress on the premises without any worry about creasing their gowns on the way to the ceremony. Giselle and Elise hadn't fallen asleep until the wee hours, since they'd had so much to catch up on. Elise was adamant that she wouldn't see Sloan on their wedding day, so she took meals in her room and never ventured down the staircase.

Guests had begun to arrive the evening before, and there was a lovely dinner held in the mammoth dining room. Elliott was there, as well as Ted and Giselle, Violette, Lord Sterling, Josef, all persons in the wedding party and, of course, the groom's parents. It had been a charming occasion, and everything went well.

It was difficult to tell what was going on with Lord Sterling and Violette. He seemed much taken with her. She'd told Elise that before the relationship moved forward, she intended to tell him her entire background. Elise begged her to wait until after the wedding, because she certainly didn't want any upset. Violette agreed. She would never have done anything to spoil Elise's wedding day.

Elise was the perfect bride. She was dressed in an exquisite gown. It was white taffeta, trimmed with white velvet. The long sleeves had soft cuffs of velvet, and the bodice was of the same fabric. The skirt billowed out into folds of silk taffeta, ending in a train trimmed with velvet braid. She wore a diadem of diamonds that Lady Celia had worn on her own wedding day. It held a gossamer veil in place on top of her golden curls. The matching earrings were a gift from Sloan. Violette gave her delicate, lace gloves, bought in Paris before the war, and Giselle provided the blue garter, so necessary for any bride. Josef presented her with a silver six-pence for her shoe, meant to bring luck and happiness. Elise's bouquet was an enormous arrangement of lilies – all varieties and all white.

Her bridesmaids were dressed in green velvet. The gowns had high waistlines, reminiscent of the Napoleonic era. Each girl carried a white fur muff, topped with a sprig of holly. Chloe was a tiny angel, dressed in white velvet, with touches of red at the collar and cuffs. She carried a basket of red and white rose petals, strewn in front of Elise as she began her walk toward Sloan. Josef was the proud brother who escorted her, and everyone in the sanctuary stood as she made her way toward the altar. Josef handed her off to Sloan and took a seat next to Violette. The two lovers stepped forward and knelt before the Rector. The organ played enchanting music, and Elise and Sloan bowed their heads in prayer.

After they stood and repeated vows, there was the exchange of rings, followed by the pronouncement that they were husband and wife. The entire chapel burst into applause, as Sloan bent and kissed Elise's sweet lips. No one in Thornton-on-Sea could say that they'd ever attended a more beautiful ceremony. Both Lady Celia and Violette wiped tears from her eyes. No one would ever know what a large part Violette had played in the coming together of the bride and groom.

Following the ceremony, the reception drew oohs and ahh's from those attending. There were so many incredible flowers that the ballroom was filled with sweet fragrance. Fountains were scattered about the room, beneath arrangements of roses, climbing on arbors and trellises. An orchestra played beautiful dance music - songs from the war years, which kindled memories for everyone in the room. A sumptuous buffet table was piled high with delicacies, and a triumphant wedding cake stood in the centre. Red roses climbed along the tiers. They rested in a pretty arrangement on the top. After receiving their guests, Elise and Sloan made their way round the room. Anne was standing with Elliott, and there was nothing for it but to acknowledge her. Before they moved on, after a chat with Elliott, Anne pulled them both aside for a private word.

"I want you to know that I truly wish you all the best. I made a terrible mistake and someday I hope you can find it in your hearts to forgive me. I'll spend the rest of my days trying to make amends. You two make a stunning couple. Thank God my actions didn't keep you from one another."

"Anne, both Elise and I appreciate your apology, and we hold no grudge. You can rest assured that there won't be any repercussions from us. Perhaps someday we can heal from the past completely. We do wish you well and hope you find happiness in the future."

With that Sloan took Elise's hand and turned away. Just as they began to move on, to speak with another group of guests, Elise spotted Violette and Lord Sterling entering the ballroom from the outer doorway. Violette looked triumphant, while Lord Sterling looked like he'd won first place at the County Fair. What on Earth could have happened? Surely Violette hadn't chosen to admit her past to him? She had promised not to do so. Elise found her way over to Violette and took her by the arm. "Why are you looking like the cat who ate the canary?" she questioned.

"Perhaps because that's the way I feel. I had to confront Lord Sterling with the truth. He began to speak about the future to me. He said he hadn't felt so romantic in ages. I had to nip it in the bud. Or, at the very least, make certain he knew all of the particulars, before getting carried away with talk about what a grand lady I am. So, I motioned for him to follow me outside, and I simply told the truth."

"Oh my God! How did you say it?"

"I just said 'There are things you don't know about me. Before you say another word about your feelings, let me be very honest with you. I operate a brothel in Brighton and have for many years.'"

"What did he say?" asked Elise, putting her hand up to her mouth.

"He said 'Is it successful? How much is your profit in a year?'"

Elise burst into laughter. "You can't mean it."

"Yes. I told him I'd grossed a little under half a million pounds last year. Her proposed to me immediately."

Elise could scarcely stop laughing. She caught Sloan's eye and motioned him to her side. When she repeated what Violette had told him, he, too, nearly bent over in hysterics.

And that was the end of that. Elise threw her bouquet; Anne caught it; Chloe danced a jig; Giselle and Ted were seen kissing in the foyer, and Violette and Lord Sterling disappeared up the stairway.

Thornton-on-Sea basked serenely in the sunlight of a winter day, while Josef Lisak sampled another hors-d'oeuvres, trying to decide whether to add it to the starter menu at '*Chez Chloe*'.

OTHER BOOKS BY MARY CHRISTIAN PAYNE

The Somerville Trilogy

Willow Grove Abbey: Book 1 of the Somerville Trilogy
St. James Road: Book 2 of the Somerville Trilogy
Serendipity: Book 3 of the Somerville Trilogy

The Claybourne Trilogy

The White Feather: Book 1 of the Claybourne Trilogy
The White Butterfly: Book 2 of the Claybourne Trilogy
White Cliffs of Dover: Book 3 of the Claybourne Trilogy

The Thornton Trilogy

No Regrets: Book 1 of The Thornton Trilogy
No Gentleman: Book 2 of the Thornton Trilogy
No Secrets: Book 3 of the Thornton Trilogy

ABOUT THE AUTHOR

Mary Christian Payne was highly successful in several management positions in Fortune 500 Companies, in New York City, St. Louis, Missouri, Orlando Florida, and Tulsa, Oklahoma. Her work included Grant writing, and designing and writing Training Manuals for Executive Training Programs.

She left the corporate world, and became Director of Career Development at the Women' Resource Center at the University of Tulsa, where she designed a program that enabled hundreds of adult women to return to college and better their lives. She received the Mayor's Pinnacle Award in 1993 for this achievement. Mary left that position when the Center closed, and then opened her own Career Counseling Center. She retired in 2008.

Mary Christian Payne became a successful, best-selling author at the age of 71, with the help of her publisher, Tom Corson-Knowles. All of her life, she had wanted to write, and had received accolades for her unpublished work. She was encouraged in college, and writing was a significant part of the various jobs she held.

In 2013, she read Tom Corson-Knowles' book about publishing on Kindle. She wrote to him and he telephoned her. The rest is history. Since that time, she has published nine books, with more on the way.

Mary lost her husband in June, 2015, after 33 years of marriage. The grief process brought a lull to her writing, but she found that putting words on paper helped immensely. She is now in the process of writing her second novel since his death. She lives in Tulsa, Oklahoma, with her two beloved Maltese dogs.

Sign up for the newsletter to get news, updates and new release info from Mary Christian Payne:

http://bit.ly/MaryChristianPayne

ONE LAST THING...

If you enjoyed this book, I'd be very grateful if you'd post a short review on Amazon. Your support really does make a difference and I read all the reviews personally.

Thanks again for your support!